THE
LIGHT
OF THE
FIREFLIES

THE
LIGHT
OF THE
FIREFLIES

PAUL PEN

Translated by Simon Bruni

amazoncrossing

Text copyright © 2013 Paul Pen
Translation copyright © 2016 Simon Bruni

Previously published as *El brillo de las luciérnagas* by PLAZA & JANES in Spain in 2013. Translated from Spanish by Simon Bruni.

First published in English by AmazonCrossing in 2016.

Published by AmazonCrossing, Seattle

www.apub.com

Amazon, the Amazon logo, and AmazonCrossing are trademarks of Amazon.com, Inc., or its affiliates.

ISBN-13: 9781503933545
ISBN-10: 1503933547

Cover design by David Drummond

Printed in the United States of America

For my father,
who gave me my first insect book.

For my mother,
who turned the veil of her wedding dress
into a butterfly net.

SIX YEARS EARLIER

I

On the night I asked my father the question, my family had been five years in the basement. Five years since the fire. It hadn't been quite so long for me. I was born just after they went down there.

"Why can't we go out?"

Dad amended the wall calendar and sat at the table, the large one we had in the main space, where living room, kitchen, and dining room merged.

"What would you want to go out for?" he replied. "All your family's here."

Mom lowered her head, her chin touching her chest. I think she also shut her eyes. There wasn't much light down there, just the bare bulbs hanging from the ceiling. Sometimes I thought of them as suicide victims, glass bodies hanged and swinging from a cable.

"Come here, son." Dad pushed his chair back and slapped his knee a couple of times. I walked over to him, dragging my feet. I could feel the cold of the floor through a hole in the heel of my pajamas. I still wore the type with feet. Dad took hold of me under the armpits, lifted me up, and sat me on his lap. As I often did in the early days down in the basement, I held my hand to his face. I liked the feel of his burned skin. From his left eye to the corner of his mouth, the irregular folds of his deformed features were appealing to a child's touch.

"Stop it," he complained, lowering my arm. "I want you to look around you. At your family." My mother, brother, and grandma turned to me. Everyone except my sister, who was looking away.

"And the one who's not facing you," said my father, "she's part of this family, too." The white mask turned on its neck then, and fixed its eyes on me.

"See them?" Dad asked. "Them, you, and me, we're all we need. There's nothing worthwhile up there. Do you remember when your mother splashed you with hot oil when she was cooking?"

It had happened a few weeks earlier, while Mom was making breakfast. The darkness of the basement and the shadows that danced around, distorting reality with each gentle sway of the lightbulbs, made some tasks difficult. The morning she splashed me with oil, I'd gotten between her legs and made her trip. It was actually my fault.

"Do you remember how much the blister hurt? The one you had here?" my father went on. He opened my hand to examine the back of it. He pointed at the exact place where the blister had been. There was no trace of it anymore.

"You're covered in drool. When're you going to stop sucking your fingers?" He barely moved his head, but looked at my mother for a second.

"Do you remember how much that little bubble of liquid hurt?" he asked again, pinching the back of my hand. "Well, the world up top is made of bubbles like that. But not little ones like yours."

He pinched harder with his fingers, making it hurt as if the blister had grown back again.

"Up there, outside, the bubbles are a hundred times bigger. You wouldn't be able to stand the pain." He began twisting with his fingers.

"Pain that would finish you off as soon as you set foot outside this basement."

I opened my mouth but said nothing. I was stopped by the pain on the back of my hand, much worse than I'd felt from the blister when it was still there, and the pain in my wrist, which my dad wasn't aware he was crushing. I remember the snotty sound in my throat, the dampness of my cheeks.

"Stop, please." It was Mom who said it, her voice barely a whisper. Dad let go. The pain lasted a while longer.

"See how you don't want to leave this place? If you can barely stand that, what would happen to you out there?" He stroked my wrist and kissed the spot where the blister had been, reddened again by the pinch. "There, there, little soldier, it's not so bad. Daddy doesn't want to hurt you, he just wants you to understand. You have to learn that this is the best place you could be. The best place in the world. Do you want to touch my face?"

He moved my hand to his scars and let me stroke them. He knew I liked it. He managed to calm me down. I used to linger on a line of hard hair that sprouted from a fold across his cheek, a place where Dad couldn't shave. It was like a scar of hair. I liked running my fingertips down it.

"Anyway," he said, shaking his head and moving my fingers away, "who said you can't go out?"

My grandmother snatched her hands back from the table. I saw them disappear underneath. Something changed in the posture of my siblings, too. They straightened up, their backs rigid. Mom kept her head bowed.

"The door's there," my father continued, gesturing at it. With the other hand he grabbed my head and forced me to look at it. "It's a few steps away. And it's open. It's always been open. Who told you otherwise?"

In silence, he looked around the table.

"Was it your mother? Your brother or sister? Was it her?" He tipped his chin at my sister. "She likes to talk too much. Because I don't think it would have been Grandma, she knows full well the door's always open."

My father grabbed me under the armpits once more to lower me from his knees and leave me standing on the ground. I felt the chill of the tiles.

"Come on." He gave me a slap on the backside. "Go over to the door, see for yourself."

I wanted to look at my mother, but Dad held my head and made me look straight ahead.

"Go on, leave if you want." The second slap on the buttocks was harder, so that I had to take a step forward to stop myself from falling. "Open that door and go. That's what you want, isn't it? So do it. Leave and forget about us. We'd rather stay here."

Behind me I heard a chair scrape along the floor, as if someone was about to get up. But nobody did. I took another step. The basement smelled of carrot. I loved that smell. It was the smell of night. The only thing that told me it was day or night was the patch of sun that went from one side of the living room floor to the other, and seeped through some crack in the ceiling. The smell of carrot always came when the patch disappeared. If I left the basement I would never have Mom's carrot soup again. An unexpected feeling of loss stopped me in my tracks. I had an urge to return to Dad's lap and scratch my fingers down his hair scar.

"Are you still there?" he yelled. "Come on, run to the door. Open it and go. Leave this basement if you're so keen to know what's out there."

I walked toward the door without stopping. I'd never been so close to it. A door loses its meaning if you don't ever go through it. It becomes a wall. Standing in front of it, I began to suck my fingers. I was sweating. I observed everyone at the table. Mom had looked up again. There was a glisten in her eyes now. Dad was sitting with his legs open, turning in his chair. He raised a hand and waved me good-bye.

Dribble was running down my forearm. I looked at the door again. I took my fingers out of my mouth and reached up to the handle, several inches above my head. The first time I tried to grab it, the spit made my hand slip off. I dried my fingers on my pajama legs and held my breath so I couldn't smell Mom's carrot soup, and to fill the void I felt in my stomach with air.

I tried again.

This time I managed to grip the handle.

THE PRESENT

THE PRESENT

2

There were two windows in the basement. One at the end of the hall and another in the kitchen. On the other side of them there were just bars, and after that, another wall. When I was ten years old, if I pushed hard and put up with the pain in my shoulder, I could stick my arm through two of the bars and, with my middle finger, touch that wall. It was just more concrete. It was the same at both windows. It was as if the basement was nothing more than a box inside another bigger box. Once, I positioned the mirror from the bathroom in the space between the bars and the wall outside. All it reflected was more darkness. Another black ceiling. A box inside another box. Sometimes I would stick my face between the bars to stare at the blackness that for me was the outside world. I liked to do it because the draft of air caressed my face. Air that had a different smell from anything there was in the basement.

"Can't you hear your sister screaming?" my father said to me the day the baby was born. "We need you in the kitchen. And close the window. Now."

He opened the door to his room with the key he always kept hanging from his neck. It immediately closed behind me. I blinked several times to moisten my eyes. They were dry from the draft. Then I heard my sister. I must have been totally absorbed by the breeze from outside not to hear those screams. They seemed to come not from the throat, but from the stomach. From somewhere deep inside the body. The door opened again, and this time my father grabbed me by the arm. He dragged me down the hall to the living room.

"Stand there," he said. "Hold that leg."

My sister was lying on the table, naked from the waist down. I recognized the sheets from her bed under her. Mom was sitting where her head was, squeezing her daughter's fist in her hands. My sister was looking down at her crotch through the mask, all white and expressionless. Just three holes showed her eyes and mouth. My brother, clinging on to one of her legs, was also peering at whatever was happening in my sister's groin. My grandmother was boiling water in two big pots. She held a hand over the stove plates to feel how hot they were. Dad went to her and gave her two towels.

"Do you think they'll do?" he asked.

My grandmother snatched them from his hands and put one in the largest pot. For a few seconds Dad just stood there, his head down and his hands in the air as if he was still holding some invisible towels.

"Come on, get over here," he said to me. "Hold her leg."

I hugged my sister's bent knee, hiding my head behind it. I didn't dare look. My sister screamed again.

Then Dad looked at the kitchen window. He rubbed the palms of his hands against his trousers, as if to dry them.

"Son, have you left the other—?"

Before he finished the question he ran out into the hall. My sister screamed once more, though this time she didn't even open her mouth. The cry escaped through her teeth. She splattered me with her spit.

"Breathe," said my mother. She was still clasping my sister's clenched fist. She moved her mouth to the ear that stuck out from behind the mask and began to breathe in a particular way, like when she'd been on the bike for a long time. "Breathe, girl . . . Don't worry . . . just breathe, like me."

My sister tried to imitate her. Her knee slipped out of my arms. I had to move away to avoid a blow to the face. She kicked out, hitting the table with her heel. When she managed to shake off my brother, who stepped back, her leg slipping his grasp, she lifted her waist until the top of her belly was facing more toward the wall than the ceiling, and she let it fall onto the table. Her tailbone hit the tabletop like a hammer. A sticky sound escaped from between her legs.

"I can't breathe with this mask on!" She screamed the words through her teeth, as if the pain and rage were phlegm stuck in her throat that she could spit out. "Get this damn thing off me!"

She continued to writhe, kicking her legs. My brother and I tried to grab hold of them and regain control. I noticed that the sheet was soaking. And slippery. A bitter smell made me retch. My mother, who'd wrapped her whole body around the fist, opened her mouth to cry out when she saw my sister lifting her free hand to the mask. She managed to snag her prosthetic nose.

My father grabbed her wrist. She stretched her fingers out as far as they would go, trying to reach the mask, until Dad's knuckles went white and my sister's fingers stopped moving. She screamed again. This time it was a high-pitched scream that hurt my ears. My father dropped my sister's exhausted hand as if it was something foul. Bones banged against the table.

"Stop being stupid. Your mother gave birth here." He glanced at me. "And she didn't make such a fuss. You're not a little girl anymore. At your age your mother already had two children."

"I was even younger," she elaborated. "Twenty-six."

My sister's legs relaxed. When she bent them we were able to grab hold of them again. My father stood there and looked her up and down. From feet to head. He smiled. "Does it hurt?"

My brother let out a guttural sound, one of his laughs that sounded like a donkey noise. Dad looked at him, not noticing the slow movement of her arm as my sister lifted it again.

This time she was able to grasp the entire mask. She closed her hand on it. The scrape of the prosthetic material alerted my father. Knowing there wasn't time to stop her from taking it off, he leapt on me, held my face to his belly so I couldn't see anything, and forced me to walk backward as he pushed me down the hall. He opened the door to my room and sat me on the bottom bunk.

"You've been lucky," he said to me. Then he turned his head toward the hall that led to the living room and shouted at my sister, "If you want the first thing that your child sees to be your deformed face, then go ahead!" He looked back at me and put his thumbs over my eyes. "But I'll decide what my son sees."

When my eyelids closed, a spot of light danced in the darkness inside my head.

Lying facedown on the living room floor, I rolled over so I could reach the patch of sun with my hand. A handful of rays that came in through a crack in the ceiling formed a circle of light no bigger than a coin. Every day it traveled along the floor of the main room from one wall to the other.

"Where does this light come from?" I closed my fingers and grabbed the empty air.

"Ask your father," Mom replied.

She was holding the newborn in one arm, washing it with the water she'd filled the kitchen sink with. My sister had been shut away in her room for a while, after Mom came out carrying the sewing box.

By the table, my brother was putting the dirty sheet and towels in a pile. Frowning, his tongue poking out, he attempted to line up the corners of one of them. In his hands, aligning the opposite edges of a towel seemed an impossible task. He let out a long groan before throwing it on the floor. He folded his arms.

I opened and closed my hand, caressing the band of orange light, like a jet of water that didn't make you wet. My skin seemed even whiter and more translucent than it normally did. I could make out all the blue and purple lines of my veins.

"What's the sun made of?"

I heard my mother take a deep breath in the kitchen. When she did so, the nostril worst affected by the fire made a strange whistling sound. Then she turned around and looked at me. "This is your nephew," she said.

The baby was crying in her arms. The palm of my hand hadn't even warmed up before the fading ray, a sliver of dust, disappeared. Like a butterfly in the fingers of an unpracticed collector. Pushing myself up with my arms as if I was doing a push-up, I stood and went over to my mother. She smiled, her burned cheek tugging the flesh and making her left eye close, as it always did. She stretched out her arms to hold the baby near me.

"I won't drop him, will I?"

Mom looked at my brother, who was watching us from the table. "I don't think so," she replied. "Hold out your arms."

I did. The baby, wrapped in a dry towel, was tightening and relaxing his lips. His tiny nostrils expanded and contracted, for the first time breathing in the air of the basement that would be his world. He had his eyes closed, very tightly. Under him, my arms trembled. "I won't drop him, will I?" I repeated.

Mom supported the baby with one arm and with the other she made me bend my elbow, forming a right angle.

I held myself in that position as still as a stick insect mimicking a twig. My mother expertly maneuvered the baby until he was resting on the palms of my hands. She edged him toward the quivering cradle that was formed by my arms. "I don't want to drop him," I insisted.

For a moment my mother stopped. Hesitated. Then she carried on. My brother grunted. The dishes stacked in the kitchen shook every time he took a step. He positioned himself behind me. I felt the heat given off by his body on my back. He pushed the baby back toward my mother.

To stop me from taking him.

The dishes vibrated again as he stomped back to the table, picked up the pile of towels, and disappeared down the hall. Mom's nose whistled.

The morning after the birth, I opened my eyes earlier than usual. I knew because all I could hear was my brother snoring in the top bunk, when normally I'd be woken up by the sound of my mother making breakfast in the kitchen. I lay awake in the dark. Something scratched the walls, on the other side. There were rats in the basement.

Between two of my brother's snores, I heard the baby whimper in the distance.

Silently I opened our bedroom door. Dad didn't like us to go around the basement as we pleased. I stuck my head out into the hall and looked toward the living room. The patch of light was there, shining on the floor, much farther to the right than I normally saw it. It must've been really early.

The baby whimpered at the other end of the hall.

Dad had put the crib in the room shared by my grandmother and sister. I waited for one of them to wake up and help the baby with whatever was upsetting him, but nothing happened. The child whimpered again.

I went into the room and approached the crib. I remembered the stack of wood that'd appeared in the basement one day and how Dad, with his box of tools, had turned it into the structure that the little boy now lay in. His eyes were open. He whimpered again. My grandmother let out a single snore. I looked over to the other bed, and in the darkness

I could make out the white contour of my sister's mask, which could've been on her face or lost among the sheets. My grandmother soon recovered the normal rhythm of her breathing. I bent over the baby and rocked him with a hand on his little tummy, and he closed his eyes.

I thought about it for a few seconds and then picked him up. I held him against my chest, his head resting near my elbow, like Mom had shown me. I walked out and took him to the dining room. I sat on the floor, near the patch of light, crossing my legs and feeling the baby breathe in my arms. I moved him into the pale yellow beam of light. It made his face glow.

"This is the sun," I told him.

We stayed there for a few minutes.

Until my sister woke up and began to scream.

3

"No one's stolen the child from you," my father said when we all sat down to eat breakfast.

My sister sniffed under the mask, which was fixed in a diagonal, indifferent stare at the ground. The eggs my mother was making for breakfast frizzled as she cracked them into the hot oil. At the time I thought they suffered when they were burned, like we do. And they screamed.

"I took the baby this morning," I said. "I woke up early and wanted to show him—" I found the circle of light on the table, but didn't finish the sentence.

"Since when are you allowed to come out of your room so early?" my father cut in. "Do you know what a scare you gave your mother and grandmother with your sister screaming?" Dad was pointing a finger at me. "She thought someone had stolen the child."

I kept quiet, ashamed. My brother tried to hold in his laughter, but it heehawed out through his nose.

The frying pan banged against the kitchen sink. My mother appeared with a plate full of fried eggs. She always said they had to stay in the pan until a black line surrounded the white. That was why there was a burning smell. With her free hand she straightened the tablecloth. As she maneuvered, some hot oil dripped from the plate and fell on her fingers, beside old scars. I peered at the seven bright orange yolks.

"I wasn't screaming because of that," said my sister. "Who would steal him from me?"

"The Cricket Man!" I replied.

"Be quiet," my father said.

"Who would steal him from me?" she repeated. Then she took a deep breath, and her nose made a bubbling sound. "The One Up There?"

My sister looked at Dad.

"I screamed because I can't wake up," she added.

The baby cried in the bedroom.

"You see?" she continued, keeping her plastic mask pointing down to the floor. "He's still here. I can't wake up."

My brother's chair shot out from under him when, without warning, he stood up and began to make his way around the table toward my sister. His stomps made little concentric waves in my cup of milk. My father held out an arm to block his path, a waist-high barrier.

"Leave it," he said. My brother grunted. "What did you mean by that?" he asked my sister.

She didn't respond, just sniffed. My father's hand shot from the table to her artificial face. He forced her to look up, grabbing her by the chin. My sister looked at me first. I could see her eyes behind the orthopedic material.

"This is a nightmare," she said.

My grandmother bowed her head. She slid her hand along the table until it rested on my mother's. She squeezed.

"You should have thought it through better," my father said. With a jerk he made my sister look toward the hall. "Whether you like it or not, that thing that's crying is your son."

My sister swallowed. The swollen veins on each side of her neck made it seem thicker. She stayed in that position until my father loosened his grip, and she let her head fall. I didn't think she would say anything else, but then she replied: "Only mine?"

"That's enough," Grandma interrupted.

The hand that Dad had sent flying toward my sister again stopped in midair.

"Join hands."

My grandmother held hers out, one on each side. Mom took her right hand, my sister her left. The rest of us did the same. When we'd formed the circle, Grandma, as she always did, gave thanks.

"We thank the One Up There for allowing us to eat each day."

She kissed the crucifix on the rosary she wore round her neck.

Mom cleared the dishes after breakfast. She tipped one of them into the trash so that a whole egg slid off it. When she took up position by the kitchen sink, I went over to her.

"If you didn't break them"—I pointed at the box of eggs that was still open on the countertop—"could a chick hatch from one of them?"

Mom lowered her gaze, looking for mine.

"A chick?"

She smiled from above, her left eye closing against her will. I hugged her waist, resting my cheek on her belly.

Dad laughed when he heard my question. He was the only one left sitting at the table. He was reading and passing the key that hung from his neck between his fingers. He put down his book, stood up, took an egg from the carton, and went down on one knee. He held the egg between his face and mine with three fingers.

"Let go of your mother." He pulled me away. Then he lifted one of my hands and made me reach out. "Let's see what's inside."

Dad laid the egg in my palm and closed my fingers around it. I was certain I was going to feel the chick's heart beating through the shell. That a crack would open and lots of yellow feathers would appear between my fingers. My father closed his hand around mine. He began to apply pressure. I tried to pull away, but he kept squeezing. I couldn't stop it. The pressure was too much, and the egg cracked open. The sticky liquid seeped out between my fingers and Dad's. He shook it off his hand, splashing me in the face.

"You don't want to bring anyone else into this house," he said. "And anyway, nothing can hatch from the eggs we eat. They're not fertilized."

He disappeared down the hall, dragging his brown slippers along the floor.

Lots of cold slime ran down my palm until the orange clot hit the floor. I stared at it blankly. Mom's nose whistled. She knelt down. I felt the damp cloth on my hand before I saw it. My eyes were fixed on the puddle of shell and death at my feet. Mom wiped my hand, working each finger. The smell of ammonia made me cough.

Her eyes moistened.

"What's wrong?" I asked.

"It's the ammonia," she replied.

"*My* eyes aren't crying."

Mom's shoulders slumped.

"I was remembering something," she said.

"Something from outside?"

She nodded.

I kissed her rough cheek.

"Don't be sad," I said. "The basement's much better than out there."

Her nose whistled. Then she whispered in my ear: "Any place where you are is much better than anywhere else."

My shoulder tickled and I wriggled away.

Mom let the cloth fall onto the floor, cleaned up the remains of the chick that never was, and went back to her work at the kitchen sink. I stood next to her, watching the damp patch that the cloth left behind shrink. Until it disappeared.

On the way to my bedroom, Mom called out my name. She asked me to come over to her. She crouched down in a very similar way to how Dad had done.

"Here." She opened my hand. "Put it away and keep it warm. That's what it needs to hatch."

"And what Dad said?"

"You just keep it warm."

I ran to my room holding the egg in both hands against my bare tummy.

My brother was sitting on his bunk, his feet hanging a yard and a half from the ground. He could spend hours there, his pajama bottoms tucked into his slippers, shaking his head and moving his feet and hands as if he was walking through a cornfield that didn't exist. He would also whistle a tune, though the result wasn't perfect since his bottom lip was split in half because of the fire. For a long time Mom and Dad didn't understand what his trance meant. Then one afternoon, when we couldn't get him to talk or stop smiling at nothing, my sister came into the room. She picked up a book from the shelf. *You read it to him when he was little,* she said, showing *The Wonderful Wizard of Oz* to my parents. *It's as though you've already forgotten we had a life outside,* she added. Since then, every time my brother traveled to that other world, there was only one way to communicate with him.

"Scarecrow, you haven't seen anything," I said. "And ask the Lion and the Tin Man to keep quiet, too."

My brother saw the egg in my hands, but he soon resumed his imperfect whistling.

I picked up a dirty T-shirt from the floor and wrapped the egg in it, in the best imitation of a nest I was able to make. Afterward I put everything in the drawer of the one piece of furniture I didn't share with my brother. The cabinet was at the foot of my bed. It had just two sections. Enough for my cactus, my crayons, and the insect and spy books that Dad gave me on cake days. I perfected the nest beside my jar of crayons.

I sat cross-legged in front of the cabinet and took out *How to Be a Spy Kid*. It was my grandmother and mother who'd taught me to read and write. There was plenty of time for it in the basement. The book contained tricks for children to learn. It taught me how to use lemon juice as invisible ink, writing secret messages that could then be read under a light. The first time I tried the trick I asked Mom to hold the piece of paper near one of the bulbs hanging from the ceiling in the living room. She had squeezed the lemon for me while I explained what I was going to do, following the instructions in the book. She doubted it was going to work, but she took the piece of paper anyway and held it near the glass bubble.

"There's nothing on here," she said, "and there won't be anything however close I hold it to the light."

Then, some brown lines began to appear on the sheet. Mom moved it around so the heat would spread evenly across its surface. New brown stains gradually emerged everywhere I'd applied the lemon juice. Finally, the secret message was visible: I TOLD YOU I WAS A SPY. Mom smiled as she read it. Her nose whistled.

"So you were right," she said.

Sitting now in front of the cabinet with the book on my legs, I was looking for a particular page. I went over the sequences of dots and dashes. With the nail of my forefinger I tapped the shell four times in quick succession. Then twice more, as the book instructed.

I held my ear to the egg.

Not a sound.

"It's Morse code," I told the chick.

I tuned in again to see if there was any reply. There wasn't, so I closed the drawer, leaving it open a slit so I could hear the chick tweeting if it decided to hatch overnight.

I put the book back in the cabinet and picked up the cactus. Two green balls covered in prickles surviving in a little pot. It appeared one day among the pile of things the One Up There sent us. Like the wood that Dad built the baby's crib with. Or the carrots that Mom used to make her soup for dinner. *While this cactus is OK, we'll be OK. We must be strong like a cactus,* my grandmother said when she gave it to me.

I left the bedroom. My brother was still whistling.

I lay facedown in the living room, my chin resting on my hands, one above the other. I positioned the cactus in the patch of light. A little cloud of dust danced among its prickles. As the light traveled along the floor, I pushed the pot with my finger to follow its course and keep the sunbeams on the cactus. If my brother could travel to Oz on a path as mysterious as the depths of his own unfocused gaze, I could imagine I was one of the cowboys from the Westerns that Dad watched.

I spent the whole day on the floor, walking through the desert among cactuses.

4

It was some time before the egg moved. "Keep it warm," Mom had said. And I had kept it warm. Now the creature was ready to be born. What Dad had said about unfertilized eggs must've been a lie.

That evening when I saw the egg in a different position from where I'd left it in the morning, I had to gulp back my urge to scream with excitement, because only Mom and I knew it was there. The fact that my brother had seen me put it in the drawer didn't mean he'd remember it five minutes later. I put my hands to my mouth and looked around, not knowing what to do.

A feeling of paternal responsibility made me act quickly. I carefully picked up the egg and held it to my belly button. The shell was warmer than usual. I felt the chick's heart beating through it. I ran to find Mom to get her to help with the hatching.

There was nobody in the living room. I swiveled around to scan the whole room. There was no one in the bathroom, either, so I went to my parents' room. Their door was metal and it didn't have a handle like the rest of the doors. From outside it could only be opened with a key that Mom and Dad hung from their necks. My father didn't want us to go near his room, but I was so excited by the egg and the chick inside that I banged on the door several times with my forehead to get Mom's attention.

"Go to your room," she shouted from inside.

"Mom, it's important," I said to the crack in the locked door. "It's going to—" Before I finished the sentence I realized Dad would be in there, too, so I swallowed my words. "I need you to come out."

"Not now," she said. "I can't right now."

"Please," I insisted.

I pictured the helpless chick hatching in front of me, and me not knowing what to do. Mom had dealt with my sister giving birth, an emergency, and this was an emergency, too. I pleaded with her with my whole face jammed into the corner of the doorframe. Slobbering on the metal. Dad didn't like it when I cried. And I knew he was about to start shouting at me from in there at any moment.

There was a short silence, then I heard my mother's steps as she came to the door. I suppose she wanted to open it a crack to see what the matter was, not knowing I was pushing against it. As soon as she turned the key, the door gave way under my weight. Mom couldn't hold it. I rolled forward, unable to hold out my arms to stop my fall as I attempted to shield the egg from harm. In a rapid succession of images I saw the ceiling of the room, the washing machine in one corner, the floor, my mother's face, my mother's feet, and a door closing. I ended up lying on my back at the foot of my parents' bed, my hands still held against my belly.

Mom looked me in the face. Then she noticed my hands. The eye that she still controlled opened in an expression of understanding. The folds of burned flesh that surrounded the other one barely moved. Just then she glanced somewhere to the right of the bed.

At Dad. Who would now ask me what I was hiding. And he'd see the egg. And he'd put it in my hand. Wrap it in his. And squeeze. Until the shell broke and a load of slime poured through my fingers. Only now it wouldn't be slime that came from the egg, but a body, with bones and feathers. It wouldn't leave a puddle on the floor that Mom could clean up with ammonia, but would hit the ground with a hollow sound. Because it would be the dead body of the chick I was waiting for, which I still had in my hands, all warm. I closed my eyes waiting to hear Dad's voice.

But it was Mom who spoke.

"Goodness, son, what's the matter? Are you sick?"

I opened my eyes as my mother bent over to take hold of my wrist. When I was up, I turned my head toward the bed.

Dad wasn't there.

Or by the wardrobe on the right-hand wall. Or near the washing machine. He was nowhere in the room. I held out the egg to show my mother.

"No, Mom, it's not me, it's—"

She put a hand over my mouth, and with the other she covered the egg. I tried to speak but instead I just sucked on the skin of her hand. Rough and irregular. It tasted like my cactus pot. Of earth.

She pushed my hands farther down to hide the egg.

"If you're sick, go and tell Grandma. She'll know what to give you. Dad's going to be really angry when he finds out you came in here when the door was locked." She led me back into the hall, keeping her hand on my mouth at all times. "And you know I'm going to have to tell him."

Unable to speak, I motioned with my hands to get my mother's attention. She turned her uneven eyes to the egg for just a second.

"Your grandmother will know what to give you," she repeated.

She pushed me out of the room.

In the hall, she took her hand off my mouth.

"It's the chi—" I started to say, but Mom shut me up again.

"Your grandmother," she said. She tilted her head to signal her room. "Don't go to the living room, your father will be there."

I wrinkled my nose. I'd just been in the living room.

My mother closed the door in my face.

She turned the key.

I opened Grandma's bedroom door by turning the handle with my chin. The egg was throbbing in my hands like a warm heart. Or like a giant saturniid chrysalis, the one where you can see the insect's blood pumping inside.

The light was on in the room. My grandmother was sitting on her bed with her back against the wall, her lifeless eyes on the child, who slept locked in the prison of shadows cast on him by the bars of the crib. In another bed, my sister slept with her sheet up to her forehead. On the bedside table lay the white form of the mask.

"The light's on," I told my grandmother.

She turned her head to me as if she hadn't heard me come in.

"I know. Leave it," she said. "It's for him. And keep your voice down."

She gestured in the direction of the baby's crib.

"What's wrong?" she whispered. "I could hear you running all over the house. Did you go into your father's room?"

"The door opened accidentally," I explained. "But Dad wasn't in there."

I went over to Grandma's bed. She always smelled of talcum powder. Sometimes when she put it on she left white patches on her face or clothes.

"It's going to hatch," I told her.

I took one of her wrinkly hands and made her touch the egg. Since the fire, my grandmother could only see with her fingers.

"It's your egg," she said when she stroked the shell. She lowered her voice even more to add, "Your mother told me about it."

"It's going to hatch," I repeated.

My grandmother frowned. One of her eyebrows had less hair than the other. There were parts of the scar where the hair hadn't grown back again. It had disappeared forever with the fire, like her vision had.

"Hatch? An unfertilized egg?" She lifted her upper lip. "What exactly has your mom said to you?"

"She said to keep it warm. That's how they hatch. Dad killed one and Mom gave me this one. And just now it moved. Look, touch it. The chick's going to come out."

Her face smoothed out as much as the furrows that had been sculpted by the flames and by time allowed.

"Oh, of course, that's right," she said. "Come on, give it here."

She pulled her bed covers down to her knees. I sat in front of her, crossed my legs, gave her the egg, and rested my chin on my interlocked hands. Grandma held the egg against her ear. She put a finger to her lips to signal that I should be quiet.

"I hear it," she said a few seconds later.

She held the egg near my face. I guided her movement to position it against my ear.

"Can you hear it?"

I couldn't hear anything.

"Can you hear it chirping?" she insisted.

Then I heard it. Chirping. A very faint tweeting, through the shell.

"Yes, yes, I can hear it!" I cried.

My grandmother shushed me.

"It's about to hatch," I added under my breath.

My grandmother nodded. She put the egg under her pillow.

"Now you have to close your eyes," she said.

"Close my eyes?"

"They don't hatch if they know someone's looking."

She put the palms of her hands on my eyelids. For a moment we sat in complete silence.

"It's here," she said.

She removed her hands but turned to the pillow in such a way that, for a few seconds, I couldn't see what she was doing anymore. When she turned back she had her hands cupped.

"See it?" she asked.

I examined her hands with surprise. They appeared empty.

"Can't you see it?" she insisted.

At first I didn't see anything.

"Look," she added, "it's here."

Then I saw it. A bright yellow chick. Feathers like cotton. And chirping so loudly I thought it would wake up the baby.

My grandmother smiled at me as she cradled the chick. Then she put it on her shoulder. The chick perched there, picking at locks of white hair, as if its first meal was in among them. My grandmother laughed and shrugged her shoulders. It was tickling her.

"See it?" she asked.

I nodded, speechless with excitement.

"See it?" she repeated, unable to see my head move.

"Of course," I now said, so she could hear me. "It's just as I imagined it would be. All yellow."

My grandmother took the chick from her shoulder in one hand. The bird's head poked out between her fingers, looking all around. It wouldn't stop tweeting.

"Hold out your hands properly," she said.

I did, and moved them toward hers until I brushed against them. The chick leapt. I felt its claws dig into my palms and its down brush my fingers. I held it to my face.

"I've been waiting for you for two rows," I told it. In the basement there was a calendar stuck to a wall in the main room, near the bike. The boxes were the days, the rows were weeks. When all the boxes had crosses in them, Dad tore off the sheet. And that was a month. The whole calendar wasn't changed very often, but when it was, a year had gone by. Years also went by when we made a cake for one of us.

My family looked at the calendar often. To me all that mattered was whether it was day or night, and for that I had the patch of sun. "I saved you from being fried in the pan," I added.

My grandmother laughed.

That was when my father shouted.

He shouted my name.

My grandma's bedroom door burst open. So hard the handle hit the wall and dented it.

I stood up with my hands behind my back, hiding the chick.

I saw one of my sister's arms come out from under the sheets. She grabbed hold of the mask and put it on with barely a movement.

The baby began to cry.

"Did you go into my room when the door was locked?" Dad asked.

"It was an accident."

I looked at Grandma as if she could back up my story, but she said nothing.

"Come here," my father said.

I hesitated.

"Now!"

I walked forward until I stood in front of him.

"What have you got behind you?" he asked.

"Nothing."

I could still feel the chick's claws and feathers between my fingers.

"What do you mean, 'nothing'?" said Dad.

Before I could react, he grabbed me by a shoulder. His hand went down my arm like an aphid toward the elbow. And then to my wrist, behind my back. When he got hold of my hand, he forced me to show it to him.

I closed my eyes, as though it would make the chick disappear.

But the hand was empty.

"Show me the other one," he ordered. "Come on."

Slowly I held out my other hand. There was nothing there, either.

Not a trace of the chick.

I was as surprised as my father.

"Explain to me why you went into my room," he said. He put his open hand on my forehead. "Your mother says you're sick."

I didn't know what to say.

I observed Dad's hair scar. His nostrils opened and closed in time with his noisy breathing.

"Are you?" he asked. "Are you sick?"

I remained silent. All I could think about was where the chick had gone.

"It's nothing," my grandmother cut in. "He's got a bit of fever, but not much. We won't need anything."

My father touched my forehead again.

"I'm going to explain to you now what a lock is," he said.

He grabbed my neck, his hand like pincers. If he had wanted, he could have closed them completely.

"Hey," said my grandmother.

My father looked at her, and I was able to do the same when he released his grip on my neck a little.

"There's not long left on that lightbulb," she said. "A few days ago I heard an electrical buzzing sound."

When Dad looked up at the ceiling where the glass body hung, my grandmother stroked her pillow so I could see it. Just where she had put the egg earlier. I understood right away.

"Thanks, Grandma," I said.

She smiled and stopped stroking the material.

"I don't know when we'll be able to change it," my father said.

"Maybe it will last a bit longer," she replied.

The pincers closed around my neck again, but I didn't care. The chick was OK and it was going to sleep with my grandmother. Smelling her talcum powder.

5

That night I was woken by a scream.

"He's choking!"

I sat up in bed. For a few seconds, I wondered whether I'd really heard something or I was having a nightmare.

"He's choking!"

The cry reached me again from the other side of the hall. The springs on my brother's bed squeaked above my head. His weight fell to the floor. The bunk frame shook. When my brother opened the door, the light from outside painted a yellow trapezoid on the floor, the longest side of the shape lighting up the exact width of my bed.

I could barely see and my eyes were sore, but two silhouettes, of my father and of my mother, joined my brother's in an improvised procession that traveled left, to where my grandmother's screaming came from.

"He's choking," the voice repeated.

It was my chick that was choking. Grandma had hidden it under her pillow and must've fallen asleep on it, squashing the newly born bird, which now couldn't breathe.

I ran over the trapezoid of light toward the door. It didn't matter if my father knew my little secret anymore. I met him in the hall, shepherding my grandmother with his hands on his hips.

"Get out of the way," he said to me.

She was carrying my nephew in her arms. But not like she normally did. She had him lying on her left arm, his head in her hand and his feet at her elbow, facing downward. With her right hand, she was slapping him on the back. It was him who was choking.

"Is he breathing?" my mother asked. She and my brother were behind Dad. They disappeared into the living room. I took the chance to search my grandmother's bed. I wanted to get the chick. Take it to its drawer. Let it grow in peace in its T-shirt nest, beside the cactus. But when I lifted the pillow I saw the eggshell. Broken. Beside it, a yellowish mark. I touched it. It was moist.

"What's that smell?" my sister asked.

She was sitting on her bed, staring at the wall. Her voice came from behind the mask, toneless. "I don't know," I replied. I felt the sticky moisture, took one of the shell pieces and dropped the pillow.

"Is the baby all right?" asked my sister, reeling off the question as if it were a single word.

"I'll go see." Before leaving the room, I stopped under the doorframe. I asked if she was coming.

"Not right now," she answered.

I went into the living room and perched on the brown sofa. Grandma was on a chair by the second window, the one at the top of one of the walls. She had the baby in the same position as before. He was making little gurgling sounds that became less and less frequent. At first they were constant, almost at normal breathing speed, but the intervals got longer and longer as my mother's erratic pacing around the chair accelerated. She was biting her thumbnail.

My brother covered his mouth to hide his laughter.

Dad approached the baby while fiddling nervously with the key hung from his neck. He let go and smacked the little boy so hard that Grandma had to raise her arm to keep him from falling off. "Not like that," she protested.

Still, after the heavy blow the gurgling ended. The baby's nose bubbled when air entered his body again. My mother interrupted her frantic pacing. My brother began to march up and down the room, lifting his knees with each step, swinging his arms. He whistled his song all the way to the table.

"Not now!" Mom shouted at him. The melody broke off. The ground stopped trembling. My brother made a scraping sound in his throat like he always did before one of his crying fits.

"Cry all you like," she said.

My brother ran out into the hall. When he slammed the door the living room lightbulb swung. The shadow from my head stretched until it melded with the chair's. There, my grandmother turned the baby around. His face was dark red now. She hunched her back to listen more closely.

The muffled gurgling continued.

"He's not breathing," said my grandmother. She shot to her feet. The chair balanced on two legs, the back resting on the wall. Grandma bit her lips, her lopsided eyebrows creased above eyes that struggled not to cry. She paced through the room's half-light, rocking the little boy, and sang to him like she did on any other day when it was time for his nap. Then Grandma forced open the baby's mouth and stuck two fingers inside. They disappeared up to the knuckles. When she took them out they shone with dribble.

"I don't know what else to do," she whispered. Then she shouted it. "I don't know what else to do!"

She turned the little boy around. Then tipped him over. She slapped his back again and again. She shook him.

The baby was almost blue.

"I don't know what else to do!" The light from the bulb reflected in the moisture around her eyes.

"We have to get him out of here," my mother said. "He's going to—"

"We won't get there in time," Dad cut in.

I looked toward the door that was on the other side of the room, near the table. The one that had always been unlocked. The one I'd approached for the first time many calendars ago, on the night when my family had been five years in the basement. When my hand slipped on the knob because of my own saliva, I'd grasped it again. But I hadn't found a reason to turn it. I didn't even try. In the basement there was my mother. And my grandmother, sister, and brother. And Dad. That night I went back to his lap, and we ate carrot soup as I swung my legs in those pajamas, the ones that have feet.

"We won't get there in time?" Grandma's sobbing became anger. And all of a sudden her eyes seemed dry. "Let's find out."

She rested the little boy against her chest, still slapping his back. She rounded the sofa, but instead of heading toward the door that was always unlocked, she walked out into the hall.

I leapt off the sofa, my feet sinking into the cushion as I propelled myself forward, excited it was me who'd come up with the final solution to the problem. I grabbed my grandmother by the elbow to stop her.

"Grandma, the door's there," I said as I ran across the room. "Come on, we can get out through here."

She raised her eyebrows halfway up her forehead when she understood. My father took a step forward with an arm outstretched as if he could pick me up just by thinking about it.

I clasped the doorknob.

And I turned it.

Or I tried.

Three times.

Dad lowered his arm. He stared at me for a few seconds. Then he spoke to Grandma. "And you're not going anywhere, either."

"I'm not going to let this child suffocate," she replied. Ignoring Dad's orders, she began walking toward the bedrooms again. He followed her, driving his heels into the floor.

"You don't even have a key to that door," he shouted at her. "Or the one up top."

At that moment the baby produced a long gurgle that ended in a cough.

He started to cry.

And to breathe.

My father stopped dead. From the constant volume of the baby's crying, I figured Grandma had stopped, too.

Mom ran into the hall.

I was still gripping the doorknob. Dad had lied to me. That door had never been unlocked.

It was just another wall.

The last wall.

There was a lot of movement in the hall and bedrooms. And in the bathroom. When Dad got back to the living room he found me still holding the doorknob. I noticed a blink of surprise. "Go to your room," he said. "Go on."

He switched off the light, leaving me in total darkness.

I heard the door to his bedroom close.

I let go of the knob, now warm, while the shapes in the room formed around me. I made for the hall, successfully negotiating all the obstacles. Before going to my room, I paid Grandma a visit.

First I went up to the crib to check the baby's breathing. It sounded so easy, so healthy, it was as if the choking had never happened. Then I went up to my grandmother. I shook her by what I thought was her shoulder under the blanket. She groaned. I jiggled her again. An almost undetectable trembling told me she had woken up.

But she didn't speak.

I shook her again.

My grandmother touched me at chest height. "Oh, it's you," she said, recognizing me by my feel. "What is it?" she asked. She moved under the covers and spoke louder. "Is it the baby again?"

"No," I said. "The baby's fine."

She breathed out. A bitter smell reached me along with the talcum powder. "Where's the chick?" I whispered.

I waited for her answer.

"The chick. Where is it?"

"So it was you who moved my pillow?" she asked.

"Yeah. Earlier. When the baby—"

"And what did you see?"

"I didn't see the chick."

"But, what did you see?"

"I saw the shell. And a yellow mark. Like the egg that Dad broke. Where's the chick?"

"It escaped," she quickly answered. "When your father came I took it from your hand. I hid it under the pillow."

"That's what you told me."

"But when Dad took you to your room, it escaped. It ran across the bed." She gestured with her hand. "And it went to the kitchen. It must have flown out of the window there."

"There's nothing on the other side of the windows. Just more concrete."

"There is for a bird," she said. "The chick was very small, it could fit through any crack. I bet you it managed to get out somehow."

I considered it.

"Is the chick OK?" I asked. I imagined it alone in that world made of blisters.

"Oh, yes." She rested a hand on my face, warming my cheek. "I'm sure it's fine. It'll be better off out there than in your—" She didn't finish the sentence.

"If I wanted to, could I go look for it?" I asked. I thought about the door in the kitchen. About the useless movement of my hand, unable to turn the knob. If I'd tried to open a wall with a knob drawn on paper nothing different would've happened.

"But then you wouldn't see me anymore," she responded. "Or your mother. Or Dad. Or the baby. Is that what you want?"

I shook my head.

"Well? Is that what you want?" she asked. She couldn't see me.

"No."

"No, of course it's not." She put her hand around my neck to pull me closer to her. Then pushed my face into some warm place between her chest and shoulder. I kissed the air. "Now get back to your room," she whispered.

"I've kept a piece of shell in case the chick comes back. So it knows where its house is."

My grandmother's chest rose. "You're such a nice boy," she said. I nodded in the warm place where my face was, smelling the talcum powder. "Now go to bed," she added. "Get some more sleep."

It was an incredible power that my grandmother gave me that night.

On the way back to my bedroom, in the hall, a gentle draft came in through the window. I put my face between the bars, closed my eyes, and breathed in, letting that different smell that came from outside envelop me. It was different from anything there was in the basement. But a bitter note ruined the moment, because the outside had just become somewhere I couldn't go even if I wanted to. The door in the kitchen was locked.

I felt another waft of air on my face.

And it brought with it the first firefly.

It flew in front of my eyes.

Then it settled on the surface that stretched from the window to the other wall, at the height of my neck. When it landed, it hid the wings that it'd used to slow its descent under its shell. Really, coleopterans' shells are just another pair of wings, hardened to protect the ones they use to fly. The insect walked toward the bars over the gravel that had built up in the space. Toward me.

And that was when it lit up.

For a second, the body of the dark bug was illuminated with a magical green light that glowed from the end of its abdomen. Just like in my insect book, the one I kept at the foot of my bed. The first time I turned the pages of the book I was fascinated by the long legs of the mantises, the perfect camouflage of the stick insects, the colors of the butterflies. But it was the firefly's glow that totally captivated me. An insect that makes light. Like the bulbs that hung bare from the ceiling in the basement. But living.

There was another flash, identical to the one in the photograph in my book, which showed a firefly perching on a blade of grass. Now I held out a finger in front of it, on the gravel, blocking its path. The firefly climbed onto it, keeping its balance by fluttering its wings.

I kept my eyes open so I wouldn't miss the next flash. When it lit up again, I had to blink a few times to moisten them.

I returned to my bedroom with my forefinger held out in front of my face, the firefly on the tip. My brother was snoring. I opened my drawer. First I put the piece of shell that I'd rescued from Grandma's bed in the T-shirt nest.

"In case you come back," I said to the chick that wasn't there.

Then I found the big jar where I kept my colored pencils. I tipped them out into the drawer, then put the firefly inside the empty container. It tried to find something to grip on to in its new world of transparent boundaries, but it slid down the glass. I put a pencil in the jar so the insect had somewhere to perch. It thanked me with a cold green flicker. There's no creature more amazing than one that can make its own light.

6

Naked, wearing only a towel around my waist, I went into the bathroom. It was a big room with tiles on the floor. They were on the walls, too, but just halfway up. Above that, it was just concrete.

I found my sister sitting on the edge of the bath in her underwear, her legs inside. The water bubbled as it filled the tub. In the basement it didn't get hot enough to make steam.

My sister undid her bra. She let it fall onto the pile of clothes on the floor. She stood up, pulled down her underpants, and took them off one foot at a time. She got them wet with the water that slid off her toes. I discovered yellow areas on her skin, bruises about to disappear, the ones she got hitting the table the day the baby was born.

From my position at the door, I could see the water level rising. It almost reached my sister's knees. The smell of soap filled the room.

She turned the water off.

Her hand spread over the mask. With the other she stretched the black rubber strap that ran across the back of her head. "I'm here," I said.

She lifted her shoulders. "Have you finished on the bike?"

"Yeah."

We all had to go on the bike three times a week. Dad had positioned it in a corner of the living room, near the calendar. It was blue and white. It never moved, no matter how much you pedaled. When it was my turn to go on it, I'd ask Mom to put a movie on the TV so I could imagine that I was cycling through the landscapes on the screen.

My sister tilted her head without letting go of the mask. The tip of an ear emerged from her black hair. "How long have you been standing there?" she asked.

"I just arrived," I lied. "It's Mom's turn now."

"Are you going to take a bath?"

"Do you mind?"

My sister sighed, letting her shoulders drop. She let go of the strap on the mask so that it tightened against her head. Then she pushed off, her hands to the side of each hip, to submerge herself in the water. She hiccupped when her chest went under. Once in, she tipped her head back to wet her hair. She ended up sitting at one end of the bathtub, her head resting against the wall.

"Come on," she said. "You can get in."

I closed the bathroom door, left my towel on the sink, and got in the water at the opposite end from my sister. I sat with my legs slotted between hers, which were open and bent. I bent mine, too, so I wouldn't touch anything with my feet.

"Smart-ass, you've left me the end with the plug," I said.

My sister laughed behind her mask. It was strange to hear her laugh. She passed me the shampoo so I could wash my hair. After using it, I gave it back.

"What are you going to do?" I asked.

"The same as you. Wash my hair," she answered. "And my face."

"OK," I said. I closed my eyes tight and added, "Ready."

My sister clicked her tongue. I heard her stretch the strap as she took off the mask, and the bottle spitting soap out onto her hands, then the sound of her rubbing the shampoo into her hair, and the water splashing her face.

"Done?" I asked after a while. She didn't answer. "Done?" I said again.

After a few seconds' silence, she answered, "Do you really not dare look?"

I covered my eyes with both hands. The bubbles in the bath crackled, floating on the water or sticking to my body. I shook my head.

"Come on," she said. "Think how Mom and Dad's faces are. Mine can't be much worse."

"You don't have a nose," I replied. "I don't want to see your hole."

She grabbed one of my wrists.

"Look at me," she said. "I know you want to." She took my other wrist as well. A tide was set off in the bathwater with our movement. The plug scraped my backside. And one of my big toes brushed against the hair between her legs.

She pulled my wrists in opposite directions. "Look at me," she said again.

When she managed to part my hands from my face, I clamped my eyelids together. So tightly that I saw colored dots floating around me. I moaned. I tried to get out of the water, but my sister grabbed hold of my knees and pushed me back down. The plug stuck into one of my cheeks again.

My sister tried to part my eyelids. I managed to resist by squeezing them shut with all my might. They hurt. Then she used both hands to try to wrench open one eye. She used her ten adult fingers to separate a boy's eyelids.

"Look at me, look at me, look at me . . ." Her voice grated in her throat.

A slit of light began to seep in through that eye. Then I could make out some colors and also started to distinguish shapes.

That was when the bathroom door opened.

"What— What are you—?" It was my mother shouting.

My sister's fingers vanished. The bathroom door slammed closed. Mom approached the bathtub and put her hand over my eyes. I instinctively blinked to relax my eyelids.

"You're lucky it wasn't your father who came into the bathroom," Mom said, spitting the words through clenched teeth. "Out of the tub. Come on, go."

My sister's legs separated from mine. The water level fell. I felt it go down on my chest. I heard the water dripping from her body as she stood.

Something touched my chest, at the same height as the water level. When I held out my hand to feel it, a shock of terror sparked at the base of my back. It was my sister's nose. A floating plastic nose pointing up to the ceiling.

"And take this with you," Mom said. There was a dripping noise in the place where the mask was floating. "None of us want to see your face."

I heard the strap tighten against my sister's head. It sounded different on wet hair.

"Suit yourselves," she replied before leaving the bathroom.

Mom stayed with me until I got out of the water. Kneeling on the floor, she wrapped me in the towel. She hugged me with the material, kissing my neck. It tickled.

"What's her face like?"

She dried my eyes with the corners of the towel. They still throbbed from the effort I'd made to keep them shut.

"Why do you want to know?" she asked.

I remained silent.

"You don't," my mother said. "You don't need to know. Your sister has always worn that mask in this house. It's your father's decision."

"Did she wear it when you lived outside?" I asked.

"You know she didn't," answered Mom. "She wears it because of what happened. The fire." When she said that, my mother's ragged gaze clouded over. Her nose whistled. Then she blinked, one eye closing just before the other one did, and returned from wherever it was she'd gone.

44

"The fire didn't affect me," I said.

"Of course it didn't," she replied while stroking my hair. "Because you were in my tummy. You were a surprise."

"What was it like, living outside?" I asked.

"Why so many questions all of a sudden?" she asked back. "You have everything anyone else has. A home to live in. And a family. The people who live outside don't have much more than that, you know."

I thought about the smell of the breeze that sometimes came in through the window in the hall.

"Why did Dad lie to me about the door in the kitchen?"

Mom let go of the towel. She looked at me for a few seconds with her arms crossed.

"Little boys are always told stories. You don't think the Cricket Man really exists, do you?"

"Shh," I whispered. "He can hear you. I don't want him to find me."

Mom dried my ears.

"And how is it you remember that night so well? You were no bigger than this," she said as she drew a small space in the air with two fingers. "That's how little you were."

I shrugged, pushing out my bottom lip. It made her smile.

"Because you're a very clever boy," she said, answering her own question. She stroked my whole face with the palm of a wrinkly hand. "And that's why you know you wouldn't go anywhere even if that door was open. Where would you go?" Mom hugged me again through the soft fabric of the towel. "Where do you want to go?" she persisted. She looked at me with her droopy eye and uneven smile.

"Nowhere," I answered.

Dressed only in my underpants, I went to the kitchen. I could hear the carrot soup bubbling on the stove. I also heard my family talking before I arrived.

"We're running out of everything," Mom said.

A utensil clinked against something metal.

"He was supposed to have come yesterday," Grandma replied.

When I walked in, I saw my mother standing on tiptoes to reach the top of one of the kitchen cupboards. In addition to the two hot plates, the kitchen had a sink, an oven, a fridge, and lots of cupboards and drawers. They were all open.

"There's nothing here," Mom said, her arm inside the upper cupboard, as if she hoped to find something that was out of sight at the back. "All we have is what's on the table."

She lowered her heels and turned around, then she saw me.

"Dinnertime. We're all here now," she said.

She approached the table, touched my grandmother's shoulder, and gestured with her mouth to Dad. They were all sitting there, under the cone of light that the bulb projected onto the table. I saw the strap on my sister's mask tight against her hair, which was still wet. Grandma and Mom tidied away some packets of rice stacked on the table. As well as cans of tuna, and eggs and potatoes. They put them in the cupboards where they were kept, which were emptier than they usually were.

"About time you showed up," my father said. "Why do you spend so long at that window? Do you want to leave or something?"

"I wasn't at the window," I answered.

"And he doesn't want to leave, either," added Mom.

"He hides things in his drawer," my brother blurted out.

"Really? What is it you hide there?" Dad asked.

My brother wanted to say something else. Before he could, the hot pan of carrot soup appeared on the table.

"Let's eat," Mom said.

She served our dinner with a ladle, filling the bowls that my grandmother had arranged on the table. She also served a seventh bowl. The one nobody would touch. And which, as ever, would end up in the trash or down the plughole.

7

The second firefly arrived that night.

Lying in bed awake, I listened to the lines in the movie my family was watching in the living room. Dad's favorite. He'd put it on so many times that I knew every word by heart, every pause, every gunshot.

I whispered the words into the darkness.

In the basement we had a television, but no antenna and no signal. There were lots of tapes on the big bookshelf in the living room, which we watched on a video recorder that had the word *Betamax* printed on one side. Dad liked cowboy movies.

Just like the cowboy would be doing on the screen, I pulled a hand out from underneath the covers, imitated a pistol with my fingers, and fired some imaginary bullets into the darkness. Just then, the baby began crying.

As if the bullets had reached his crib.

I heard my mother's footsteps in the hall. Behind her, my grandmother's. Since the night he almost suffocated, every time the boy cried they ran to his crib, scared they'd find him turned blue.

I opened my bedroom door to see what was happening. The TV screen flickered light into the hall. I pictured Dad in his striped armchair. My brother sitting on the brown sofa, laughing when he wasn't supposed to at a violent scene, or frowning, not fully understanding what was happening behind that window of images. My sister sat on the floor, using the sofa as a backrest, her legs crossed and her interlinked hands resting on her stomach, watching the TV like someone staring at an aquarium.

"Shut that baby up!" Dad shouted from the living room. He made himself heard over the noise of the gunfire and my nephew's inconsolable crying.

I crossed the hall in the direction of his room. Something hurt my foot. It was a little screw from Dad's toolbox. I thought it'd stuck into me, but it fell away by itself, rolling along the hall floor.

As soon as I walked into the room I smelled Grandma's talcum powder. By the crib, my mother was rocking the little boy in her arms. Seeing me, she held a finger to her mouth so that I wouldn't make any noise. When there was more light from the screen because an especially bright image in the film had come on, a pan shot of a sunny day in the mountains, for instance, I could make out her features. But when the screen went dark with a close-up of a cowboy's dirty face, she wasn't more than a black shape in front of me.

I felt my way up my mother's body, over her stretched T-shirt, to the baby.

"Easy now," I whispered.

Mom sighed. My grandmother put her arms around me, resting her hands on my bare chest.

That was when I saw it.

A spot of green light floating in the hall. A few flashes left a trail from the ceiling to the floor. I pushed Grandma's hands away so I could go find it.

"Hang on," my mother said. I thought she was talking to me, that she'd seen the firefly, too, but then she switched on the bedroom light and the insect's green flicker disappeared.

Dazzled, my eyes stung.

The baby stopped crying.

Mom hit the switch once more.

In the dark, the baby started crying again.

When my mother turned the light on for a second time, it was as I guessed.

"Same as him," Mom said, pointing at me with her chin. "It's the dark that makes him cry."

"Same as me?" I asked.

My mother passed the baby to Grandma. Then she sat me on the bed.

"When you were little you were frightened of the dark," she explained. "The first few nights, you wouldn't stop crying until someone turned on a light."

"But I'm not scared of it anymore."

Mom smiled and an eye closed. "Of course you're not."

"And how did I stop being afraid?"

"Like all fears are overcome," she answered. She stood and went to the door, then held a finger over the switch and added, "By facing up to it."

She turned off the light.

The baby cried.

Grandma shushed him over his crying while my eyes readjusted to the absence of light. I looked toward the hall, but the firefly was gone.

"Are you going to let him cry?" I asked.

My nephew screamed with all his might, grating his throat. The two dark shapes that were my mother and grandmother approached the crib. One of the figures shortened. It was Grandma bending to put the baby down inside.

"It's all we can do," she replied.

"Anyway," added Mom, "the dark isn't so bad."

The baby was crying louder and louder.

Dad's voice came from the hall. "Shut him up, please!"

I approached the crib and peered in. My grandmother, or my mother, was rocking the frame to lull the baby to sleep.

"Don't be afraid," I whispered. "The dark isn't so bad."

Mom's nose whistled as she heard me repeat her words.

But the baby kept crying.

My father's armchair scraped along the living room floor. The changes in light on the television screen marked out his silhouette in the doorway. In the movie someone was playing a harmonica.

"What's wrong with the child?"

"It's the dark," my mother answered.

Dad turned on the light. I closed my eyes in time.

"And what's he doing here?" he asked. I knew he was referring to me. "You, what are you doing here?"

"I couldn't sleep. I wanted to see what was happening."

Dad hit the light switch twice, seeing that the baby was quiet when it was on and cried when it was off. He left it on.

"Then we'll leave it."

"We have to turn it off," said Mom.

"Do you want us to leave the light on all night?" Grandma said. "How's your daughter going to sleep? She has to sleep in this room, too."

"And anyway, the baby has to get used to the dark," my mother added. Dad sighed. He flipped the switch again.

We were left in darkness.

The baby began to cry again.

"You, go to bed," he ordered me. "You know what the Cricket Man does to boys who misbehave."

Before letting go of the crib, I whispered to the baby, "Don't worry, I have an idea."

My father waited for me to go out in front of him. Then he went back to the living room. The striped armchair scraped along the floor as he turned up the volume on the television.

I walked down the hall with my eyes scanning it for the new firefly. I stepped on the screw again. Next to my foot the insect's greenish light came on. It flew to the jar as if visiting a relative in an entomological jail, the two of them communicating with light signals from each side of the glass. I opened the lid to usher it in there. Both fireflies accompanied the action with flashes of green light.

I smiled when I thought of my nephew, who I could still hear crying.

"Hang on," I whispered. I got back in bed, impatient. I parroted the lines from the movie that my father never tired of watching, my brother never fully understood, and my sister probably hated. Until the same old music had ended. The saddest melody ever sung. That woman's voice filled the basement with a much deeper darkness than the mere absence of light.

My brother came into our bedroom and climbed onto his bunk. The springs squeaked under his weight when he lay down. Then they squeaked again, rhythmically, for a few minutes. First slow, then faster. Faster and faster. Until my brother groaned. And the springs stopped squeaking.

Soon he was snoring.

I waited a while longer, to make sure everyone was sleeping. When I couldn't hear anything except the cistern's dripping and the baby crying, I got out of bed and picked up the firefly jar.

In my sister's room I could hear my grandmother's slow breathing.

I leaned into the crib.

"Give him light," I whispered to the fireflies. "He's still scared of the dark."

I positioned the jar beside him and covered both of them in the sheet. Two green flashes illuminated his face.

Before I left the room, the baby stopped crying.

8

The next morning, I sat up with a start in bed as I remembered the jar with the two fireflies. There was already a lot of noise in the house. The toaster went off a few times in the kitchen, the chairs scraped the floor around the dining table, and the cistern filled in the bathroom.

I arrived in my grandmother's room dressed in the same underpants as the night before. I bent over the crib, but it was empty. No trace of the baby or my jar. I lifted the sheet I'd covered them with. Nothing.

Mom called my name from the kitchen, the smell of toast in the air. First I went to the bathroom to wet my face and hair. It was always on end when I woke up.

"Come on, sit down," Mom said when she saw me, getting the butter out of the fridge. "We're having breakfast now. See what happens when you stay up so late? Then you don't wake up."

My brother was waiting with cutlery at the ready for my mother to serve breakfast. He pointed at the chair next to him with his knife, then made a face that lowered his scarred bottom lip to reveal his gums. I sat down. In front of me, Grandma was smiling at nothing. She drank coffee with the tip of her finger in the cup to check the level. To her left, my sister breast-fed the baby. Dad stared at him.

"He slept in the end," he said.

My sister turned her mask toward Dad. When she found him looking at where the baby was suckling, she covered the visible part of her nipple with her hand. Dad frowned.

"See?" my mother said from the toaster. "He just needs to get used to the dark."

My sister looked at me without turning her head.

"Or not," she said.

I thought I could see a smile on her lips. I thought about the jar with the fireflies.

"What do you mean by that?" Dad cut in.

"Nothing," she answered.

"No, tell me, what did you mean by that?"

Grandma stopped smiling. My brother contained one of his heehaws.

"I didn't mean anything by it," she insisted from behind the mask, still looking at me.

"What did you mean?" Dad said again.

The baby cried when the nipple escaped its mouth. My sister pinched it with two fingers to offer it to him again.

"I meant that it can't be all that good for these children to get used to the dark," she said, gesturing at the baby and me with slight movements of her head. "These boys need sunlight."

"We take all the vitamin D we need," my mother reasoned from the kitchen.

"But they need air," continued my sister. "They need life. They need—" She took a deep breath as if she was about to say something important, but closed her mouth and fell silent.

"What do they need?" Dad prompted her. "Say it. What is it they need?"

My sister fixed her eyes on my father's.

"I've said what I wanted to say."

"Are you sure?" he asked. "I don't think you finished your sentence. Go on, I dare you to say what these boys need again."

My sister helped the baby in his wrestling with her breast.

"Come on," Dad persisted. "I dare you. They need air. They need sun." My sister's lips tightened behind the mask.

"Go on!" my father shouted.

My sister straightened her back. The baby began crying again when he lost the nipple. She put her breast back in her blouse and buttoned it up.

"What this child needs more than anything is a father," she said.

With care, she laid the baby on his back on the table.

In front of Dad.

The blow he dealt the wood with his fist made all the plates and forks jump. The baby waggled arms and legs. Grandma found him, guided by the sound of his crying. Mom took her cup in both hands as if it were about to fly off the table. Dad's fist opened and closed three times. His knucklebones crunched the first two times. He blew out as he shook his head.

After punching the table again, he stood up and left without saying another word. During the short walk to the hall, he stared at my sister. The metal door to his bedroom closed behind him.

Mom began passing out the toast. She served everyone except my sister.

"And me?" she asked.

"The last slice is over there." She indicated the kitchen. "The toaster's in the cupboard."

Sitting on the floor with my legs crossed, I pushed the cactus along with my finger to follow the sun's trajectory.

"Here, vitamin D."

I remembered what my sister had said that morning and formed a bowl with both hands, holding it under the shaft of light, in case the pills that Mom gave me weren't enough. I turned them over under the sun and then lay down. With my eyes at floor level I scanned the main room of our home. I looked under the dining table. Under the cupboards and fridge in the kitchen. Mom was washing some clothes in the sink. There was a washing machine in the basement, but she preferred to do the laundry by hand. She said it was good exercise. Then she'd hang the clothes out in her bedroom, by the washing machine she never used. I also looked around the bike. And under the brown sofa and Dad's striped armchair. And under the cabinet the television sat on, and the shelves filled with tapes and books. My jar was nowhere to be seen.

First the chick had escaped.

And now the fireflies were escaping.

"At least I know you won't go anywhere," I said to the cactus. When I sighed I smelled the detergent Mom used. It was one of my favorite smells in the basement.

Dad came back into the living room for the first time that day since the incident at breakfast. He'd even skipped lunch. He walked up to my mother at the sink.

"He still hasn't come," he said to her. "And we're out of eggs. We knew this could happen one day, but not—"

"The boy's here," my mother interrupted. "Look, there, on the floor. With the cactus."

Dad turned around. "You're like a ghost," he said. "You're always so quiet."

I went up on my knees.

"Leave it," whispered my mother.

"Come on, get out. I need to speak to your mother."

I showed him the pot with the cactus.

"And?" he said after glancing at it. "That plant's had more light than it could ever need."

I left the living room. My parents waited until I was far enough away before carrying on with their conversation. Before I could open my bedroom door, a hand grabbed me. It was my sister. Her pretend face rested on my shoulder from behind.

"Come with me," she whispered.

She pulled me to her bedroom. The baby was sleeping in the crib. Grandma was on her knees, by the bed, with her forearms resting on the mattress. The rosary danced in her fingers, the beads advancing with their familiar rattle. She murmured her prayer with her eyes closed, an indecipherable cooing. My sister held a finger over the hole in her mask where her mouth was. We continued to her bed. I could see a shape under the covers. She pulled them off, revealing what was under them.

It was my firefly jar.

I breathed in, about to say something, but my sister silenced me again. Grandma opened her eyes, still saying over and over the name of the One Up There. My sister and I kept still. The rosary beads continued to chink together and against my grandmother's fingernails. We tiptoed back to the door, accompanied by the hum of her prayer. Just before we left the room, Grandma said, "Close the door on your way out." My sister did so. In the hall I looked toward the main room. My parents were still talking in low voices by the sink. My sister gave me a slap on the backside and pointed to the bathroom.

When we were in, she squatted down, pushing the door with her back to close it. She rested the jar on one knee.

"What's this?" she asked.

I looked at the jar.

"What the hell is this?" she repeated. "And what was it doing in the baby's crib?"

I bent to put the cactus on the floor. Then I tried to take the jar. My sister snatched it away from me, holding it high above her head.

"Why did you put this in the baby's crib?"

I didn't respond.

"Do you want me to call Dad and tell him? So *he* can ask you why you did it?" She turned her face so that her mouth was nearer the door, still staring at me. She gave me a few more seconds before shouting, "Da—!"

I covered her mouth with both hands, touching the orthopedic material of her mask. She stuck out her tongue and I felt a moist slug between my fingers. It made me take my hands away.

"What is this?" she asked again. "Tell me. It'll be our little secret. You know this is dangerous for such a tiny baby, right?" She shook the jar. The pencil knocked against the container's transparent walls.

"Careful," I said. "You'll hurt them."

My sister studied the jar. "I asked whether you know how dangerous this is for a baby as tiny as that one is."

I hung my head, ashamed. I hadn't thought of that.

"Don't get like that now," my sister said. "Look at me. You've put the baby's life in danger."

My lips wrinkled up.

"Don't cry. As long as no one finds out, it doesn't matter. And if you behave yourself, nobody has to find out. It'll be our little secret."

"I won't do it again," I said.

She laughed, then pushed the jar against my chest and let go of it without warning. I managed to catch it before it fell onto the floor. My sister opened the bathroom door and disappeared. One of the fireflies flashed green. The other responded right after it.

I felt the back of my hand burning. Perhaps I'd held it under the sun too long. I discovered a red mark on my white skin. So white that I thought maybe Dad was right.

Maybe I was a ghost.

I climbed onto my chair at dinnertime.

"Is this all we're having?" I asked.

I combed the mashed potato with my fork and rummaged through the heap of peas. A couple of them fell onto the floor. I waited, shoulders hunched, for Dad to tell me off.

"Eat," he said.

I didn't argue.

"Eat this as well," he then ordered. He pointed with his knife at the potato skins that he'd set aside on his plate.

"We've never eaten mashed potato like this."

Mom's nose whistled.

"Well, it's much tastier this way," she said.

She searched for some scraps of skin in her potato and put them in her mouth. She chewed with a smile that made her cheek wrinkle in an irregular way. My grandmother ate her skins, too. To my right, my brother was gobbling the yellowish substance. Some pieces slipped through the gap in his bottom lip and returned to his plate all chewed up. Just like flies when they vomit their saliva to regurgitate the solids they feed on, transforming them into a liquid substance, which they then suck up with their horn-shaped mouth.

I ate everything on my plate, but I was still hungry.

"There's no more?" I asked. I heard Dad rest his cutlery on his plate. In quick succession, my grandmother's hand moved from her forehead to her stomach to each side of her chest and to her mouth.

"Sure there's more," Mom replied. She reached for the seventh plate, positioned as always between my grandmother and my sister. When Grandma heard her, she grabbed Mom's hand.

"Not yet," she said.

Mom looked at me and bit her bottom lip.

"Please," Grandma whispered. "Not yet."

Mom left the plate where it was with a sigh. Dad offered me his. He held it with his arm stretched out, the plate in the air in the middle of the table.

"That won't solve anything," my mother said.

"It solves the boy's hunger."

"Only tonight," she added. "What will we do tomorrow?"

"What's happening tomorrow?" I asked, chewing a piece of skin.

"Nothing," whispered Mom very close to my face, trying to smile. Then she looked at Dad. "What will we do tomorrow?"

"I don't know," he answered. "I really don't know."

That night, Dad let me stay and watch a movie with them. I watched while I played with the two peas that had fallen from my plate.

9

Back in my room after the movie, I knelt in front of the cabinet at the foot of my bed. When I opened the drawer I found two more fireflies near the jar. When I unscrewed the lid to put them in, my brother appeared in the bedroom. He climbed onto the bunk, making everything shake. The lid fell onto the floor. After I recovered it and closed the jar, only three fireflies were inside.

One was missing.

I heard the heavy metal door to my parents' bedroom close. My sister pulled the chain. I heard her footsteps traveling from the bathroom to her bedroom. My brother turned off the light in our room. The cistern's dripping was clear in the sudden silence.

I remained still, looking into the darkness.

A spot of light hovered about the room. I left the jar in the drawer and the green glow flickered twice before landing near the door. I crawled toward the firefly, still glowing in the same place.

"Come here," I whispered. But just before reaching it, the spot of light slid under the door. I opened it a crack. The firefly took off in the hall, heading in the direction of the living room. I came out of the bedroom on tiptoes, feeling the draft from the window on my legs. The two new visitors must've flown in through there.

I followed the trail of light in total silence. In the living room, the pilot lights on the TV and video shone, like two more fireflies trapped inside the appliances, dead. The living one flashed three times before perching on my father's armchair. I leapt on it, forming an upside-down bowl with my hands. I thought I'd missed, until four green lines glowed between my fingers. I closed my right hand, trapping the insect inside. It tickled when it beat its wings.

That was when I heard a bang.

My heart thumped in my ears.

There was another bang.

And then another.

I broke into a sweat because I knew what it meant. "Please not for me. Please don't have come for me," I whispered into the darkness.

The first night I heard those noises I cried in my bed with my muscles so frozen with terror I couldn't move. When I mentioned it at breakfast, Mom told me that I must've imagined it. That there were no monsters up above, or in the wardrobe, or under my bed. But Dad told me the truth.

"What you heard was the Cricket Man's footsteps," he explained.

"He's an old man with giant black eyes whose knees bend the wrong way." And he tried to dramatize what he was saying by walking in a squat around the dining area. "He also has two big antennae, so big they rub against the ceiling when he goes in a house."

"Why does he go in houses?" I asked.

Dad turned a chair around and sat on it with his legs open, holding the backrest. "Because he hunts for children with his antennae." He held both arms against his forehead and waved them. "With his antennae, and the light from an oil lamp, he searches underground for badly behaved children, to stick them in his sack."

"And what does he do with them?" I wanted to know.

Dad moved his face so close to mine that he scratched me with his hair scar. "He eats them," he said. "He starts with the feet, then the legs, and then the belly, until he reaches the head." He made a chomping sound with his teeth. "And while he eats them, he rubs his back-to-front knees together to chirp like a cricket."

Now, positioned by Dad's armchair with the firefly beating its wings inside my hand, I felt a shiver as I remembered the chirping I'd heard just after he told me that story, the chirping of a real cricket.

There was another bang in the darkness.

The Cricket Man was coming for me. He wanted to stick me in his sack because I'd put the baby's life in danger when I hid the firefly jar in the crib. And because I'd begun to ask myself what there was outside the basement.

I held my breath.

I looked up at the living room window. The bars killed off any idea of escape. I also looked at the door that had never been open. I had to make a big effort to move my body numbed with fear, but managed to cross the living room in the direction of the hall. I saw the half-open door to my bedroom. I wanted to run to my bed and disappear under the sheets, to feel the soft material inside my pillow between my fingers.

That was when the hinges creaked on my parents' door.

I pressed myself against the wall, to one side of the threshold that led to the hall.

Then I heard it.

A knee clicking. The back-to-front knee of the Cricket Man. I imagined his antennae vibrating, searching for my scent, scraping the ceiling. His giant black eyes capturing what little light there was in the basement to make my silhouette multiply in lots of hexagonal cells.

More clicking. Nearer this time.

With my head pressed against the wall, I made out his silhouette in the hall, to one side of my field of vision.

I heard the patter of his feet on the floor. Until I realized it was the sound of my teeth chattering. I bit my bottom lip to stop them.

The Cricket Man opened the door to my grandmother's room. I knew then that he hadn't come for me. He wanted to take the baby. The stony feeling that locked my joints prevented me from moving.

When the door closed, I couldn't contain the hot liquid that now dripped down my legs.

After a space of time that I was unable to measure, the silhouette emerged from the room. I imagined my nephew in the sack, his face scratched by the Cricket Man's hairy legs.

The baby cried.

But the crying came from inside the bedroom. The little boy was safe.

The hinges on my parents' door creaked again, making my body finally react. I emerged from behind the wall and ran to the bunk bed. I threw myself onto the mattress, sheets up to my forehead, firefly still in my fist.

"I'm sorry, I'm sorry, I'm sorry," I whispered. "I didn't mean to hurt the baby. Please don't have come for me."

The sweat that covered my body went cold. I could sense someone looking at me inside the room. I could hear breathing. When I heard the first guffaw I closed my eyes. And then I recognized the laughter. That guttural sound. My brother's heehaw got louder.

"You're scared," he said. He made another donkey noise.

"Shut up, or he'll find us."

"Who?" he asked, still laughing.

"The man who comes sometimes," I whispered.

My brother went quiet.

"Did Dad tell you about him?" he said after a few seconds.

"Yeah," I answered into the darkness. "Ages ago."

"Age—" He swallowed. "Ages ago?"

My brother fell silent again.

"Didn't you know?" I asked. "The Cricket Man hunts children who live underground, if they misbehave."

My brother laughed again.

"Oh, yeah," he said. "He told me, yeah."

He exploded into guttural laughter while I tried to shush him.

"Shut up," I said. "Shut up, or he'll find me."

My brother laughed until he choked. Then he started coughing. The springs on his bunk squeaked with every cough.

Then the bedroom door opened.

The Cricket Man had found me.

The light came on. I covered my face with the sheet.

"What's wrong?" Mom asked from the door.

I sighed with relief, and took a breath before answering. "I'm scared."

"Not you, your brother." He was still laughing and coughing. "Will you be quiet?" my mother ordered.

She approached the bed. I poked my head out from the sheet. I could see Mom's body up to her chest. The rest was above my brother's bunk. He wasn't laughing much anymore. He was coughing in a frantic way that was making him choke.

"Stop!" my mother shouted. I heard her slap my brother's back a few times.

"You have to stop!" she persisted. "Your brother mustn't be kept awake."

The coughing fit gradually subsided.

"What brought this on?" my mother asked him. Receiving no answer, she turned to me. "How long have you been awake? What have you heard?"

I hesitated. The key hung from her neck like a pendulum. "I saw the Cricket Man," I said.

"Have you been out of your room?"

The firefly I'd gone to rescue was still fluttering in my closed hand.

"No," I lied.

"Then where did you see him? In this bedroom?"

I shook my head.

"Of course you didn't," she said, "because he doesn't exist. You know that."

"He does exist!" my brother shouted from above.

My mother cuffed him.

"Be quiet," she told him. "He doesn't exist."

Mom pinched her stretched T-shirt between her legs and sat on the side of my bed. She put a hand on my tummy.

"That man doesn't exist," she repeated. "No one's going to take you away. This is your home and you're safe here. Now I'm going to bring you a glass of milk, you're going to drink it, and you're going to sleep. Understood?"

I nodded, unconvinced.

Mom left the room. Above me, my brother said, "He does exist."

I remained silent, remembering the silhouette I'd seen in the hall. The two clicks of his back-to-front knees. Then I heard a cricket's chirp. Like I had just after Dad revealed the Cricket Man's existence to me. A real chirp, like the one I'd heard in documentaries. Like when night fell in the movies.

A shiver ran down my back, as if a real cricket walked down my spine.

Mom returned with the glass of milk. She offered it to me, and I took it with my free hand. I didn't want her to discover the firefly.

"I want to see you drink it," she said.

I drank it in one gulp.

"It tastes strange," I said.

My mother looked away for an instant. "The glass must be dirty," she replied. "Now, sleep."

She took the glass and waited for me to lie down. She tucked me in.

"I'm still scared," I said to her. "What if I can't sleep?"

I had to wait until she went and my brother started to snore before I could put the firefly back in the jar. I would've liked to have changed my wet underpants, too. But I must've fallen asleep right then, because when I opened my eyes again, my family was talking in the kitchen. The house smelled of coffee and toast. In my hand there was a squashed pea.

10

The toaster went off to welcome me to the kitchen. Mom was warming milk. Beside her, twelve eggs sat on their throne of gray cardboard.

"Doesn't it all smell great?" she said. "I knew he wouldn't let us down."

"The boy's here," my father warned her.

Mom turned around.

"Come here so I can give you a hug," she said, kneeling by the oven.

My brother, sister, and father were also hanging around in the kitchen.

"That doesn't go there," Dad said. He took out a packet of rice my brother had just put in the top drawer and stored it in the third one down.

When I pulled my chair out from under the table, I found a sack of potatoes on the seat.

"Wait," said Mom. She came over and took it off so I could sit down. "See how you were able to sleep?"

I nodded, rubbing an eye with the back of my hand.

"Don't listen to your father," she whispered in my ear. "That Cricket Man's an invention to scare kids and make them behave."

"But I saw him," I responded.

Dad spoke from the fridge. "I can hear you both," he said. "You bet you saw him. Because the Cricket Man exists. And he moves like this." He crossed the kitchen in a squat and put a string of onions on the extractor fan. "The difference is his knees bend backward."

Mom held my chin and shook her head. Then she straightened with a groan, hefting the potatoes, and she stored them in a low cupboard.

The rest of my family sat down one by one.

"So someone was scared last night," my father said as he took his seat. "And it seems it wasn't the baby," he added, gesturing at my sister without looking at her.

"First the baby cries, then the next night it's the boy. What is going on in this house?"

"I didn't cry," I answered.

"You didn't? So why did your mother have to go to your room and comfort you?"

"I actually went to calm your other son down," Mom cut in. She put down a bowl of boiled eggs in the middle of the table before sitting. "He wouldn't stop laughing."

"Can we eat?" my sister interrupted. "I'm hungry."

Dad waited with his wrists resting on the table's edge, without picking up his cutlery.

"Why isn't Grandma coming?" Mom whispered. "Shall I go fetch her?"

My sister stretched out an arm to take an egg from the bowl.

Dad smashed his hand down like he was killing a mosquito. "No one eats until Grandma's here," he said.

"And how do we know she's coming?" Mom asked.

My grandmother's voice came from her room. "I'm coming out," she shouted.

"She's coming out," repeated Dad.

"They understood me," she added. "I don't need a translator."

The sound of her slippers dragging along the hall preceded her appearance in the doorway. She was wearing the nightgown she always ate breakfast in, which she then changed out of and wouldn't put on again until nighttime. Her white hair, which combed in a certain way hid the bald areas made by the fire, was now brushed forward, covering her face. On either side of her head the bare patches of scalp could be seen.

"Your hair," said my father. "We're all here."

She sorted it out as best she could. Mom wanted to get up, but my grandmother stopped her. "Don't worry, I'm fine on my own."

When she sat down, she tidied her hair a bit more and tried to smile, but the result was nothing more than a big crease across her swollen face.

"How are you?" my father asked her.

"What's wrong with your eyes?" said my brother.

Grandma took a deep breath. She felt for her plate with her fingers. Then a hand slid across the table to her right. She touched the seventh plate. She always smiled when she found that Mom had served it, but this time her chin trembled.

"Let's eat," Dad said.

"Let's eat," Grandma repeated. Her lips were reddened, her eyes swollen, the tip of her nose raw.

"Why are you so sad?" I asked her.

She put her cup down on the table, and dried her lips with a cloth napkin full of holes. Mom had explained to me that moths made the holes, so for days I'd searched for caterpillars all around the basement. I wanted to feed them with my clothes, see them grow, and witness their metamorphosis. But Mom filled wardrobes and drawers with mothballs. For days the basement smelled of nothing else.

"Can't you see how sad she is?" I said to everyone.

Mom lowered her head.

Grandma put her napkin on her lap. A strained crease of flesh spread across her face in the worst imitation of a smile.

"Did the Cricket Man do something to you?" I asked. "I saw him go into your room."

Her normally cloudy eyes filled with tears.

Then the baby's high-pitched scream came from the hall.

"Have you left him in the bedroom?" asked Dad. Grandma blinked as if she'd just remembered there was a baby in the basement.

"Go get your son," Dad ordered my sister.

She put the sugar jar down on the table. The teaspoon clinked against the edge of the glass. She looked at Grandma, then held a finger to her temple and moved it in circles.

"Don't do that," Dad said.

"Do what?" asked Grandma.

"Nothing," replied my sister, "I'm not doing anything. I'll go see what's wrong with him."

She tipped a final spoonful of sugar into her coffee and closed the jar as she got up. Then she was still for a moment and sat down again. She lifted the jar with her elbow resting on the table. "Would you mind going?" she asked me.

"Me? Why me?"

She looked at the jar. Then tipped it up. It was just like the firefly jar.

"Well, if you don't want to . . ." She left the jar on the table and ran her finger around the edge of the lid. "I could—"

"All right," I interrupted when I understood she was blackmailing me, "I'll go."

She smiled and took her finger away from the lid.

"If he's crying because he's hungry, bring him here and I'll feed him."

My brother pushed his chair out to block my path.

"*She* has to go," he said.

I tried to dodge around him but he moved again.

"*She* has to," he insisted.

"I don't care who goes," Dad said, "but go now. I can't stand that child's screaming."

In the crib, the baby was crying with his arms stretched out toward the ceiling, as if he wanted the Cricket Man to find him and take him away. I put a hand on his tummy and rocked him. His crying began to subside. When I put a finger near his mouth, the baby caught it and began to suck. A mistaken look of peace lit up his face.

That was when I noticed the bulge under the sheet.

It moved near his feet. At first I thought it had been his legs thrashing about as he cried, but the bump was too far from the baby's body, like a stretchy limb that wanted to escape from its own anatomy. The bulge moved to a corner of the crib. I went on tiptoes to grab hold of my nephew. Before I could lift him and get him away from the thing that moved under the sheet, the bulge positioned itself on his chest. Like a second body.

I felt the tickling of whiskers before I saw anything. A gray, pointed nose, twitching, appeared between my hands. It bumped against the baby's chin, and my nephew just managed to turn his head to escape the thing.

The rat came out from under the sheet. It walked over the little boy's cheeks, sinking its feet into the flesh. One of the front ones found purchase on his nose, the other near the ear. The rodent's claws opened little cuts on the skin. The baby opened his mouth to scream again. The animal's tail slithered between his lips, and its snout stopped for a few seconds on the boy's left eye, sniffing, the whiskers quivering over it like grotesque eyelashes.

I pulled on the baby with trembling hands. A muscle in my back sent me a stab of pain. The animal clutched the boy's head, bending the neck at an unnatural angle, before jumping back into the crib. It escaped between two bars. The tail disappeared into a corner of the room.

I kissed the baby's forehead, which was resting on my chest. I held his head from behind to keep the neck straight. Two drops of blood slid down his face.

"Is that child going to shut up, or what?" my father yelled from the kitchen.

I sat on the floor, my back resting against my grandmother's bed. With one of my thumbs, I cleaned the drops of blood from the baby's face.

"How hard can it be?" Dad asked from the other room.

"If he's hungry, bring him to me," shouted my sister.

My throat was so tight from the shock I couldn't answer.

I sat there waiting, until I heard my grandmother's footsteps in the hall.

"What is it?" she asked as she walked in.

She bumped into me. A sparse eyebrow arched, taut with worry.

"Hey, what is it?" She knelt beside me. She searched for the baby with her hands. "Is he OK?"

I swallowed. I opened my mouth but couldn't utter a word. I swallowed again.

"A rat," I managed to say.

"No," she responded. She pressed the little boy's head against her chest. "Where?"

"In the crib," I said. "A huge rat, it came out from under the sheet. It walked over his face. Grandma, it scratched his face."

Mom appeared in the room. Behind her, my dad and my brother. They crowded around us.

"What's happened?" Dad asked.

"What's happened, you ask?" My grandmother held the baby out for my mother to take him, then she stood up. She spoke very close to Dad's face. "Rats. I told you they'd end up giving us a fright."

"Rats?" Mom covered her mouth.

"There's poison in every corner," Dad explained. "Maybe with the delay it took a bit longer for—"

"Sure, blame it on him," my grandmother broke in. "Is there any more with today's things?"

My father left the room without answering.

My sister then appeared in the doorway. She parted a lock of hair caught in her mask's artificial nose and examined the tips. "What's happened?"

My brother grabbed my sister's arm. He pulled her toward the baby, which still cried in my mother's arms. He pushed her till she was down on her knees.

"Don't touch me!" she yelled. "Get off me. Don't touch me."

My brother's fingers went white around her arm. "You should have"—he choked on a syllable—"have been looking after him," he said.

She groaned.

"Leave her," Mom said as she stroked the baby's face. "It was an accident."

"It was an accident," my sister repeated. "This place is full of rats."

My brother let go of her arm. She massaged it.

Dad returned to the room. "We've got another box," he said.

He shook it so my grandmother could hear it. It was red, smaller than a cereal box, but the same shape. The black silhouette of a rat was printed on one side, inside a yellow circle.

"Someone bring me the antiseptic from the bathroom," Mom asked while blowing on the baby's face.

My sister sat on the bed. She chose another lock of hair and smoothed it using two fingers like scissors.

"He's your son," my mother said. "Won't you go?"

"How about his father goes?" she replied.

I ran to the bathroom to find the first-aid kit. Screams came from the bedroom. I also heard a slap.

***

In the afternoon I sat by Mom on the brown sofa in the living room. She was mending one of Dad's shirts. On the sofa's arm was the sewing box she'd used to help my sister after she gave birth. It was really an old Danish cookie tin. That was what the lid said. Behind us, my brother was riding the exercise bike, the pedal clipping the metal frame once every five seconds.

I observed Mom's face. Her profile sculpted by the fire. Once I found her in the kitchen looking at a photo. She was touching it with her fingers. It was her before going down into the basement. She was standing on some rocks, gripping her skirt between her legs. Surrounded by the white spray from a massive wave that must've soaked her an instant later. Mom knelt to show it to me. When I saw that face of smooth skin and perfect features, like an orthopedic mask over Mom's scars, I seized the picture frame and threw it to the floor. The glass broke.

On the sofa, I stopped the needle and thread. I kissed my mother's cheek. I liked her eye that was almost shut. I liked the rough feel of her skin when she kissed me on the forehead before I slept. And I liked the clumsy eyelid that wrinkled up when she was concentrating on mending a shirt's elbow.

Her nose whistled after I kissed her. I pressed my mouth against her ear. "Did the Cricket Man come for me last night?" I asked.

She let her shoulders fall and folded the shirtsleeve on her lap. She put the thread, needle, and thimble back in the sewing box. I stroked the wrinkly fold between two of her knuckles. The circle of burned skin at the base of the thumb. The wide, smooth scar near the wrist.

"For you?"

I nodded.

"Why would he come for you?"

I thought about the firefly jar hidden in the drawer. About how I could've suffocated the baby when I put it in his crib. The questions I'd begun asking myself about the world outside.

"Because . . ." I hesitated.

"And anyway, how's an old man who doesn't even exist going to stick you in a sack?" She pinched my nose.

"I saw him."

"Are you sure?"

I nodded with my eyes wide open.

"Sure you're sure you're sure?"

She said the words in a funny way to distract me. But I remembered the bangs. The antennae scraping the hallway ceiling. The clicking of his back-to-front knees.

"I'm sure," I insisted. "Maybe he came for the baby."

"For the baby? What has the baby done?"

I shrugged, unable to find an answer.

Then I got it. "Mom," I said. I gave a long pause before continuing. "Mom, is the Cricket Man the baby's father?"

Her head fell forward, as if the neck had turned to mashed potato. She glanced at my brother on the bike to make sure he wasn't listening.

"You do say some silly things," she whispered. "If your father heard you . . . Son, you have to listen to me. The Cricket Man doesn't exist. You're safe here."

"But I saw him."

"The Cricket Man doesn't exist," she insisted. "Anyway, you don't even know how babies are made. We're not on that page yet."

"I bet it's not so different from how insects do it," I responded. "And I've read a lot about that in my book."

Mom smiled. One eye involuntarily closed. "Believe me, son, it's very different."

She picked up the shirt and took the needle and thread from the sewing box again to resume her work. A circular container made of transparent plastic fell onto the sofa. I examined its contents, moving it in my fingers.

"What are these?"

"They're your milk teeth." The container slipped. It rolled along the floor until the lid came off. The teeth scattered. My brother heehawed from the bike.

"Go on, go," Mom said. A black thread joined her mouth to the shirt on her knees. "I'll tidy that up. But go before this needle has your eye out."

I took two of the teeth without her noticing.

I ran to the hall. Dad was speaking to my sister from the bathroom door. The faucet was running. "Put it on," he said.

"I need to wash my face," she responded.

"And I need to lay this stuff in the bathroom." Dad showed her the box of rat poison he had in his hand.

"Lay it, then."

"I don't want to be looking at your face while I'm doing it." Dad saw me and registered my hand pinching my underpants.

"And nor does your brother," he said. He winked at me. "He needs to use the bathroom, too. He can't come in if you have your nose hole out."

I stood still.

The faucet kept running.

My sister's arm emerged from inside the bathroom. I was about to close my eyes. She took the box of poison. Dad was left with his arm outstretched.

"I'll lay it," she said.

Then the pedaling noise stopped in the living room. The floor reverberated when my brother began one of his marches. He whistled the same melody as always.

I sucked in saliva, squeezing my underpants.

"Your brother needs to come in," insisted my father. His tone darkened. "Put your mask on."

I heard the strap adjusting.

"There's a good girl," he said, and he let me by. "You can go in now."

Dad waited for me to position myself in front of the toilet bowl.

My sister clicked her tongue.

From the living room, Mom called to my father. "Make him stop," she yelled, referring to my brother and his march around the kitchen.

Dad took the box of rat poison from the sink and put it on the cistern.

"You lay the poison," he told me. "I don't trust this one in the mask. One cube behind this cupboard." He touched the unit under the sink. "Another behind this one." He laid his hand on the towel cupboard. "And another behind the door. Understood?"

I nodded.

"And wash your hands properly afterward," he added. "I don't want to find you dead in a corner." He disappeared off to the living room, where my brother was still marching.

I took the cubes of poison from the box. They were light blue. I positioned them where Dad had told me. My sister was looking at the reflection of her mask in the mirror. She hit the jet of water a few times to make it splash onto the glass. Her image blurred. When I put the last dose of poison down behind the door, she asked, "Can I wash my face now?"

I nodded as I left the bathroom. My sister kicked the door shut.

I handed the rat poison box back to Dad, who was now on the bike. He snatched it from my hands as he pedaled and jammed it between two parts of the frame.

On the way back to my bedroom, I discovered two green spots of light behind the window. I looked back toward the living room. Mom's hand appeared for a second in the rectangle of the doorway into the hall. It was pulling on black thread. My grandmother's door was still closed. She hadn't come out all day since breakfast.

The two new fireflies hovered in a playful way behind the glass, like a giant, cross-eyed insect looking in. When I opened the window, they landed on my hand.

"You're from outside, aren't you?" I said.

In my bedroom I found my brother sitting on the edge of his bunk. He was whistling his march through his broken lip with his pajama bottoms tucked into his socks. Seeing me, he stretched out his arms, like the man on Grandma's rosary cross. He stood very still in his cornfield.

11

Grandma didn't have dinner with us. We waited like we did at breakfast, but when the soup stopped steaming in its bowls, Dad gave us permission to start. This time it was Mom who gave thanks to the One Up There. When Grandma finally came out of her room, she found us on the sofa, illuminated by the intermittent light from the snow on the television. It was time for the movie.

Grandma dragged her slippers to the sofa. She sat with her hands in her lap. Lying on the floor, I breathed in the smell of talcum powder. Dad followed her movements from the striped armchair. He was sitting with one leg crossed over the other, a foot resting on the opposite knee. He was shelling peanuts in a bowl on his stomach, breaking the shells with his thumb. My brother asked if he could be the one who inserted the tape in the recorder. He waved it in the air like a trophy before letting himself drop near the Betamax machine. The ground trembled. He managed to get the tape in on the third attempt. My sister applauded. She was sitting on the floor, rocking the baby in her arms. The little boy was asleep. Mom, who was drying a plate near the sofa, flicked my sister's head with the dishtowel for making fun of her brother.

"Mind the baby," my sister said. She bent her back over in an exaggerated way, shielding the child as if protecting him from an explosion.

"Oh, come off it," my mother responded, and she hit my sister again with the dishtowel.

"Mom!" she protested.

But Mom smiled and went over to the kitchen sink. She rarely sat down to watch the movies. She might follow them from start to finish, but did so resting against the sink, drying the dishes. Or from the table, talking to Grandma and choosing potatoes for the next day's lunch. Or standing by the sofa, biting her nails with enough skill that they wouldn't fall on the floor. She kept them in her mouth till she'd finished. Then threw the clippings in the bin. It made her fingernails jagged, like little saws. "You can start," she said now from the kitchen. "I'll come and sit down soon." But she wouldn't sit down.

"Can I watch?" I asked. I was lying facedown, my chin resting on the floor and my arms stretched out to the sides. I liked feeling the cold of the tiles in the main room.

Dad stopped shelling peanuts. "Which one did we put on in the end?" he asked my brother.

He looked at me from the video recorder, and grunted. The light now coming from the screen painted blue brushstrokes on his face. He got up and went to Dad's armchair. He whispered the movie title into my father's ear.

"No, you can't," Dad said to me. He tossed up a shelled peanut and caught it in his mouth.

"Can't we put a different one on?" Grandma asked.

"No. Anyway, it's his bedtime. He'll just fall asleep on the sofa."

Grandma turned her face toward Mom. I could see the dark skin of her neck, thick and rough.

"He's right," my mother answered, a nail clipping dancing between her lips. "It's his bedtime." She came over to me.

"Come on." She ruffled my hair.

My sister sat up. "Take the baby with you, then," she said. As if he'd heard his mother name him, the little boy began to cry.

"What's wrong with him now?" She held the baby out in front of her to get a better look at him. In the holes in her mask, her eyes narrowed. The baby's feet hung over the floor. He coughed, waggled his legs, shook his head.

My grandmother quickly bent down. She felt for the baby with her hands and picked him up, resting him against her chest. She gently patted him on the back.

"What is it?" Mom asked. I sensed a hint of alarm in her voice.

Grandma continued to assist the boy.

She gave him four gentle slaps on the back.

On the fifth, the baby burped.

It was a loud burp, almost like an adult's.

My brother was the first to laugh. Then my sister. Dad cleared his throat with a first attack of laughter and then continued to guffaw with his mouth wide open. A piece of peanut skin detached from his lip and returned to the bowl it came from. Mom smiled, letting air escape through her nose. I laughed with her. Even Grandma smiled, this time for real, showing her teeth and raising the eyebrow with less hair.

We laughed like the family we were, accompanied by the orchestral symphony from the television, which showed a woman wielding a torch among the clouds.

"OK," Dad said then, "that's enough. It's about to begin. Go on, and take the baby with you."

"*She* can take him," my brother said.

"Don't start," Dad cut in. "Your brother's taking him."

I took the baby from Grandma's arms. She stroked my face.

"You're such a good boy," she said in a voice I could just hear. "And don't worry about me. I'm almost back to normal."

I left the room with the baby in my arms. I knew what movie it was as soon as I heard the first line over the noise of peanut shells breaking.

***

I stopped at the door to the little boy's room. A storm of light broke in the living room, behind me. I looked at the closed window at the end of the hall. When the light flashed, I discovered my own reflection in the glass. I walked toward it. The changing light made the shadows dance and the space change shape. As I advanced, for a moment I couldn't see the hallway anymore. Then the light returned, and I discovered myself again in the glass. Like the ghost that Dad said I was.

A ghost looking into the house from the outside.

The baby moved in my arms. He pressed his forehead against my chest and made a nice sound with his throat, like cooing. We continued until I reached the window. I opened it. I repositioned the little boy so he faced the outside, so he faced the darkness. Another flash of light from the television allowed me to see the nothingness on the other side of the bars. A box inside another box.

A soft breeze came in through the window, reaching the baby's face and making his eyelashes flitter. He moved his lips in a sucking reflex.

"It's from outside," I told him. I lifted him to my face, pressing one of my cheeks against his, and added, "It smells different. But I don't know what of. Smell it."

I closed my eyes, feeling the heat of my nephew's skin on my face. His little heart was beating on the hand I had on his torso. I was holding him from behind with my other hand. I felt his body rise and fall, filling itself with the air that came from somewhere neither he nor I would ever know. I breathed that moisture in deep. The baby's chest expanded under my fingers.

We breathed together.

After opening my eyes, I took hold of one of the little boy's hands, his fingers closing around one of mine. Then he gripped one of the bars like it was another finger, but then let it go. He stretched out his arm, wanting to reach whatever there was beyond. He tried it with his other arm as well. He opened and closed his little hands in an attempt to reach behind the window.

"You can't go out," I whispered to him.

The boy's face wrinkled up, and he showed the corners of hard flesh that were his gums. His eyes became mounds of wrinkled skin, the first stage before an outrageous scream. I put my hand over his mouth.

"Shh, Dad can't see us here."

The baby kicked his legs. He squirmed with his head, trying to free his nose and mouth so he could cry. I shushed him again in his ear. From the living room a woman's screams came from the movie.

"Wait, I have an idea." I closed the window. "Look, there's no need to cry." I made him face the window. The flashes of light in the living room reflected our image in the glass. "Look at us," I repeated. "We're outside now."

The baby's eyes opened on the other side of the glass. I smiled at the only part of me that didn't live in the basement. And he smiled back.

The white light suddenly vanished, making us disappear.

We were left in the dark again. Trapped in the basement.

Then Mom's nose whistled.

"Do you really want to leave?" she said from just behind me. The fright made me unable to answer.

From the living room, Dad asked Mom if she wanted him to pause the movie.

"No, it's all right. I'm going to the bathroom. I wasn't watching it, anyway." Mom took the baby from my arms.

"Wait for me in bed," she whispered.

In my room, I said goodnight to the fireflies with a few taps on the glass of their jar. They answered by filling the drawer with their magical light. I also checked that the eggshell was still there. No sign of the chick. I got into bed with the green glow of the fireflies still alight.

It went out before Mom came into the room. She sat on my bed and tucked the sheet in on each side of my shoulders, at chin height. Then she kissed my forehead, her skin rough as always.

"Is there somewhere to go?" I asked. The pressure from the material on my chest was a cozy feeling.

Mom blinked in her usual unsynchronized way. First the eye least affected by the burns, and then the other. There was very little difference between the movements of each eyelid, but it was a characteristic mannerism of my mother's.

"What?" she asked.

"Is there somewhere outside I could go?"

"Do you want to go to the bathroom?" She looked at the hallway.

"No, Mom." I knew she was playing dumb. "You asked me if I want to leave."

"What does it matter if there's somewhere to go?" she now said, answering my previous question. She smoothed one of my eyebrows with her thumb. Then she lowered her voice as quiet as it'd go, down to a whisper.

"Man took off to the moon without knowing exactly what he'd find. Would you do that, too? Would you leave the basement if you could?" Some of the consonants were no more than whistles.

"By myself?"

"Just you."

Like it was a reflex action, I spoke in a low voice as well. "With the baby?"

Mom fell silent for a while.

"No," she finally said.

"And how would I get out?" I asked. "There're bars on both windows. And Dad lied to me about the door in the kitchen. It's always been locked."

"Son, that wasn't my question," she whispered. "Imagine you could get out. Imagine I have this magic chalk." She held an imaginary object

84

between two fingers. "And I can paint a door in the ceiling. Straight to the surface. Would you go?"

I could only see Mom's face when the light reached her from the hall. "Could you come with me?"

"No."

"What about Grandma?"

"No, not her, either."

"Dad?"

"You'd have to go alone."

I considered it with my eyes closed, feeling the material inside my pillow with my fingers. I could almost make out the smell of carrot soup that spread through the basement in the evenings. I could feel the softness of the towel that Mom hugged me with when I got out of the bath. I remembered how just now we'd all laughed together as a family in front of the television. I thought about Grandma. I breathed deep to smell her talcum powder by memory. I opened my eyes. It was one thing seeing my reflection in the window and imagining myself out there. It was quite another to leave for real.

"No," I answered.

"You wouldn't leave this basement if you could?" A flash lit up the room. Mom's eyes observed me from two deep shadows.

I shook my head.

"Are you sure?" she persisted.

"I'm sure," I replied. I fought against the sheets that pressed against me to sit up and hug my mother. "I want to live with you forever."

Her chest rose under our hug. Her nose whistled with a bubbling sound and she sniffed up snot. I separated myself from her. It was dark again, and I could see only the silhouette of her head. I touched her eyes. They were wet.

"Why are you crying?" I asked.

"I'm not crying," she answered. She waved a hand in front of her face to move my fingers away, like she was swatting a fly. "Come on, sleep," she added, and she sniffed in snot again.

"You *are* crying," I insisted.

Then she hugged me, and very close to my ear, she whispered, "I'm crying with happiness."

I wanted to touch her eyes again, but misjudged it. I felt the folds of burned flesh on her cheek.

"Enough now," she said. "Go to sleep."

The pressure on my chest returned when Mom tucked me in. She left the room. I lay awake, repeating every line in the movie.

12

More fireflies appeared in the following days. Whenever I peered through the bars on the window at the end of the hallway, something I did more and more often, at least one would drop down. Others arrived by themselves at the jar where I kept the rest. I found two one afternoon near Dad's toolbox. A few calendar boxes later, I ended up with nineteen specimens in the jar. I could turn off the light and illuminate the whole room with my firefly lamp. Sometimes, lying in bed at night, I'd peek out over the sheet. There was a green glow beyond my feet. It emanated from inside the drawer even when it was closed, through the crack. My brother snored, oblivious to the light dancing in our room, but I'd be hypnotized by it, imagining it was sunbeams that the fireflies brought from outside so I could see them. Though I knew that wasn't true: fireflies make light using chemicals from their own body.

It was on one of those nights that the rat walked over me.

First I felt something strange on my chest. Then on my belly. Then the unexpected sensation reached my groin. I knew what it was before its feet found my bare foot. The rat walked over me, scratching me with its claws. It jumped off the bed and fell with a muffled thump, which was followed by the rattle of its feet on the floor. Its silhouette moved along the line of orange light that came under the door. Someone was awake.

When I went out to get help, I heard voices in the living room. It was just a murmur. I recognized my grandmother's voice and my mother's. I walked toward them and heard another, deeper murmur join the conversation. It was my father. I stood still, not knowing what to do.

Standing in the middle of the hall, among the indecipherable murmuring I heard a word that caught my attention. My father had said my name. Then my grandmother said something back, but I couldn't make it out.

Involuntarily, I took a step forward.

And then another.

And another.

I snuck forward, keeping balance with my arms, holding my breath. Three shadows were cast against a wall of the living room. Now the conversation reached me more or less clearly.

". . . moon. But he doesn't want to leave," Mom was saying.

"What did I tell you?" Dad asked. "We knew this moment would come."

"And we've dealt with it very well," said Mom. "He's happy here."

"But now comes the difficult part," Dad added.

"Has any of this been easy?" Grandma sobbed.

The rattle of the rat's feet on the floor started up behind me, passed by me to one side, and went into the living room.

"The rat!" screamed my mother. A piece of furniture was dragged over the tiles in the living room. Grandma hiccupped. My father shushed everyone, as if that would keep the sudden commotion under control, but Mom was already running around the room following the noise the animal was making as it scuttled among the chairs. I saw her appear under the arch that led to the hall, whacking the floor with the broom. She was after the rat, but what she found was me, standing there in the hallway. She looked at the sofa, where their conversation had taken place and where my father would now be sitting. She came toward me, hitting out with the broom.

"Get out of here," she said as if speaking to the rat. She kept hitting the floor with the broom until she reached me, and then she swept at my feet.

"Don't let your father see you," she whispered to one side of me.

I fled to my bedroom. As I went through the door, I ran into a hot, soft barrier that made me fall. I landed on my backside, softening the impact with both hands. I heard a heehaw. My brother turned on our bedroom light before going out.

"Why are you shouting?" he blurted out down the hall.

"Nothing. It's nothing," my mother said. "Go back to your room, or you'll wake your sister. And the baby."

"I can hear it under the fridge!" my grandmother yelled.

Then I heard cupboards opening. And the bottles of ammonia rattling about.

"Another rat!" my brother then concluded. He said it as if it were news that should be celebrated.

I poked my head through the doorway.

The baby started crying.

"There you go, you've done it," my father said.

The little boy's screams got louder.

"Hey!" my father screamed from the living room. "I don't think you're sleeping with this racket! Tend to your son!"

The line of light that emerged under her bedroom door confirmed that my sister had woken up. But Dad, who couldn't have seen this, continued to yell.

"Hey!" he shouted again, then waited a few seconds before adding, "Damn it!"

I heard his footsteps before he appeared in the hall. When he discovered me, there was surprise in his eyes, but he had more important things on his mind.

He opened the door to my sister's room. The baby fell silent for a moment before taking up his screaming again at a higher volume than before.

"Make him be quiet," Dad said.

"I'm going," my sister mumbled from inside the room.

"And put your mask on," he ordered. He looked at me to make sure I was still paying attention to him. Then he raised his top lip and stuck his tongue out. He bent forward contracting his stomach, pretending to retch, as if seeing my sister's uncovered face had made him want to throw up. "The baby will never stop crying if he sees you like that." He smiled at me, wanting to make me complicit in the joke. I remained serious, looking at the horrid grin spread across his disfigured face. As his smile faded, the hair scar on his cheek slowly regained its usual straightness. The wrinkles around his eyes, including the fold of sunken flesh that he had as a lower eyelid, also relaxed. Inside the bedroom, the baby's crying eased up.

"The rat's gone," my mother said from the kitchen. Then she appeared in the hallway. She rested both hands on the end of the broom handle.

"What are you doing here?" she asked me.

"I just came out," I answered.

She knew I was lying, which was why she quickly changed the subject.

"What happened with the poison?" she asked. "Didn't we lay it all over the house? How can we be overrun with rats again?"

Dad dashed off into the living room. I heard him walking all around the main room. He moved some furniture. Then he reappeared in the hall and went into my sister's room. "That's what I like to see," I heard him sneer. "Your little mask where it should be, covering that face."

He moved around in that room, too, before crossing over to me and my brother's bedroom. He pushed me by the head into the room to get past. He knelt by the bunk bed and looked under my bed. Then he searched in the three other corners of the room. My heart beat faster when he went near my drawer, near the firefly jar and the chick's abandoned nest.

He came out of there, and then used the key hanging from his neck to open his own bedroom door. He emerged a few seconds later and moved on to the bathroom. I recognized the metallic rattle of the shower curtain as he drew it back. He also opened the cupboard under the sink, rummaging through the towels and first-aid kit. Then he returned to his position in my sister's doorway and looked at me from there with a serious expression.

"Who was it?" he asked. He turned to my sister. The question was for her as well.

Neither of us answered.

"Who?" he pressed. My brother arrived from the living room and stood behind my mother.

"Leave them," my grandmother shouted from the sofa.

Mom twisted the broomstick in her hands. "What do you want to know?" she asked my father.

Dad huffed. He looked at both of us. "Let him tell you what's happened to the rat poison," he said, pointing at me with his chin, before doing the same at my sister. "Or her. It's everywhere in the house. Everywhere I laid it. Everywhere except the bathroom. There's only one cube in the bathroom. Who did I tell to lay it in there?" he asked. "Who decided to go against the rules of this house?"

Neither of us answered.

"Come with me," he said then. He went into my sister's bedroom. "Leave the baby."

My mother passed the broom handle to my brother and quickly went in to take the little boy. Dad came out seconds later dragging my sister by the arm. Before I knew it, he'd grabbed me, too. He took us to the bathroom. "I remember giving you the box right here, and I asked you to put cubes there, there, and there." He pointed to three places. "Why's there only one behind this door?"

"The rats eat it," Mom intervened. "Perhaps—"

Dad silenced her with a stare.

"It was him," said my sister. Her lips smiled through the hole in the mask. "You gave the box to him in the end."

I remembered the box on the cistern while I peed. And I remembered my sister standing in front of the mirror. Splashing her reflection with water so she couldn't see it anymore.

"*Was* it your job?" Dad asked.

My sister wasn't lying. So I nodded. I did it in the manner of someone admitting guilt: looking down at the floor. But then I lifted my head again and looked my father in the eyes.

"And I did it," I said, "everywhere you told me to. I put a cube in each place. Dad, I swear, I did what you told me to do."

"Don't lie to me."

"I'm not lying."

One of my sister's contained laughs bubbled in her throat.

"He must be lying," she said. Then she imitated a pair of legs with two fingers, making them walk. "Those cubes can't grow feet and walk off on their own, you know."

"You be quiet," Dad cut in.

From the hallway, my brother started to sing to himself. "He's lyyyyyyying! He's lyyyyyyying! He's lyyyyyyying!"

"I swear I laid them, Dad—"

"He's lyyyyyyying!"

"—I remember it perfectly."

This time my sister couldn't contain her laughter. She laughed until my father grabbed her by the neck and squeezed, forcing her to be quiet. Then he dragged her down the hall by her head. "You're hurting me," I think she said. It was hard to understand her. Dad shoved her into her bedroom. Mom came out after Dad beckoned her with his head. He slammed the door closed. The baby started crying again.

"And shut that child up," he yelled at the closed door. "This door won't open until—"

"May I?" Grandma had appeared at some point. She wrapped one of her hands, wrinkled by time and the fire, around the same door handle that Dad was gripping. "May I?" she repeated.

She was speaking in a calm way, gently defying my father's authority. "I need to get in. I sleep here, too."

Dad hesitated for a few seconds. Then he came away from the door to let her past.

Grandma turned the handle. The baby's crying emerged from inside the room. "Thank you very much," she said. "And goodnight."

She closed the door with great care.

Dad glared at me. "I can't ask you to do anything." He reached me with one stride and knelt in front of me. With a finger outstretched, he turned my face until we were both looking into the bathroom.

"How do you think you'll sleep in that bathtub?" he asked.

"Please," Mom said, "there's no need for any of this."

He pushed me inside the bathroom. The floor was cold. "Tell me, how do you think you'll sleep in that tub?" he said again.

I shrugged.

"Well, you can tell me tomorrow," he announced. And he closed the door.

13

The banging woke me up. With my eyes open in the dark, my legs pressed against the cold ceramic of the bathtub, I attuned my ears. I expected to hear the Cricket Man's sack, too, dragging along the ground up above.

More bangs. One after the other, but soft. On the door. Someone was knocking. I waited for a few seconds before poking my head out. I lifted a corner of the shower curtain, carefully, so the metal hoops it hung from wouldn't make any noise. The door opened then without the hinges making a sound, as if whoever had opened it only wanted to leave it ajar. My eyes, accustomed to the dark, made out a new shape beside the door. Whoever it was moved, and I heard the familiar sound of fabric rustling. I smiled.

I got out of the bathtub in the direction of the door, the shower curtain rattling when I went through it. With my arms held out in front of me feeling the air, I reached the place where the shape was.

I touched it.

It was what I'd imagined.

My pillow.

I felt the material, searching for whatever was holding it up. I found a hand. I stroked it with my fingers, recognizing its bumps. The wrinkly fold between two of her knuckles, the circle of burned skin at the base of the thumb, the wide, smooth scar near the wrist. It was my mother's hand.

I squeezed it gently to tell her she could let go. Her nose whistled from the other side of the wood. The door closed.

I went back to the bathtub.

I closed the curtain again and lay back.

I hugged the pillow inside that cold white ceramic bed.

I slept.

The pipes whistling woke me up again. The water was running in the sink. On the other side of the curtain, someone had turned it on, but the light in the bathroom was still off. Only Grandma would use the bathroom without switching on the light. I breathed, trying to smell her talcum powder.

Then I heard a cough that I recognized. It wasn't my grandmother's, but my sister's. She hadn't seen Dad punish me by making me spend the night in the bathtub. Maybe she didn't know I was there. Which was why she hadn't knocked on the door. But why hadn't she turned on the light?

There was another cough. It was actually a wetter sound than a cough. A retch. I waited to hear the vomit hitting the sink, but it didn't. She just hawked the spit and snot from her throat.

She also groaned in a way I could barely hear. When she sighed a few times, I thought she might be crying. There was a high-pitched screech when she turned the handle again, followed by a louder flow of water. If the shower curtain hadn't been closed, the drops I heard splashing against the plastic would've reached me. Then the gargling started. A gurgle and then the mouthful of water falling into the basin. Followed by a moan, or rather, a stifled whimper. She repeated the exercise several times. I wanted to peek out by lifting a corner of the curtain, like I had before, but the sticky sound of the skin on my hand when I peeled it from the tub ended any attempt to move. If my sister didn't know I was there, if she thought I was sleeping in my bunk like I did every night, she may not be wearing her mask. In the darkness of the room I might not manage to see her deformed face, but I could perhaps make out some grotesque contour. The flat profile of a noseless face.

I recognized the sound of the soap dish sliding a little. It was fish-shaped and it gripped the soap with plastic scales. Its three resting points squeaked when they slipped along the ceramic sink. The bubbling and friction I heard next told me that my sister was washing her hands. It was for longer than even Mom spent washing hers after chopping garlic in the kitchen. The sound of my sister washing her hands was followed by a flicking sound that was repeated five times. Then the curtain moved and a piece of material landed on my chest.

I used the hand I'd peeled from the bathtub to touch it, feeling the circular contour of a button. It was the blouse my sister slept in. I understood that she'd undone the five buttons before leaving the blouse on the edge of the bathtub. Where I was.

There was also an elastic sound, but not the one made by the strap on her mask. I remembered her taking off her bra the afternoon when we'd had a bath together. The garment fell onto the blouse. One of the straps brushed against my shoulder. The soap dish skidded again. It was followed by some kind of friction sound. It wasn't two hands soaping each other. It was different. There were more muffled whimpers, like the ones Grandma gave sometimes when she was sitting in the living room, her face in the direction of the wall for an entire afternoon.

Another noise broke through the darkness of that bathroom that my sister and I shared without her knowing it. A noise from out in the hallway. My sister drew in her breath. The bar of soap hit the washbasin. The bra strap and bottom of her blouse escaped from the bath as fast as wasps retract their sting after using it. The quick movement made the hoops holding up the curtain tinkle. I also heard the door latch clicking into place.

My sister had left.

The bathroom was silent again.

The apparent peace lasted a few seconds.

Until the bathroom light suddenly came on. I held my hands over my eyes to ease the pain from being dazzled.

"So," I heard my father's voice say, "how's your night going?"

The curtain was thrown open with a metallic racket. The sudden light and deafening noise made it hard to believe I was in the same place where a moment before a fly would've given away its position just from the noise of its heartbeat. Even if a fly's heart is nothing more than a throbbing organ that pumps hemolymph and not blood.

"Sleep well in there?"

I opened my eyes and could only make out stripes of light through my hands. The curtain rail made its noise again. Dad was shaking it. When my vision finally got used to the bright light, I could see my father's silhouette, a diagonal line that ran from the left of my field of sight to the center. Like how a corpse would see the figure of its burier.

I blinked to focus better. At first I thought he was naked, his torso marked by the flames like a choppy sea of dark flesh, but then I saw the worn elastic of his sky-blue cotton underpants. I looked at him without saying anything, detecting a smile on his face from the shape his hair scar had taken. "Where did you get that pillow?" he asked.

I didn't answer. In response to my silence, Dad let go of the curtain, which then dangled between us like a plastic barrier.

I tucked my legs in as I raised my back until I managed to sit myself up in the bathtub. Then I lifted the corner of the curtain to poke one eye out without making the hoops jingle. I saw Dad standing in front of the toilet bowl, his back to me. He had the key hanging from his neck on his back and the elastic on his underpants down, so I could see part of a vertical line of black hair. I saw him use toilet paper to dry himself with in front, as Mom insisted I did whenever I'd finished peeing, although now I hadn't heard a trickle. He did it while looking down and then to one side, looking out perhaps for any movement of mine behind the curtain. I was scared that my hand's trembling would be reproduced in the portion of material on which he kept watch.

I discovered two pairs of scratches crossing his back diagonally, from his spine outward. Two new wounds on creased skin. He didn't seem bothered about them at all.

He threw the piece of paper into the toilet and pulled the chain. He stood watching the mechanism work. We had to stay to the end to make sure it drained out properly. It often didn't, and Dad would get angry if he found dirty water in there when it was his turn to use it. Once it was broken for a few days, so we had to use the washbasin to get rid of liquids. For the other, we used the bin.

The last sucking noise preceded the dripping that filled the cistern. Dad pulled up his underpants, which was when I carefully lowered the corner of the curtain. It didn't make a noise. I sat looking at the plastic.

His voice came from the other side.

"I discipline you so you learn to follow the rules of this house, and you break them a minute later?"

I didn't know what he meant.

His fingers appeared at one end of the curtain. He pulled it. I sat there looking at him.

Dad was holding the pink bar of soap in his free hand.

"When you use this"—he raised his eyebrows to look first at the soap and then at me—"you put it back where it belongs."

He let go of the curtain and returned the soap bar to the dish. The same fish-shaped dish whose sliding I'd heard in the darkness before my sister had again and again washed her hands, mouth, and whatever else she'd washed.

"It's not so hard, is it?" my father said.

I wanted to tell him it had been my sister, but Dad didn't even give me time to speak. With a snort of contempt he closed the curtain. I heard him turn the water on once more before the light went out and the bathroom door slammed shut, followed just after by his bedroom's metal door.

I stayed sitting in the bathtub for a few minutes. With my eyes open looking at nothing. I got up, grabbed a towel, and dried all the water that had been splashed on the washbasin, curtain, floor, and mirror.

That way Dad wouldn't find a reason to tell me off.

I got back in the tub and made myself comfortable. If I lay on my side and bent my knees a certain way, hugging the pillow, it wasn't too bad. I lifted a corner of the pillowcase to pinch the material inside. I stroked the soft fabric between my fingers again and again.

Then I heard the chirp of a cricket. A few chirps. A shiver ran down my back each time.

I covered my ears. I thought of my fireflies, on the other side of the wall. I couldn't see it, but I knew they'd be glowing.

14

My mother came to see me in the morning. "You can come out now," she said.

And I must've been deep asleep despite how uncomfortable my hard, curved bed was, because somehow I absorbed her sentence into the dream I was having, where I saw myself standing in front of the locked door in the kitchen. Scratching the concrete. Then my mother had said the sentence, and a vertical line of yellow light had appeared around the door's edge, growing wider and wider.

The beam of light kept getting thicker as the door shrank.

It was opening.

"You can come out now," my mother said again.

And then the door disappeared completely. And I looked through it with my face reddened by the bright blast of light that came from outside. Like what happened to my cactus under the spot of light in the living room. The same particles of dust that danced between its prickles while I pushed it with my finger along the floor now danced between my eyelashes. I could feel the light's heat on my cheeks.

But that second time, my mother's sentence was followed by a rattle.

A noise that couldn't be absorbed into the dreamworld I was in. Because it was a very familiar noise. The shower curtain as it was drawn back. Reality began to take shape around me while the light that illuminated me from the other side of that dreamed door went out.

The cold pressure on my leg replaced the heat from the light that didn't exist.

The white of the ceramic bathtub blanked out the yellow from the outside as soon as I opened my eyes.

"I said you can come out now," said my mother for the third time. One of her hands rested on my face. I smiled. That warmth was much better than the one from the nonexistent light in a dream that I was already beginning to forget. I rubbed my cheek against her wrinkled palm. Her nose whistled.

"Thank you for bringing the pillow," I whispered.

"A pillow?" she asked, holding back a smile. "Me?"

I stroked her hand the same way I had in the night. The wrinkly fold between two of her knuckles. The circle of burned skin at the base of the thumb. The wide, smooth scar near the wrist.

She received the message. "Come on, give it to me so I can take it to your room. Dad mustn't know," she said. She took hold of the pillowcase that emerged from between my legs and pulled. I sat up in the bathtub to make it easier for her.

"Dad already knows," I told her. "He was here last night."

My mother's eyes opened in an expression that I couldn't identify. Her cheeks went red.

"I'm not going to get angry over a pillow now, am I?" My father's voice surprised us from the bathroom door.

Mom spun around. She hugged the pillow as if she could make it disappear.

"And did you have to wake up the boy?" she asked.

"Well," Dad said, "the kid was sleeping there in the bathtub. And I had to turn the light on. He would've woken up anyway."

He spoke as he walked over to the toilet, the lid still up from when he last used it. He positioned himself in front of the toilet bowl and stood with his legs a little apart.

"You make it sound as if it was the boy who decided to sleep there," my mother said.

He let out a short groan of pleasure when he started to urinate. "That's irrelevant."

A tremor began on the other side of the bathroom wall. Then some quick steps advanced through the bedroom and hallway, almost like the clatter of a train. The half-open bathroom door hit the wall when my brother burst in.

"Dad," he complained when he discovered my father at the toilet bowl. "I have to use it."

My brother was gripping his crotch with both hands.

"So use it," Dad replied as he made space for my brother.

"But I have to do it kneeling down," he explained.

Dad let out a snigger. Mom gave him a slap on the shoulder.

"I know, I know," he answered, turning his neck to look at my mother. "Sorry."

When Dad finished, he made way for my brother, who knelt by the toilet bowl. He let out a groan of pleasure, too, when he started to urinate, but much louder. His stream of pee traveled upward before falling. I saw it as I stood up in the tub.

Dad was already washing his hands. When he'd finished, he said to me, "Watch and learn." He picked up the bar of soap, the same one my sister had used in secret in the night, and placed it carefully on the blue fish.

"You put it back in the soap dish," he told me. "You. Put it back. In the soap dish."

"Come on," my mother broke in, "get out of the bathtub now."

My brother pulled the chain.

My sister appeared in the doorway. Her face, those two eyes like creatures that had fallen into her mask's traps, scanned the inside of the bathroom. I examined her blouse. The five buttons I'd heard her undo in the night. I remembered the wet sound of her retching.

"Come on, son," my mother insisted.

I took the hand she held out to me.

"What's the kid doing there?" asked my sister.

"Don't call him *the kid*," my father corrected her. "He has a name."

"What's he doing there?"

My father put the towel back in its place. "Sometimes a telling-off isn't enough. A child has to be punished."

My sister stood in silence. She didn't seem to quite grasp the explanation.

"He made him spend the night in the bathtub," my mother spelled out as she pulled me toward the door. "Because of the thing with the rat poison."

I brushed past my sister. A spider of fingers clutched my shoulder.

"You spent the night in the bathtub?" she asked me. "You were here? All night?"

I nodded. Something shifted underneath her mask. The light in her eyes changed.

"And . . ." She paused to swallow before continuing. "Were you asleep the whole time?"

I understood the real meaning of her question.

"Well," Dad replied on my behalf, "he was poking about around the washbasin. Like one of those rats. When I came in I found the soap down there." He pointed at the inside of the sink.

My sister ran her fingers over her blouse buttons, as if looking for one she could do up. From her mouth escaped the unconscious murmur triggered by a bad thought. She tried to catch my eye again, but Mom was pulling my arm and managed to get me out of the bathroom before I could say a word. The white mask disappeared from my sight behind the wall.

"Did you wake him up?" was the last thing I heard my sister say. She was asking my father.

Mom led me to my room. We put the pillow back where it belonged. She peered at my brother's empty bed, felt his sheets, and wrinkled her nose, before pulling one of them off and rolling it around her arm.

"Go to the kitchen," she said. "I'm making breakfast now."

When she left the room, I opened my drawer. The eggshell danced in its T-shirt nest. The fireflies greeted me with random flashes of green light. "No," I responded in Morse code, tapping the lid five times, "I haven't left the basement."

When I came out, I found Grandma in the hall. She was carrying the baby in her arms. "Good morning," I said to her. I approached her to give her a hug, to squeeze her soft body, sink my face into her clothes, and smell the talcum powder, but she walked off before I could catch up with her.

"Not so good," she replied, and when she was in the living room she added, "The baby won't wake up."

I heard something behind me and turned around. I saw a corner of my sister's mask, poking out into the hallway from inside the bathroom. One eye still behind the door. When she saw me looking at her, she disappeared as fast as a dragonfly takes off.

"What do you mean, he won't wake up?" my father asked. He was sitting in his striped armchair. In the afternoon and evening he turned the chair toward the television, but in the mornings it normally faced the kitchen. From there Dad watched Mom making breakfast. He usually asked if anything needed fixing. If there was a cupboard door that was starting to come off. If it'd be better to change the height of some of the shelves. That way he could use his toolbox and have something to do for a few hours. Once I caught my mother loosening some hinges herself, so she could then ask Dad to fix them.

Mom dropped two eggs whose shells she'd already broken into the frying pan. She dried her hands on her apron, and ignoring the little explosions of oil, she approached my grandmother, who was pacing around the dining table. Grandma was hissing and tapping the baby's mouth with a finger.

"Come on, wake up," she said.

"Let the baby sleep if he wants to," Dad blurted out from the armchair. "He cries enough as it is without anyone encouraging him."

"But what's the matter with him?" asked my mother. She stopped Grandma, grabbing her by the waist. She made her sit down. Mom sat opposite her.

"He's not sleeping," my grandmother said.

My mother's back straightened. My father leaned forward in his armchair. I ran to the baby.

"What do you mean, he's not sleeping?" asked my mother. She took the little boy from his great-grandmother's arms.

"He's not sleeping," she said again.

The eggs spluttered in the frying pan. The smell of burning began to spread around the living room.

Mom lifted up the baby. She gave him a puzzled look and then touched her lips to his forehead, before holding him near her ear. She sighed with relief.

"You say such silly things," she chided my grandmother. "Of course he's sleeping. His breathing's perfect. He doesn't even have a fever. You must stop scaring us."

"So why won't he wake up?"

"He's a baby," I answered. "He can sleep all he likes."

Mom laughed when she heard my reply.

Grandma's expression stayed the same.

"Go on, wake him up."

Mom put the baby on her legs and shook his little face with two fingers. There was no reaction.

"It's him who wakes me up every morning," my grandmother continued. I noticed a trembling in her throat. She took the crucifix from among the folds of her nightgown and spun it around in her fingers.

My mother began jolting her legs, rocking the baby. Her heels came out of her slippers, like Dad's had when he played with me when I was little, gripping my hands and making me trot on his lap. I'd look at the spot of light in the living room and become a cowboy riding a horse through one of the deserts in those movies that Dad never stopped watching. If I felt brave, I'd yell and free my arm to crack an imaginary whip. Until my father decided I was too heavy to keep riding his legs like a horse.

"I still can't hear him crying," my grandmother said. "Something's wrong with the boy."

We sat in silence. All that could be heard was Mom's slipper hitting the floor, and the constant sizzle of the eggs burning in the frying pan.

From the entrance to the living room, my sister said, "Is something wrong with him?"

She came over to us and picked up her son, then rocked him in her arms. There was no response. She pointed at the kitchen with her chin. A column of smoke was coming from the pan, where the eggs were now totally burnt.

"We're going to set ourselves on fire," she said. "Again."

Dad shot to his feet and stood there for a few seconds, before clicking his tongue and leaving the room. My sister watched his movements. Something happened behind the hole in her mask. A smile.

I had an idea. With the baby still in his mother's arms, I took hold of him.

"Can I?" I asked. I waited for her to let go. When she did, I took the baby like Mom had shown me, his head near my elbow, and I went to the spot of light in the living room.

"Be careful," Mom said. "What're you doing?"

"What *is* he doing?" Grandma also wanted to know.

I sat in the spot of light as I had done the day the little boy was born. I positioned myself so that my back faced the others, hiding the baby.

"What are you doing?" my mother repeated with curiosity.

I moved the baby on my lap until the beam of light fell on his face. "You don't know about locked doors yet," I whispered. "Feel the sun."

The baby opened his eyes and started crying.

"See?" I heard my sister say. "There was nothing wrong with him."

15

That night, while I was cleaning my teeth, my sister's mask appeared reflected in the mirror.

"Were you in the bathtub?" she asked me.

She gripped my free hand, then picked up her toothbrush and dipped it in the froth I'd spat out. There were some days we had to share the foam, use baking soda, or even brush our teeth with just water, but in the end we always had toothpaste again. Among all the pills that Mom made us take there was one, a white one, called calcium. It was good for our teeth.

My sister began moving the brush inside her mouth. She had to manage with just her left hand. During the process, we looked at each other in the mirror, without saying a word. I spat. Then she did. A string of red saliva hung from her mouth, joining her bottom lip to the small puddle of blood and drool she'd spat out. When she lifted her head, the thread broke and stuck to her mask. "Is that normal?" I asked when I saw the blood.

"Living like we live, yeah."

She quickly washed the froth and blood away, before drying the saliva on her chin with the five-buttoned blouse. Then she let me rinse my mouth out, before rinsing her own and turning off the water. She pulled on my wrist to lead me out of the bathroom, much like Mom had done that very morning. I resisted until I managed to put my toothbrush back in its place. I hadn't used it, but I also made sure the soap was firmly in the blue fish.

We went into my sister's room. She sat me at the bottom of her bed and went to the baby's crib. The rest of my family was still in the living room after dinner. She turned around, resting her backside on the edge of the crib.

"Tell me, were you in the bathtub?"

I nodded. I squeezed my hands between my bare knees. I was wearing a pair of my white underpants.

"And?" she said. She noticed she'd left her bedroom door open. She closed it without making a sound. Her mask turned on her shoulders to look at me. "What did you see?"

"I didn't see anything." It was true.

"Did you wake up when I came in?"

I took a bit longer to answer that question. My sister had time to come sit beside me. I felt her breath on my neck, the mask almost touching my face. I nodded.

"What did you hear?"

I shrugged.

"Tell me what you heard."

The mask moved even closer.

"You threw up," I said.

"Don't lie," she replied. "I didn't throw up."

"I heard you . . ." Instead of saying it with words, I imitated the retching.

"But I didn't throw up."

"And you washed."

"I was washing my hands," she explained, "and what else?"

"You ran out when there was a noise in the hall."

"It was Dad, wasn't it?" My sister's mask came away from my face. "What did Dad go into the bathroom for?"

"You left the soap in the sink," I complained.

"That's not what I asked. Why did Dad go to the bathroom?"

"I don't know," I replied.

"Did he go to see what I'd been doing?"

"He told me off," I reminded her. "He didn't even know you'd been in there."

"Why was he there, then?"

"He had scratches on his back," I said. "But he didn't put anything on them."

"Scratches," my sister repeated. She ran her left thumb over the curve of the fingernails on her right hand.

"I also saw him wash himself." I wasn't sure how to say it. "You know . . ." I pointed at my underpants. "Then he pulled the chain. And he told me off for the soap."

My sister continued to run her thumb over the edges of her nails. She sat in silence.

For a long time.

So long, it was me who carried on the conversation.

"What?" I asked.

The baby moved in the crib. He made the special cooing sound he made when he got himself comfortable.

"What is it?" I said again.

It was another few seconds before she began to speak. She lowered her face until her plastic chin almost touched her chest. She checked the door was still shut.

"Do you know what Dad was washing?"

I shook my head.

"Have you got to the book in Mom's lessons about how children are made?" she continued.

"I know how children are made."

My sister breathed out. She took ages to finish taking a deep breath. "Dad's not as good as you think," she said.

"I know. He made me sleep in the bathtub."

She smiled and took my hand.

"That's nothing," she said. "He can do worse things." She pulled my hand to position it on her stomach. Then she looked at the crib. She waited for me to do so, too, before continuing. "That baby there came from my tummy."

As if he'd heard us talking about him, the little boy kicked the air with both legs.

"I know he did," I said, "I saw him come out." I remembered how I'd gripped my sister's leg while she struggled, naked on the dining table. How she'd fought to free herself. And to get the mask off her face. I heard in my mind the sound made by her wrist bone when Dad let her hand drop.

"And who put it there?" she asked me. At the same time she pressed my hand against her belly. A bone in her neck clicked. A tear appeared on her lower eyelid and got trapped on the edge of the mask's hole. For an instant it sparkled when it reflected the light from the bulb hanging from the ceiling. In the end it fell inside, behind the orthopedic material.

I thought about the answer to the question she'd asked. All I could do was reply with another question. "Was it the Cricket Man?"

She shook her head with a click of her tongue. She rested the hand that was still free on mine.

"No," she whispered. Another long out-breath prepared her for what she was about to say. She moistened her lips before speaking. "It was Dad."

She blurted it out. The baby kicked behind the bars of his crib. Bars like the ones on the basement's windows. My sister looked at me. She held my gaze for just a few seconds. Twice her eyes glanced toward the door.

"Dad?" I asked. The skin on my arms and thighs tightened and was suddenly covered in dozens of dots, as if a creature inside me wanted to get out.

"Yesterday wasn't the first time," she continued.

"Yesterday?"

My sister let go of my hand. She rested one of hers on my back. She ran it up and down, digging her nails into my flesh. Tracing scratches much like the ones I'd seen the night before on Dad's back.

"Was it you?" I asked.

She nodded.

"What did he do to you?"

"He hurt me."

"And, a baby?" I asked.

Her eyes went out of focus. "No, not that," she answered. "I hope not." Her chest rose as she breathed in. Then she shook her head as if waking herself up. She repositioned herself on the bed, tucking a leg in and sitting on it. The mattress springs squeaked with the movement.

"Promise me you won't say anything," she said. Her voice took on a sudden hardness. "You must promise. Not to Dad, not Mom, not Grandma. Not even your brother."

"Does he do it to you a lot?"

"What?"

"Dad. Does he do that to you a lot?"

My sister showed me a fist. She unfolded her fingers one after the other. After opening a full hand, she closed it again and continued to count. She stopped when she closed her fist for the second time.

"Does Mom know Dad hurts you?"

"If you know how children are made," replied my sister, "then that baby makes it pretty obvious, doesn't it?"

A shiver ran through my whole body.

"But you have to promise you won't say anything. You have to swear it on the baby's life. And on . . ." My sister looked around her.

The orthopedic nose pointed to various parts of the room as the mask scanned the space. Then she got up, took something from Grandma's bedside table, and returned to her position on the bed. She took both my hands in hers and then untangled what she'd taken from Grandma's bedside table. It was a rosary. She wrapped our fingers in the maroon-colored beads.

"Swear on the One Up There," she said. She squeezed the rosary until my hands hurt. "Say after me: I won't say anything about this to anyone." My sister was breathing in a strange way, her eyes fixed on the door. "I won't say anything about this to anyone. I swear on the One Up There," she reeled off. "Repeat it." She spat out the last words, spraying me with saliva. "Repeat it!"

She squeezed the rosary even tighter, twisting it to strangle one of my fingers, which turned bright red.

"I won't," I started to say. A white band appeared on my skin around the beads. "I won't say anything about this to anyone. I swear . . ." I tried to remember the words. "On the One Up There."

"Not anyone," she repeated. "You've sworn on it."

I nodded.

"And not just because of that." A different light appeared in her eyes. "But also because otherwise I could tell all your secrets." She was referring to the firefly jar with which I could've suffocated the baby. "Not anyone," she said one last time.

"Not anyone," I repeated.

Then she untangled the rosary. She got up to put it back in its place, but stopped. All of a sudden I felt the crucifix against my lips. "Kiss the One Up There," she ordered me. "You have to, to make your oath real. If you break it after you kiss the One Up There, the punishment will be a thousand times worse."

She pressed the cross against my mouth with such force that I could barely move my lips. Even so I managed to give it something resembling a kiss.

"Good," she said.

The bedroom door opened just as my sister put the rosary back. With a leap, she let herself fall onto my grandmother's bed. She pretended to laugh.

"What's going on in here?" my grandmother asked.

My sister was still laughing.

"Nothing," she answered. She moved on the bed so that it made a sound. "I'm playing with my brother."

My grandmother's sparse eyebrow moved up her forehead.

"Where are you?" she asked into the air.

"Here," I answered.

My voice served as a guide so she could face me.

"What's going on?" she persisted.

I looked at my sister, at her eyes behind the mask. The same eyes that had just cried, even if the tear had fallen inside. She forced another chuckle out and bounced on the bed again in an improvised imaginary game. I looked at the baby. The sound of the springs was making him stir. He began to cry. The scratches my sister had just made on my back were burning. Scratches like the ones that would already be healing on Dad's back.

"I don't know," I replied. "I don't know what's going on."

And not even my grandmother, who usually heard much more than just the words, realized that I'd said that from the bottom of my soul.

The first tear fell on my bare leg.

Then I cried like the little boy I was.

I cried like I was beside my nephew, in his crib.

16

After that, Mom came to see me in bed.

Sitting with my back against the wall, the sheet up to my waist, I was flicking through my insect book looking at the photographs. Thanks to that book I knew what a dragonfly was before I ever saw one. And a cricket. And a saturniid. I learned the names of almost all the species that appeared in those pages. Once I tried to make Grandma believe I'd learned Latin by reciting to her a long stream of scientific names of bugs. *Actias selene, Inachis io, Colias crocea.* I said them to her one after the other, but voiced them as if I was speaking normally. I even asked a question with the name of one species and then answered it with another. *Saturnia pyri? Acherontia atropos.*

You won't fool me, Grandma replied after hearing the list of names. *I bet you got all those from that book of yours on bugs.*

When Mom opened the door, I had the book open on the page that showed a photo of a firefly. In the picture it clung onto a blade of grass growing beside a lake. Its light was reflected, more weakly, on the water's surface. It became my favorite insect from the first time Dad let me see the book. There's no creature more amazing than one that can make its own light.

"Grandma tells me you cried," Mom said from the door. She was poking her head through the narrow crack she'd opened. From the living room the irregular flashing from the television now reached my room like lightning bolts on the floor.

I didn't answer. I was absorbed in the photograph of the firefly, in the magical green glow emitted from the bottom of its abdomen. *Do these bugs really make light?* I asked Dad the day he got the book down from the top shelf for me. It was when he still let me ride on his legs. When he didn't punish me by making me sleep in the bathtub.

Well, he explained, *I think they actually steal it from the sun. In the day they absorb its energy and then at night they let it out.*

Then I'd asked if the sun was that light that came in through the ceiling in the living room. He got up and left me alone in the room. That afternoon I discovered that Dad was wrong, that fireflies make their own light with chemicals in their body. Not everything my father said was true.

"I want to know if you've been crying," Mom said.

I shook my head.

"Grandma found you crying in her bedroom," she went on.

I touched the green glow in the book. It was no more than a bit of ink printed on a piece of glossy paper. Another artificial light.

Mom came over to my bed. "Are you going to tell me what's wrong?"

My finger touching the picture of the firefly was the same one my sister had strangled with the rosary to make me swear I wouldn't repeat anything she'd just told me.

"Nothing," I replied.

I thought of the baby. Of the day my sister gave birth on the kitchen table. Of how much the little boy's crying annoyed Dad. How he had never held the little boy in his arms. My throat tightened.

"Hey, what is it?" my mother asked. "Why are you crying now?" She made me shuffle along under the sheet to make room for her. She almost hit her head on the bunk's metal frame before sitting under my brother's mattress. Mom stroked my face. "Is it being here?"

I shook my head.

"This is my house," I replied. "I want to live with you all."

Her nose whistled. "So what is it, then?"

I thought about it for a few seconds, before answering, "You're tricking me."

"Why do you say that?"

No one had explained to me who the baby's father was.

"You all know whether or not the Cricket Man exists. You all knew that the kitchen door has always been locked. You all know much more than you tell me."

"Well, that's what parents do. It's our job," she responded. "Parents always know a lot more than their children."

"Well, I want to know everything."

"Believe me, there are things you don't want to know yet."

"Like what?"

Mom sighed. "All in good time."

"See? You only tell me what you want to tell me. You're tricking me all the time." I laid the open book on my chest, crossed my arms, and looked away, at the wall.

"All right," my mother then said, clapping her hands together. "Ask me whatever you want. Anything you can think of. And I promise I'll answer only with the truth." She gripped my chin to turn my face to her, her smile making the usual eye close. The light from the ceiling cast shadows under the irregular folds of her skin. "But just one question," she added.

I lifted the book from my chest and turned a few pages. "Do all these insects live outside?"

She nodded.

"All of them?"

She nodded again.

"Will I be able to see them one day?"

Mom stretched out a finger. "You were only meant to ask one question," she sang.

"Will I be able to see them one day?" I insisted.

She swallowed, then combed my hair with her hand.

"You're already seeing them," she answered. She touched the firefly picture in front of me.

"I mean really *see* them." I put the stress on the second-to-last word so she'd understand what I meant. But she already knew.

"You wouldn't see them even if you were out there."

"Why not?"

"It's impossible to see everything. People know about things through books. Like you do."

Mom had taught me to read and write. With my sister's help I also learned mathematics. Geography was my dad's thing.

"So the fact you don't actually see these bugs," Mom said, "doesn't mean they don't exist. If they exist here"—she put her finger on my temple—"and here"—she moved it to my chest—"that's all that matters."

I smiled.

"Up there, there are people who die without seeing the sea," she went on. "And many of them live very close to it." She rested a hand on my chest. "If we lived outside, right now we'd be no different. I'd still tuck you in at night, you'd be reading your insect book, and I bet you'd be asking me why you've never seen any of those strange butterflies."

She ran her thumb around a corner of the book and opened it at one of the first pages, where there was a light-green moth with two long tails on its lower wings. *Actias luna.*

"Who has actually seen one of these butterflies?" Mom asked. "Look, it's like a kite. I can promise you I never saw anything like that out there. Do you think anyone has seen them?"

I shrugged, pushing out my bottom lip. "The person who took the picture did," I said.

Mom laughed, curling her lips, and she managed to make me laugh, too.

"Why are we here?" I surprised her with the question, and knew she'd heard me by the way she looked at me, even if she tried to hide it by laughing for longer.

"Why are we here?" I repeated.

"You were only meant to ask one question," she finally replied. "And you've already asked a few."

"Why are we here?" I said for the third time.

The laughter died in her face. She closed my book and got up to put it on top of the chest of drawers. Then she came back beside me, but this time didn't sit on the bed. She just crouched down to give me a kiss on the cheek before heading to the door. From there, her head against the frame, she said, "Because we can't be anywhere else."

She turned off the light. The glow from the television in the living room silhouetted her from behind. Before leaving, she added, "Same as everyone else." She closed the door, leaving me in total darkness.

17

The next evening, before dinner, Dad picked up a knife from the middle of the table. Mom left all the cutlery piled there so we could help ourselves. Grandma always stroked one side of her knife along her forearm to know which way to point the blade. Dad now took one of the big ones, one with a brown handle, and spread his other hand out on the table, his fingers wide apart, the palm pressed down on the tablecloth.

"Look, son," he said to my brother, "like in the movie last night." Dad began to stab the tip of the knife between his fingers. At first he did it slowly, but he gradually increased the speed until the noise of the knife hitting the table sounded like a horse galloping like they did in the Westerns.

My brother's laughter got louder and louder, with guttural spasms that almost made him choke. He was rocking in his chair and banging on the table. Twice he tried to clap, but his hands missed each other, and he ended up hitting himself on the shoulders. My sister stared down the hall to detach herself from the spectacle.

Mom brought the soup bowl. The white steam danced in front of her face before disappearing. She put it down at one end of the table and caught my father's hand in midair as he pretended to be some dirty cowboy gambling in a saloon.

"Done?" my sister said when she couldn't hear the cutlery trotting on the tablecloth anymore. She waited a few seconds to make sure.

Then the white mask turned on her shoulders.

And it was just then that she started to bleed.

The blood appeared suddenly.

A dark red stream, as if the orthopedic material were bleeding. My sister was the last to realize. She stretched out her arm to reach the soup as if nothing had happened as the blood emerged on the edge of the hole she had as a mouth.

"What is it?" she asked. She must've seen the surprise and horror on our faces.

She screamed when she saw the blood spots on the tablecloth. Little apples on the branches of the trees printed on the material. Dad dropped his knife. He pulled his other hand away before it could stab him.

"You're bleeding," my mother said.

My sister felt the mask with her hands. Searching for the source of the flow, with her fingers covered in her own blood, she made fingerprints all over the white plastic.

"Bleeding?" Grandma asked, moving her head in several directions. She felt for my sister's artificial face with both hands. When her fingers met the liquid that covered the mask she snatched them back as if they'd touched something hot. Then she held them to her nose and smelled them.

"It's blood!" she yelled.

My mother went to help my sister. She made her stand up and then examined the contour of the mask. Twenty fingers touched it like a colony of ants with their antennae cut off.

"We have to get it off you," said my mother.

Dad's hand shot out from wherever it was and caught one of my wrists.

"Come on, come with me," Mom said as she guided my sister toward the kitchen sink.

"Do you have to do it here?" my father asked.

Mom didn't answer. She just positioned my sister with her back to me. I could see the strap running from one side of her head to the other. Despite my mother's precautions, Dad's warm hand pressed against my eyes.

He closed them for me.

I heard a chair scrape along the floor.

"You don't have to go," said my father. I knew he was saying it to Grandma.

"What's happening to me?" my sister asked.

"Let's take a look," Mom replied.

"It's this basement," added my sister. "It's going to kill us all."

Although I couldn't see anything, I assumed that my sister had taken off her blood-soaked mask, showing Mom the face the fire had made. And that Mom would be examining her old wounds to find the source of the hemorrhage.

She quickly found it.

"It's nothing," I heard Mom say. "Just a nosebleed."

Dad's hot breath whispered in my ear, "If you can call it a nose."

I heard the water come on.

"Wash it until the bleeding stops," my mother instructed her.

"She should tip her head back," Grandma added from the table.

"That's a really bad idea," Mom answered.

"I did it with your husband every time he fell off a sled or got hit by a ball," she responded. "I know about these things."

The water fell in a different way in the sink. My sister was taking Mom's advice. "Keep going, until it stops," my mother said. "It has to stop sometime."

I heard my sister rubbing her face. A very similar situation to the one I'd experienced two nights before, when Dad made me sleep in the bathroom. When she'd snuck in to wash. When I remembered that, Dad's warm hand on my face made me recoil.

The water was still running.

"It won't stop," my sister said after a while. "The blood won't stop coming."

"Then plug your hole with your fingers," Dad said. "Do whatever you want. But we should eat, the soup's already cold."

My grandmother's chair scraped against the floor.

"I said you don't have to go," repeated my father.

This time she ignored him. I heard her short steps approaching the kitchen.

"Get one of those cloths we keep around here," Grandma said, "and press it hard to her face. The pressure will make it stop."

There were a few noises I couldn't identify.

"That's it," said my grandmother. "Now let's eat."

More footsteps came toward the table, which vibrated when everyone sat down. Dad pressed harder on my eyes.

"You can't eat here without the mask on," he told my sister. "The boy's here." He moved my head with his hand, as if that was necessary to prove I was there.

"Who is it who my face really bothers?" my sister asked. "The kid? Or you?"

A piece of cutlery hit the table. The high-pitched screech of a chair's legs against the floor was followed by the muffled footsteps of someone heading to the hall.

"How are you going to eat your soup without a spoon?" my mother asked.

"I'll make do," my sister replied. She slammed her bedroom door shut.

"You can eat now," my father said.

As he took away his hand, the air dried the veil of sweat with a cool feeling. The first thing I saw when I opened my eyes was my sister's mask on the table. A bloody, empty face looking up at the ceiling, praying to the One Up There, perhaps.

My sister didn't come out of her room to return her bowl to the kitchen. It was my grandmother who fetched it, when she went to the room to bring out the baby. She sat on the sofa beside my mother. She was humming a song and rocking him in her arms. She was about to change him, and a big bottle of talcum powder sat on her lap. The smell was even stronger than the dirty diaper that she'd set aside on the floor.

I climbed onto the sofa to sit next to Mom. I saw that she had something in her hands. It was my sister's mask. She was wiping it with a gray cloth. The smell of ammonia told me she was cleaning off the bloodstains. She'd wedged the orthopedic mask onto one of her knees, and was holding it in place, rubbing the forehead hard. The brown color of the dry blood gradually dissolved, fading to an orange and then a pinkish cloud, before finally making way for the white. The corner of the cloth was stained brown. She turned it around a few times to find another part of the material that was still clean, and did the same with the nose bump. It was as if her knee were looking forward.

"What is it?" she asked me. "Are you going to sit there watching me all night?"

I shook my head. "I came to give you a kiss goodnight."

"Go on, then," she said. "And another for your grandmother. Then go to bed. Dad will want to watch a movie."

She waited for the kiss as she continued to handle my sister's mask. When I gave it to her, she was going over the false lips.

"Why does she have to wear it?" I asked.

"What?"

"Why does she have to wear the mask all the time and you don't?"

Mom's hand that held the cloth stopped. "She doesn't always wear it," she explained. "She sleeps without it. She washes without it."

"But here," I said, waving my finger around the living room. "She always wears it here. When I'm around."

Mom sighed.

"The fire affected us all differently," Grandma broke in. While she said it, she stroked the baby's pink face.

"It wouldn't do you any good to see what her face is like," added Mom. "It could frighten you. She doesn't have—" Mom ran a finger over the curve of her nose. "You know."

Then I touched Mom's face. I stroked the creased skin around her eyes. "Your faces don't scare me," I said.

Her nose whistled. She seemed touched.

"I want to have a face like all of you," I added. "I don't want to be different."

Mom suddenly snatched my hand from her cheek. "Don't ever say that. You have a face that people would like to look at, with those two beautiful moles." She touched one of them, then the other, under my right eye.

"What people?" I asked.

Mom took in a deep breath.

"There are no people here," I said. "Just us. It wouldn't matter if my face was burned."

"No, son, it *would* matter." She continued to stroke my face.

"It would matter," she said again.

Grandma wanted my attention.

"Come," she said. "Come over here."

I went around the back of the sofa to the other end and sat by Grandma. She rested the baby on her knees and put her two hands on my face. She kneaded my flesh with her fingers as if molding it. I felt my eyelids stretch, my lips contract. One nostril opened wider than the other when she pulled the tip with her thumb and forefinger. She also pinched my eyebrows and bent them out of shape.

"There you go," she said when she'd finished her work. "Now you're just like us."

I tried to smile but my grandmother's fingers were clutching my face and it was impossible.

"Am I handsome?" I asked, but I hadn't mastered the different shape of my lips and pronounced it with an odd lisp. "I talk like my brother!" I joked.

"Very handsome," said Grandma.

"You can't see me, that doesn't count," I responded. "Mom, am I handsome?"

I could barely make out an unevenly colored blob when she leaned over to look at me. A form lit from above by the bulb that hung from the ceiling. My stretched eyelids meant I couldn't see much.

"Am I handsome?" I repeated.

"Let go of him, will you?" my mother said. "I don't like seeing him like that."

My grandmother took her hands away from my face and my features went back to normal. Like the new skin of a caterpillar after it sheds its old one. Back to how it always was.

"You were lucky enough to be in here on the day of the fire," my mother said, indicating her belly. "Don't wish that away."

I crossed my arms as my only response.

"Anyway," Grandma murmured beside me, "you're not different, in actual fact." She lifted the baby up from her lap. "He's the same as you," she said.

I heard Mom's nose whistle.

I looked at my nephew. At his little face full of light and shade. A pink face, smooth and uniform like mine. He blinked as if he knew I was looking at him.

Dad returned then to the living room dragging his brown slippers, which already had a hole in the bottom from the rubbing.

"You, the house ghost. Don't you have a book to read? Or some experiment to do with a lemon?"

I didn't answer.

"Or even better," he continued, "go find your sister. Get her to come take the boy. I have to speak to your mother and grandmother."

I got off the sofa. Halfway down the hall, I heard one of the kitchen cupboards opening behind me. "We're having everything we're meant to have," Dad said.

"Yep," Mom replied, "all the essentials."

Then I remembered something. I retraced my footsteps. Dad stopped talking when he discovered me in the living room.

"Didn't I tell you to go look for your sister?" he asked.

"I can't," I answered.

"And why not?"

"Her mask's here," I said, pointing at the sofa.

"I'll go," Grandma said. She felt for the mask with her hand until she found it. Then she got up from the sofa, knocking off the bottle of talcum powder. A white cloud rose for a second over the basement's floor. Grandma trod in the powder and left two white footprints on a tile, but luckily she dodged the baby's dirty diaper. She continued down the hallway.

"Are you planning to stay there all night?" Dad asked me from the kitchen. He was resting his hand on one of the cupboards, the one where Mom kept the tons of pills she made us take. "Can you go, for goodness sake?"

In our bedroom my brother was whistling his song. I took the opportunity while he was in his trance to say goodnight to my fireflies. When I went to get into bed, the legs that hung from his bunk blocked my path.

"Out of the way, Scarecrow," I said.

He laughed with a heehaw, separating his legs to form an upside-down U. I passed between them while he continued to laugh. His bedsprings squeaked with each spasm.

Then a train's clatter reached me from the living room. Along with the high-pitched whine of a harmonica. Dad had put on his favorite movie again. My brother stopped laughing and jumped down from the bunk, making the floor shake. He left the room in the direction of the living room, where he would sit to watch the film with Dad.

I lay looking up at the mattress I had as a ceiling.

Repeating the movie's lines one by one.

The dark around me became denser when the same old melody started up, the unhappiest melody I'd ever heard. My eyes moistened when the orchestra's sound swelled and the singer hit the highest notes of her sad song.

I was forcing myself to stay awake. I had to ask my sister something, and I had to ask it that night.

Mom was the first to go to bed. The floor creaked as she went past my door. The bathroom pipes whistled when she turned on the water and then emptied the cistern. I heard her close her bedroom door. My grandmother closed hers a few minutes later, making as little noise as possible.

My brother was the total opposite. As soon as the movie ended, he got up from the sofa, making it scrape on the floor, and ran down the hall, not caring whether anyone was asleep. When his shadow dimmed the light that came in under our bedroom door I covered my face with my sheet, ready for the earthquake. The bunk's metal frame shook as he climbed the ladder. Dozens of springs squeaked as they took his weight. Then the frame vibrated for a few minutes. The trembling got more intense as my brother's breathing did. He groaned just before the movement stopped. Straightaway he began to snore.

Later it was Dad who was moving around in the bathroom. I heard him brushing his teeth and then opening his bedroom door with his key.

The house was silent. Except for the cistern's dripping and my brother's snores.

Only my sister hadn't gone to bed yet. She was still in the living room.

I stayed in bed looking into nothingness, trying to hear any suggestion of movement in the living room. I listened so intently that I could hear the fireflies' legs climbing the colored pencils inside the jar.

After my brother had changed positions a few times, I got out of bed and tiptoed down the hallway. Luckily the floor didn't creak like it had with Mom. My eyesight adjusted to the dark, and the colored pilot lights on the television and video, those dead fireflies, were almost as bright as lightbulbs. Before going through the entrance to the main room, I closed my eyes, in case my sister had decided to take off her mask.

A cold blade tore at my stomach when I realized my mistake.

It had all been a trick of the Cricket Man's. He'd come in the house attracted by the smell of my sister's blood. He'd hidden somewhere in the living room without any of us noticing. Disappearing into the shadows of a corner. Watching us with his giant black eyes. His long antennae vibrating and brushing against the ceiling. He'd trapped my sister in the living room and was using her as bait to lure me there.

And it'd worked. There he had me, defenseless in the middle of the room, my eyes closed. I hunched my shoulders waiting to hear his back-to-front knees as they bent. Waiting for his legs to touch my face.

But nothing happened.

The sweat on my back evaporated, leaving me with an icy sensation.

I half opened my eyelids. I could make out the usual contours of the living room: the sofa, Dad's armchair, the shelves for the books and tapes. The television's red pilot light made a silhouette.

Lots of hair.

I closed my eyes so tight my top lip was pulled in.

"What on earth are you doing?" whispered my sister.

"The Cricket Man," I answered.

She rasped the roof of her mouth. "Going chirp-chirp?"

I heard the strap tighten against her head. I opened my eyes. The red light from the television outlined my sister's artificial features. She was sitting on the floor with her legs crossed and her back resting on the sofa legs. Inside the holes in her mask her eyes seemed as black as I'd imagined the Cricket Man's to be.

"What're you doing here?" I asked.

She just let her head fall. I noticed some remains of blood that my mother must've missed or which perhaps she'd been unable to clean off. I sat on the floor next to my sister, brushing against her with the left side of my body. I could feel her breathing. I wondered whether I should ask her anything, or just let things happen around me like I always did. Just observing, and accepting Mom's and Dad's explanations. And Grandma's.

"Was it Dad?" I asked then.

My voice was no more than an out-breath, just air that my lips molded in letter form, like the smoking caterpillar in *Alice's Adventures in Wonderland*. I read that book and watched the movie in the basement. It was one of the tapes that Dad kept on the lower shelves.

"Da . . . d?" In a single syllable my sister managed to change her voice from a whisper to normal volume. "What about Dad?"

"The nosebleed," I said.

My sister swallowed. I went to stroke her face, but stopped my hand in midair. She noticed. Her eyes moved behind her mask like bee larvae inside a honeycomb's cells. She grabbed my wrist to pull my hand to her face.

"You can touch me," she whispered. "If you want, you can touch me."

"I don't want—"

But my sister squeezed my wrist harder. The first thing I touched, just with the tips of my fingers, was the curve of her false cheekbone. I kept my hand cupped so it wouldn't span more surface. She rested her left hand on mine while keeping hold of my wrist with her right. The gentle gesture made me stop resisting. I laid my now-relaxed hand on the right side of her mask.

The white wall that hid my sister.

She closed her eyes and took a deep breath.

"I can feel your warmth," she said.

And although what I was touching was a cold, rigid surface, I could feel the throb of something living underneath, like an eggshell with the chick still inside.

"Was it him?" I persisted.

The bee larvae squirmed. She examined my face, our intertwined hands resting on her cheek. She swallowed.

"Yes," she answered, "everything's his fault." She squeezed my fingers and separated them from the orthopedic material. Pain burned in my thumb. "But you can't tell anybody," she said. "On the One Up There."

I remembered the oath we'd made with Grandma's rosary. She made me renew it. The red light from the television gave the mask a different glaze. New, darker circles appeared under her eyes.

"Nobody," she said again.

The shadows changed inside the hole she had for a mouth. My sister pushed my hand away and got up without giving me a chance to reply. Her socks crept off down the hallway while I sat still rubbing my thumb. Her bedroom door closed before I had time to get to my feet. She'd suddenly gone, like the spot of sunlight between my fingers at the end of each day.

I tiptoed back to my room.

I got into bed under the thunderstorm of my brother's snores. I reached up and felt the curved contour of his bunk. Then I ran two fingers over the palm of the hand that'd stroked my sister's face. A face that could've been sculpted from the bone of her own skull.

An inside-out face.

With the sheet up to my chin, I asked the One Up There not to be hard on me if I decided to break the oath and tell my mother everything I knew. I also asked him not to let my father do anything bad to my sister.

"You don't have to bring me any more potatoes," I murmured as an offering.

Then I remembered the wood from which Dad had built the crib. It had appeared in the basement just a few days before my sister gave birth on the kitchen table. Grandma had been saying how urgently we needed the crib, including it in her prayers, I bet, since my sister had started to sit with her hands resting on the bulge on her tummy. But even so, that wood hadn't appeared until my sister was complaining of pains down there.

The One Up There had to be asked for things ahead of time. Being nailed on Grandma's cross meant he couldn't do everything right away.

So for the time being, it fell on me to protect my sister.

18

The next morning, while Mom explained to me with a textbook that Earth had lots of tectonic plates that moved and smashed against each other to form mountains, I was thinking about another book. *How to Be a Spy Kid.* It would give me all the tricks I needed to protect my sister.

Mom told me about the liquid core, the strata, the crust, and the atmosphere. "Have you understood everything?" she asked.

I nodded.

"Let's see whether you have." She pushed the book toward me on the page where there was a picture of Earth, with a corner cut into it like an orange.

"A practical example: Where do we live?" She handed me the pencil she'd been using to underline part of the text.

Kneeling on the chair, I drew a rectangle, the place where we lived. The basement.

Mom's nose whistled when I showed her the drawing. "Son, that's the center of the Earth. You've put us next to the core."

I looked at her without understanding where I'd gone wrong. She snatched the pencil from me.

"We live here." She drew an arrow pointing at the blue-and-white part of the ball.

"Really?" I asked.

Mom nodded.

"That's good. I thought we were deeper down."

Her bumpy hand rested on mine. She sat looking at me.

"What?" I eventually asked. "Why are you looking at me?"

She smiled, making one eye close.

"Come on," she said, "lesson's over."

I ran to my bedroom.

I threw myself onto my bed to reread the chapters of the book that would help me that night. Heading one of them was the motto that should guide any good spy.

"No one must know you are there," I read out loud. "No one will know," I whispered to the pages.

The book said I should familiarize myself with the terrain. That wasn't a problem. I knew every last detail of my sister's room. An illustration of a spy kid in uniform showed him dressed in black. The closest thing I found in the wardrobe was a black T-shirt and gray pajama bottoms. I hid them under the sheet. The young spy also had his face covered in a piece of clothing that only showed his eyes. I searched my bedroom, knowing I wouldn't find anything like that in the basement. He also had a thing called a walkie-talkie in his hand, which he'd use to alert headquarters if he was in danger. I shook my head because I didn't have any gadgets like that, or a headquarters to contact. In the other hand, the boy held a flashlight. I only knew of a couple of candles and a box of matches. Mom kept them in one of the highest cupboards in the kitchen.

When I was little, Dad showed me a trick that always made me laugh: he built a structure with five matches, lit one of them, and when it'd burned away, the rest went flying into the air in an explosion of little sticks. He stopped doing it as I grew older. I touched the book, my finger falling on a circle of light with which the young spy illuminated a footprint on a muddy track.

"I need a flashlight," I murmured.

I heard one of the colored pencils move inside the jar. The fireflies must have shifted it as they climbed up. I smiled. I might not have a walkie-talkie. I might not have a balaclava. But I did have my own flashlight. When I opened the drawer, the firefly jar glowed bright, lighting up the inside of the cabinet and the chick's shell that lay empty beside it.

"But you'll have to stay off until I say. We don't want my sister to see us. Or Dad, especially not Dad." The fireflies went out. I watched them walk around the jar's transparent walls. Then, out loud, I reread the motto of a good spy, printed in orange capital letters: *"No one must know you are there."*

I spent the day trying out movements on my bedroom floor. Rolling from one side of the room to the other. By dinnertime I was so nervous about the mission I was about to embark on that I could barely eat. My mother hit her head on the bulb when she stood to clear up the plates. The shadows stretched and shrunk, distorting the shapes on the table. Dad grabbed the lamp socket to stop it swinging.

"Not hungry?" he asked me. "You've left half your food."

With my fork I tore the peak from a mountain of mashed potato and put it in my mouth. I chewed without enthusiasm.

"Come on, hurry up. Your mother shouldn't have to make three trips."

I swallowed.

"That's what I like to see," Dad said.

"I don't want any more." I pushed the plate into the middle of the table, dragging the tablecloth with it.

"Do you know that there're children dying of hunger in other parts of the world?" said Dad.

"I don't know any other parts of the world."

"Oh yes, you do," my mother cut in. "Today we found out about the strata, the core . . . Did you know he drew the basement as if we were in the center of the Earth?"

Grandma's eyes lit up.

My sister laughed. "Wait, let me show you something," she said before getting up.

"Are you going to eat some more or not?" asked Mom.

I shook my head. She picked up my plate and put it on top of the tower she'd built as she spoke, squashing the food left on the seventh plate that nobody had touched.

"I'm going to bed," I said.

Dad gave an exaggerated gesture of surprise. "You don't even want to know what movie we're watching tonight?"

"It doesn't matter," I answered. "It's bound to be one I can't watch."

"Because you're younger than me," my brother said beside me. Two drops of spit fell onto the creased tablecloth.

"Why don't we watch a cartoon one tonight?" Grandma asked.

My brother groaned a complaint.

"Don't worry, Grandma," I said. "I'm tired."

"Your voice doesn't sound very tired."

The mashed potato was stuck in my throat. Grandma had uncovered my lie. The mission was in jeopardy before it'd even begun. I'd never be as professional as the spy kid in my book with his uniform, flashlight, and gadgets. I would have to stick to writing secret messages in lemon juice and communicating in Morse code with chicks and fireflies.

I felt my family's eyes on me as if they were giving off heat. Or maybe it was the heat from the blood rising to my face. I looked away as if I could escape it and saw my sister by the living room bookcase. Crouching, she was searching for a book, running her finger over the spines of the ones on the bottom shelf.

"Here it is!" she blurted out, attracting everyone's attention, except my grandmother, who still faced me, with new wrinkles of curiosity.

Something hit me on the shoulder.

"Look," my sister said, holding a book in front of my eyes. "This is the center of the Earth. Where we are is just a basement."

Dad clicked his tongue. "Leave him alone."

I read the title of the book out loud. *"A Journey to the Center of the Earth."*

"There's something to read in bed until you really are tired," said my grandmother. When she winked an eye the suspicion disappeared from her face.

I left the book on the floor, by my bed, open on the first pages. Like a tent for the basement rats. I pulled back the sheet and got dressed in the uniform I had to wear to copy the spy kid in the book.

I heard footsteps in the hall.

I threw myself on the bed and covered myself up to my chest. Just before Mom appeared through the door, I grabbed the book from the floor and pretended to read.

"Since when do you go to sleep without giving me a kiss?" Mom sat on the bed, wagged a finger feigning anger, and with the same finger pushed my book downward. "And since when do you sleep with a T-shirt on?"

Unable to think of a reply, I distracted her attention with another question. "We don't live at the center of the Earth?"

"You've seen that we don't."

I wanted to tell her everything I knew. That the baby was Dad's son. That Dad didn't treat my sister well. And that it was Dad's fault that her nose bled.

"Mom . . ."

But I was left voiceless as I remembered the oath I'd made to the One Up There. The way in which Grandma's rosary had strangled my finger. The feel of the figure molded in metal on my lips.

"Ye—es?"

The One Up There could stop sending us stuff. Might punish the whole family by making us go without food if I said something.

"Can a family of mammals have babies among themselves?"

Mom didn't answer. "Why do you ask that?"

I shrugged.

"I read in an animal book that they can't," I made up.

"Well, no, they can't." She bent over to kiss me. And then corrected herself: "It's not good if they do," she whispered. "But sometimes it happens."

Then I knew my sister was right. Mom knew about everything.

"I think someone hasn't brushed his teeth," Mom said. "I can smell mashed potato from here. Come on. Go. It'll take you two minutes."

"Do other mammals' pups clean their teeth?" I improvised.

Mom smiled.

"You win," she said. "But I'll only let you off this once. I don't know what's with you today with all this talk of mammals. I thought it was those strange bugs that you liked."

From the hall she asked me if I wanted her to leave the light on.

"Yeah, I'm going to read a bit more."

I put down the book as soon as she closed the door. I got out of bed and put my pillow under the sheets, hitting it to mold a shape like my body. My brother wouldn't notice my absence if my bed disappeared and his floated in the air on an invisible frame, but my parents might look in on me. I took the firefly jar from the drawer. They were glowing at different times in an irregular way. They were as nervous as me about the mission.

"Let's go," I said to them.

I turned off my bedroom light before opening the door. The water was running in the kitchen. There was still movement in the living room. My brother was talking loudly to my father about the movie they were going to put on. I crossed the hallway with a leap. There was total darkness in my sister's bedroom, but the baby wasn't crying. Mom was right: the best way to overcome a fear was to face up to it. I tapped the jar's lid. The fireflies lit up part of the room. Copying one of the book's basic movements I'd practiced in the day, I rolled along the floor. Before I reached my sister's bed I rotated myself so that my feet went under the bedsprings first. Then my legs and torso. With the help of my free hand I got my head under, too.

I put the jar near my face, with my arms bent and my hands pressed against the floor. I rested my chin on them.

"Off," I whispered to the fireflies. "We have to get used to the dark."

For a few seconds the world turned black, but I soon began to make out some forms. I could see vertical lines in front of me, in the background. After appearing to float in the air, they finally took shape. They became the baby's crib.

The baby himself was a dark blob behind them.

I also located the legs of Grandma's bed and even some of the cracks that time had made in the bedroom floor. As if the floor was the basement's skin and time was the fire that damaged it, just like my family's faces. I felt it. Grit and dust.

I took a deep breath.

I waited.

Until the door opened.

19

I recognized the sound of Grandma's slippers on the first footstep. And the smell of her talcum powder. I held my breath so she wouldn't hear me. Her feet moved in front of me like two frightened rodents. They stopped by the crib before continuing their slow walk to the bed.

The springs squeaked when she sat down, and I took the chance to take in air.

I heard her opening the drawer in her bedside table, straightaway recognizing the rattle of the rosary beads between her fingers. She prayed with a constant murmur, like the wings of a hummingbird hawk moth. The noise allowed me to breathe easily.

Before finishing, Grandma said out loud, "Take from me the days you give to him."

I identified the wet sound of a kiss and knew that Grandma was making her own oaths to the One Up There.

"You don't need to ask that," Mom's voice said, surprising me. She'd appeared in the room during Grandma's prayer. She turned on the light.

"I'm sure he has plenty of days left. You'll see." She sat on the bed beside my grandmother.

"I hope to God you're right," Grandma replied. "But he's old now. We're both old. The doctors have made it very clear to him what he's facing. He's been making all this effort for ten years and—"

I saw Mom hug Grandma when her voice failed.

"—and I don't want to be here when he's gone," she said between sobs.

I had no idea what they were talking about.

"Everything will be fine," Mom said. "I'm sure he has years left in him. He's strong."

I heard a kiss.

"And your son's certain of it, too. That's why he wants to start organizing Grandpa's replacement. So he can make the decision himself. None of us know what the best way will be, but—"

The baby started crying, interrupting the conversation. Mom got up to tend to him.

"What's up with him?" asked Grandma.

Mom shushed the baby. The screaming fit subsided, reduced to an almost inaudible gurgle.

"Do you know what?" Mom said. "The boy asked me something very odd today."

I pricked my ears even more when I heard myself mentioned.

"Odd?" Grandma asked, still sounding sad.

"About animals. Something about . . ." She paused as though trying to find the right words. "Something about whether a family of mammals can have babies among themselves."

I heard the drawer in Grandma's bedside table close. "Did he ask it because of the baby?"

"I don't know what to think," Mom answered.

When Grandma burst into tears again, Mom went back to the bed beside her. I saw that the crib was empty, so she must've had the baby in her arms.

"What's wrong now?" she asked. "What did I say?"

Grandma sniffed.

"Nothing. It's not you," she said. "It's this baby. I swear . . . I love him more than I love myself. I swear that's the truth. But every time I hold him . . ." She took a deep breath. "Every time I hold him, I feel the weight of every bad decision we've made."

She cried but kept speaking, letting her words out in a howl rising in pitch. "I see in him the worst of the sins committed in this basement. The worst of our sins."

Under the mattress, I, too, let out silent tears. I again felt my sister's scratches on my back imitating the ones I'd seen on Dad's. I remembered the single tear that she'd shed when she told me the truth about the baby. The tear that'd fallen behind the mask.

"How could we have let it happen?" asked Grandma.

Mom took a while to respond.

"We could punish ourselves every day," she said, "but there's no point."

Grandma blew her nose.

"And you know why?" continued Mom. "Because we have a healthy baby. And a baby as lovely as your grandchildren were. And we're going to look after him like we do them. Because he has his whole life ahead of him. Plus," Mom went on, "it's us, me and you, who have to love this baby most."

She lowered her voice. "This beautiful little thing that's fallen asleep. Such a gorgeous little boy whose mother doesn't want him."

As Mom got up to put the baby back in the crib, Grandma added, "His father doesn't want him, either."

Mom took a deep breath. "But that's not the same," she replied from the door.

"Goodnight." She turned off the light, barely making a noise with the switch. We were left in the dark again.

"Goodnight," Grandma whispered.

In the total silence of the room, I slowed my breathing until Grandma's slowed, too. I found a thousand meanings for the words I'd just heard from my hiding place.

When I knew Grandma was asleep, I took the chance to change the position of my arms.

My sister soon arrived.

The door opened, and the room was filled with flashes from the television in the living room, which disappeared as soon as she turned on the light. I put a hand over my eyes to give my pupils time to get used to the new reality. When I took it away, I saw her legs by the crib. I pressed my chin against the floor to expand my field of vision. My sister had a hand resting on the baby's tummy. She rocked him. The little boy carried on sleeping.

The mask turned on my sister's shoulders. I could see an eye hole, the curve of the nose, and a corner of her mouth. She was still. Perhaps listening to the rhythm of Grandma's breathing like I had minutes before. By the way her chest rose and fell, I could tell her own breathing had quickened.

She rocked the baby again.

She waited.

Then the hand she'd rocked the baby with went to one of the pockets she had on each side of the five-buttoned blouse. She undid the toggles with her eyes fixed on the baby. The movement of her fingers inside the pocket made it look as if it was full of life, as if cockroaches were crawling around in there.

Wood creaked on Grandma's bed. "It's not time yet," she said.

My sister's fingers stopped. They shot out of the pocket with the speed of real cockroaches.

"Feeding him now won't get you out of having to wake up later, you know," Grandma added.

My sister's white mask looked at her and at the baby. At the baby and at her.

"And switch the light off, will you? It's been hard enough as it is trying to get him used to the dark. It's taking him longer than it did your brother."

I smiled under the bed when I heard that, as if I'd won some sort of prize.

"How do you know I turned on the light?" my sister asked.

"Do you think I don't hear it when you flick the switch?"

With one step, my sister reached the door. She hit the switch hard, so it made a sound. "Did you hear that?"

"Excellent," Grandma replied, ignoring my sister's provocation. "Lights off."

The floor, crib, and bed legs gradually materialized in front of me in the darkness. Two moving blots, my sister's feet, approached the bed. Something touched my back. It was the mattress I was hiding under, dipping now under her weight as she sat. I laid the jar on its side and pressed a cheek against the floor. I remembered how Mom had explained to me what noodles were by squashing spaghetti on the table.

The blouse fell to the floor. It made another irregularly shaped patch in front of me. The bulge on my back changed shape and position, dividing itself bit by bit until it became a slight contour stretched along the mattress. I heard the mask strap stretch, and the elastic click as it was released. Then a hollow sound that told me she'd put the thing down on the bedside table.

My sister's breathing gradually fell in time with my grandmother's.

I listened to them for a long time, until my own breathing imitated their rhythm. I blinked a few times to stop myself from falling asleep. The dust gave the floor a rough texture, like the hair scar on Dad's face. I closed my eyes just for a second.

But it wasn't a second.

And what woke me was the sound of footsteps.

Someone was walking around the room.

When I opened my eyes I thought the Cricket Man must've come back to the basement to take away the baby he'd been unable to snatch on his first visit. Or to put me in his sack for spying from my hiding place under the bed. After blinking a few times I remembered the mission. It must be Dad walking around the room. He wanted to make my sister bleed, or put another baby in her belly.

The mattress lifted above me in one corner.

I was about to ask the fireflies for light.

Then the footsteps dragged along the floor near the crib. I heard my sister humming a tune, the music becoming a string of *mmm*'s that came from some place between the roof of her mouth and her nose.

It was the music from Dad's favorite movie. The saddest melody I'd ever heard. The orchestra's swell was now reduced to my sister's almost inaudible murmur. I recognized the silhouette of her feet by the crib.

The melody broke up in her throat when she arrived at the highest note.

The baby began to cry.

"I told you," I heard Grandma say. Her voice sounded deep, as if it'd traveled light-years to reach the room from the planet of dreams where she'd been. "Turn on the light."

My sister didn't reply, but she took Grandma's advice. I pressed my eyelids together when she flicked the switch. Then gradually relaxed them while she hummed the sad tune and the baby's crying rose and fell.

I was about to peer out, but then I remembered that my sister left her mask on the bedside table when she went to sleep. So I fixed my eyes on her feet. I climbed her legs with my gaze, stopping at her hip, her blouse pocket, her chest. The baby's legs hung at belly height. She held him with her left arm, the fingers lost in the folds of the diaper.

Still humming the song, she undid the top two buttons of her blouse. Her breast popped out from the material. I saw a purple circle around her nipple.

I pushed myself forward to expand my field of vision. I did it carefully: I stopped when the bed frame above me still blocked the view of my sister's face.

The humming broke off. I thought she'd heard the dust crunch under my hands. But then she continued with the melody, unaware of my presence.

Now I could see her bare breast and all of the baby's body. His little face was wrinkled up and his eyes were closed. His mouth wide open as if he was crying, but he wasn't. He bit my sister's left breast through the blouse.

"Not that one," she said. With a movement of her shoulder she pushed the little boy's mouth away, and that was when I noticed another movement lower down. In the blouse pocket. The imaginary cockroaches had returned. My sister's hand was moving around in there. Her wrist emerging and hiding behind the folds of fabric.

My heartbeat boomed in my ears. It seemed as if the whole house would hear it.

The hummed melody reached its highest point again. Once more my sister's throat gave way. She took up the song again from the beginning.

That was when her hand came out of her pocket.

Straightaway I noticed the sky-blue crumbs between two of her knuckles. The same color as the cubes of rat poison. She stroked her bare nipple with her fingers. She circled it a few times with two fingertips.

She hummed as she did it.

The brown skin turned bluish.

Then she lowered her fingers. She rubbed them together over the pocket like when Mom added salt to a salad.

"Is everything all right?" Grandma asked.

My sister stopped humming to answer. "Everything's fine," she said. I stared at her. At the blue powder that'd spread over her nipple.

"That's it," my sister whispered to the baby. "This one's yours. You can eat now."

She guided the little boy's head to her bare nipple stained blue.

20

I hit my head against the boards that supported the mattress as I tried to come out. My chin hit the floor. The firefly jar rolled. I kicked as if swimming, trying to make as much noise as possible. I couldn't find the strength to scream.

When I managed to get my head out, I steadied myself by anchoring my hands to the floor. I looked up toward my sister, not caring what face I'd find. Her hair flapped on her shoulders, free without the strap that always held it to her head.

"What's going on?"

It was my grandmother who shouted that. She shot up and waved her arms in the air as if a swarm of wasps attacked her.

My sister ran off around one side of the crib, heading for a corner of the room. An escape very similar to the one made by the rat I'd found in that very crib. She crouched in the corner, nowhere else to go.

The little boy started crying again. It sounded muffled coming from the small space where my sister had confined him, between her breast and the wall. When I reached them, I tried to get my hands in around her hips, but she stopped me with her elbows. She was pumping her arms as if they were a praying mantis's big legs.

"Let go of the baby!" I screamed.

A rough hand covered my mouth. I could taste the talcum powder. My grandma held me around the middle and pulled me. I stretched out my hands in an effort to grab hold of my sister. And my nephew. My fists closed on the air. Grandma turned me around and knelt in front of me. Locks of white hair were falling down her face, getting caught in the eyelids, in the scars on her skin, and in the corners of her mouth. I could see some bald patches. "What is it?" she shouted. She pressed my face between her hands. "You have to describe it to me."

I breathed.

Behind me I heard my sister squirming in the corner.

Drops of sweat slid down my forehead.

I let out a wild moan. It was a while before I was able to say a sentence.

"She's giving the baby rat poison," I finally said.

My grandmother's two eyebrows joined at the top of her nose to become one. She moved her lips but said nothing.

At that moment a tremor started in my bedroom. The earthquake advanced up the hall toward us. The door opened, the handle hit the wall, and my brother appeared in the room.

Grandma put him to use.

"Get the baby from her," she ordered him. She pointed at the corner where my sister still crouched.

I took a step back to get out of my brother's way. My sister's elbowing was no bother for him. Neither was her kicking. He took a few blows before he was able to grab her by the arms. He pulled her shoulders back, making a bigger space between her body and the wall. My sister's attempts to defend herself were reduced to spasms.

My brother yelled at us, "Take him!"

My grandmother stepped forward. She felt the contours of my siblings, searching for a gap between them where she could reach the baby, until she managed to get her arms over my brother's shoulder.

"I've got the baby," she said to my brother. Then, to my sister, she said, "Let him go."

My sister thrashed about.

"Let him go," my grandmother said again.

The thick veins on my sister's ankles changed shape when she went up on tiptoes. The baby's red face emerged from behind my sister's back. My grandmother grabbed him under the arms, my nephew's feet hanging in the air. She rocked and shushed him.

She sat on the bed.

My mother then came into the room.

"Leave her!" she shouted at my brother, who was still overpowering my sister in the corner. She leapt into the corner with her bent elbow pointing outward. She rammed it into the bottom of my brother's back when she fell on him. "Leave her!"

His response was just a grunt.

"It's not what you think. He hasn't done anything this time," Grandma said. "It was your daughter."

Mom stopped her attack. The baggy T-shirt she slept in reached her knees and showed the cleft in her chest.

Dad appeared in the doorway.

His face wrinkled up when he saw my mother with her legs apart, shoulders slumped and hands hanging on each side of her body. And my brother pushing my sister to trap her against the wall.

Sitting on the edge of the bed, Grandma held out her arms, offering the baby to anyone who could see him.

"Is his mouth blue?" she asked. "Is his little mouth blue?"

The baby kicked and cried.

"What do you mean?" My father looked at me, searching for an explanation. "What's your grandmother saying?"

Instead of answering, I went up to Grandma. I touched her arms so she knew I was there. She lowered them to my height. I took the baby like Mom had taught me. Then I sat on the bed, beside my grandmother.

"What's this about a blue mouth?" asked Dad.

I opened the baby's mouth with two fingers. Bubbles of snot exploded on his nose and splashed my hand. I separated his lips and discovered the ridges of flesh that were his gums. I examined them, and the inside of his lips. Another loud scream allowed me to peer into his mouth.

Tears gave me away. I sniffed.

Grandma touched my eyelids before I could say anything.

"No . . ." It was Mom who said that. It must've been the moment she understood what was happening. Perhaps, like me, she remembered the cubes of poison that'd disappeared. And she grasped the meaning of my grandmother's question. And the meaning of my tears. And why my brother was trapping my sister against the wall.

"What have you done to him?" she yelled at the corner. She knelt beside me to look at the baby and stroked his face with a finger. Then she pinched him hard. Twice. Three times. I wanted to get the baby away from her, but when he started crying again, I understood what Mom was trying to do. She kept his mouth open until she, too, could see the tip of his blue tongue. She snatched the baby from my arms and pinched it between two fingers.

"We have to make him sick," she said.

My sister spoke from her prison in the corner, her voice choked. "Don't worry—he—he won't die." Her breathing rasped in her chest. "Never—he never dies."

The hair scar on Dad's face moved to a straight angle I'd never seen before.

"You can't make me—" She choked on her own words. "You can't make me love that child. That baby's an abomination."

"Shut up!" Dad screamed. "The boy's here."

My parents looked at each other. Then their eyes rested on me just for an instant. Grandma straightened her back so suddenly I heard the muscles in her neck tense. Mom left the bedroom with the baby in her arms, heading toward the bathroom.

Dad approached the corner, pushing my brother aside.

"What've you done to the baby?" he asked my sister.

She covered her ears, her hands over her hair, and shook her head, pressing it against the wall. Dad forced her to turn around.

I closed my eyes and covered them with my hands before she faced me.

"And the mask?" Dad asked. "Can't you see the boy's here?"

"I wouldn't worry," she replied. "You have your son perfectly trained. There's no way to make him look at my face."

"Good. He shouldn't have to see it."

My sister moaned with pain.

"Tell me what you've done to the baby." Dad spat the words out.

"I gave him a little bit of this," she replied. I heard a sound I couldn't identify.

"Put that tongue away," said Dad. "And tell me why it's blue."

"And why do you care so much—*Dad*?"

She said the last word in an exaggerated way. I understood the meaning behind it. I heard the first slap. Then there was another.

My brother's guttural laugh exploded somewhere near them.

Grandma took me by the wrist. "Let's go," she whispered.

There was another slap.

This time my sister groaned.

"Are you trying to disfigure me?" she said. "Even more?"

My grandmother guided me across the bedroom. When I remembered the firefly jar under the bed I wanted to stop, but Grandma yanked me out of the room. The door closed behind me. On the other side, my sister screamed.

***

In the bathroom, my mother was holding the baby to her chest. A wet mark covered a bit of her T-shirt.

"I did it," she said. "He's been sick." She ran a finger over the wet material, picking up some white and blue residue. She shook her finger over the washbasin. "See?"

"What is it?" asked Grandma.

I described it to her.

Mom held the baby out in front of her to inspect his face.

"Will he be OK?" my grandmother asked.

She examined him, looking for any unusual symptoms. "He looks all right. I think he got everything up."

"Have you washed his tongue?"

"I had to pull on it. That's how I made him be sick."

"He couldn't have had much," I said. "I came out from the bed before he started sucking."

"Why were you hiding there?" Grandma asked.

Mom rocked the baby. "Hidden?" she asked. "And why are you dressed like that?"

I thought about my secret mission. The idea to protect my sister from Dad. When really it was the baby who needed protecting from my sister.

I left the bathroom without answering Mom.

"Hidden where?" she asked again, but I was already setting off down the hall toward the kitchen. I heard my grandmother explain what'd happened in the bedroom. I hit the switch, and a cone of orangey light illuminated the main room. It still must've been several hours before the spot of light would appear. I pressed the back of a chair against the oven in the kitchen and climbed onto it to reach one of the highest cupboards. I opened it. It smelled of dry rags. There were bottles of bleach and ammonia, two half-used candles, matches, scourers with the green side worn away, and, at the back, the box I was looking for.

The box of rat poison. I jumped off without bothering to put the chair back. I observed the picture of the rat in a yellow circle.

In the sink, I pulled back the flaps on the top of the box, shaking it so the cubes that were left would fall out. I turned on the water. I crushed the poison with a big wooden spoon, pushing the pieces down the plughole so they'd dissolve and wash away.

I cried thinking what could have happened. Imagining how I would never have been able to hold the baby in my arms again or enjoy the spot of sunlight together in the living room. Or stand by the window in the hall, breathing in the air from outside. Or how we would never have grown up together so that I could tell him about the night I left the firefly lamp in his crib so he wouldn't be scared of the dark.

My sister was wrong when she said that what the baby and I had in the basement wasn't a life.

Of course it was.

It was our life.

The only one we had.

The poison finished dissolving in the sink.

A door opened in the hall.

I heard my sister crying. There were thumps against the walls.

"Make her throw up as well," my father said. "She's swallowed the lot."

The water started running in the washbasin.

While the whole family was seeing to my sister, I took the chance to go back to the baby's room. I searched my hiding place under the bed. I found what I was looking for. The firefly jar had been hidden when it rolled away before the incident. This time I concealed it under the black T-shirt. It was obvious it was under the material, but I knew no one would pay any attention to me right then. In the hall, my brother was craning his neck to watch what was happening inside the bathroom from the door.

Before closing my bedroom door, between my sister's groans, my brother's donkey noises, and my grandmother's instructions on how to make my sister sick, I heard Dad say: "I'm not dealing with another dead body."

21

I quickly put the firefly jar in the drawer and undressed. I moved the pillow I'd hidden under the sheets to simulate my body, and took shelter in my bed, covering up to my chin.

I heard my sister throwing up in the bathroom.

She let out a cry of pain.

Similar to the one I'd heard once, when I discovered how my sister's belly button had popped out when she was still pregnant. It happened one night as we got ready to take a bath, waiting naked for the tub to fill. "Is the baby going to come out?" I'd asked when I saw the belly button sticking out.

"I hope not," she answered, looking at herself in the mirror while massaging her breasts.

I'd knelt down so my face was at the same height as the baby.

"Is it dark in there?" I asked the tummy. I pressed my ear to my sister's skin, waiting for an answer that never came. "Do you have any light in there?"

My sister pushed me away.

"Come on, get off," she said. "How's there going to be light inside my stomach? Where would it come from?"

"We don't know where the light that comes in through the crack in the ceiling comes from."

She blew out behind the mask. "Doesn't Dad know?" she asked.

I shook my head.

I put a leg in the bathwater to test it. I snatched it out with a spasm.

"What?" asked my sister. "Is it cold?"

"Freezing," I replied. Although the water in the basement was never hot, turning the faucet all the way to the left made the temperature reasonable. My sister had now turned it all the way to the right.

"Why did you fill it like that?" I asked.

"Get out," she said to me.

"I have to take a bath, too."

"Get out," she repeated. "Or I'll take my mask off, if you want."

"Dad will tell us off if we take separate baths."

"You can come in afterward."

She surged forward to push me out with her giant belly. She got me out into the hall and poked her head out, looking both ways.

"Count to ten then come in." She closed the door, leaving me naked outside.

I began to count.

One. Two. Three. On four, I heard my sister's body go into the water. On six, I heard her let out air through her mouth, and she gave that special cry of pain. On nine I heard her teeth chattering. And on ten I opened the door. I saw my sister struggling to breathe, submerged to the neck in the freezing bathwater. Just her belly rose out of it like a mountain of flesh.

I stepped in the puddles that'd formed on the floor.

I dipped a leg into the water, but I pulled it out with another spasm. The cold cut through my skin.

"It's too cold," I said.

My sister's mask, soaked, turned to look at me.

"It's perfect," she replied. Her teeth chattered as she spoke.

The wet mask and her teeth making that noise was something I never forgot. For the first time I understood the reality of what'd happened that evening in the bathroom. It was the same thing my sister had tried to do now with the poison. Get rid of the baby.

The sound of a dry, rough retch reached me from the bathroom. My grandmother was still forcing my sister to be sick.

My bedroom door flew open.

From the doorframe to my bed, a rectangle of light appeared on the floor. Inside it two long shadows were cast, those of my father and my sister. He was holding her by the shoulders, her back to me. A piece of pink material from the blouse emerged like a handkerchief from each of my father's fists. My brother's face was floating somewhere in the background. It was him who turned on the light. My mother appeared with the mask. "Put it on," she told my sister.

Mom held it to her face, but she pushed it away. "It hurts."

My father shook her using those handles of fabric. He gripped them hard when her legs bent. Her head danced on her shoulders, the hair moving from side to side.

"I've barely touched you," said Dad.

"You're fine," Grandma added from somewhere in the hallway. "You deserved much worse for what you've done. To a poor defenseless baby."

Mom held the mask to her face again.

"Come on," she said, "your brother's in the room. You can't sleep in here without this."

She managed to get the mask on. She stretched the strap until it was around the whole head and then let go of the elastic.

"You'll sleep with your sister from now on," Dad said to me. "We can't risk leaving her with the baby."

Dad pushed her into the room. She twisted her body to stop herself, and then let herself fall. She hit the floor with her backside. I felt the vibration in the bed frame. Dad was left with her blouse in his hands, with my sister's arms stretched upward, her face hidden behind the material. The garment's neck was turned inside out at the chin. Her breasts, naked, fell in opposite directions.

"Do what you want," said Dad. He let go of the material. The buttons hit my sister on the head. The blouse partly found its way back onto her body.

She sat there for a few seconds.

Then she dropped to one side.

I jumped out of bed to help her, but my mother and grandmother were there first. They knelt beside her. "Is it the poison?" Grandma asked.

"It can't be, she threw it all up," replied Mom.

"What's wrong with her?" Dad broke in. "Is she breathing?"

He put his hand on my sister's chest.

"Of course she's breathing," he said. "She's just fainted. Again."

I couldn't remember her ever fainting in the basement.

"Wake up, girl!" my father yelled.

She moaned.

"Ha, there you go," added Dad.

My sister was lying belly-up. Her white face prayed to the ceiling like the empty mask had done from the table the night of her nosebleed. She murmured something I didn't understand. She moved her head from side to side.

My father stopped the movement, grabbing her by the forehead. "Try doing something to the baby again and—" Although he didn't finish his threat, his fingers pressed against the orthopedic material. My sister bent her legs and twisted her waist.

"I hope I've made myself clear," Dad added.

She nodded.

He pulled her up by the armpits and took a few steps back to keep his balance. Then he checked that she was keeping herself up on her own feet. Her waist buckled, and it looked as if she'd fall again, but in the end her legs straightened.

"Help me get her into bed," he said.

My mother approached, going around them and looking like she didn't really know what to do.

"Come on, out of the way," my father said to her. "Pull the sheets back."

Mom climbed two rungs of the bunk's ladder and peeled the cover off my brother's bed. Dad pushed my sister forward. She dug her feet into the floor. Her toes wrinkled up. They shrank as they offered resistance.

"Not in his sheets," she muttered.

Dad pushed harder. She resisted by skidding on her heels.

"Not in his sheets," she repeated in a tiny voice, still drowsy from fainting.

Dad blew out to get her hair away from his face. He spat out a lock.

"This isn't necessary," Grandma cut in.

"I'll fetch some other sheets," my mother said.

When Dad continued to push, my sister let out one last scream. "Not in his sheets!"

Her body relaxed. Or rather, it deflated. As if the scream had taken away the last of her strength.

"Not in his sheets . . ."

My sister fell to one side. Dad bent his legs trying to keep her up. When he found himself unable to hold her dead weight, he let her fall to the floor. Lying on her side at the foot of the bunk bed.

"Suit yourself," he said.

He rubbed his palms together as if he'd relieved himself of an annoying burden. And it was that simple gesture that set off an explosion of sadness in me, a sadness made by everything that'd happened that night in the basement. Because I imagined my dad could've made a similar gesture a few nights before when he got rid of my sister after she'd had to defend herself scratching his back. I thought about how Grandma had described the baby as a shameful sin. And how my sister had tried to poison him so he wouldn't live with me in the basement.

Right then an unknown emotion was set off inside me. A spark that fought to catch fire.

I felt tears well up in my eyes. My family moved around the room as blurry blobs. Dad's slippers dragged on the way back to his room. Mom changed the sheets on the top bunk. She gave the pillow a few final slaps to fluff it up.

"Come on, back to sleep," she said to me.

She left the room without noticing my state. Two streams of snot flowed to my mouth. I resisted the urge to sniff because the sound would've alerted my grandmother. She was last to leave the room. She felt the air until she found the top of my head. I opened my mouth so I could breathe, tasting the salty flavor of my snot. My throat felt blocked by the effort I was making not to show that I was crying.

"Tomorrow I'll tell Mom to make you a special breakfast," she said. She ruffled my hair and added, "What do you want? Eggs or toast?"

I moved my tongue inside my open mouth. I couldn't speak.

"Eh?"

"Eggs." I pronounced it with no *g*.

"Eggs it is, then," she said. "And don't worry about your sister. What she did was much worse."

She ruffled my hair again before leaving. The smell of talcum powder vanished with her. At last I could relax my throat. I dried my snot with my forearm.

My sister was no more than a heap of clothes by the bunk bed. She was making a strange snoring sound.

The spark inside me caught light.

I knelt in front of the drawer.

I swallowed saliva.

I took out the firefly jar.

"I need you to glow," I told them. "I need to see the light from outside." I held the jar in front of my eyes.

It stayed dark.

"Please . . ."

I looked into the emptiness between my hands, wishing I could see the rays of sun they'd brought me from the world up top. Even if that wasn't really what it was. Even if their light was no more than another artificial light in my life, a load of chemicals in the abdomen of an insect.

"Take me away from this darkness."

A tear rolled down my cheek to my mouth.

I shook the jar.

"I want to go to where you come from."

I blinked, preparing myself to be dazzled. I closed my eyes. I waited. I wanted to give them time to light up. I opened them again, expecting the room to be colored green.

But I found the same darkness.

I shook the jar again. "Come on," I begged them.

The clinking of the pencils against the glass grew louder as I increased the speed of my hands.

I shook the jar until the tiredness in my shoulders made me accept what had happened.

I rested the container on the chest of drawers. This time I cried freely, remembering the magical moment when the first flash of green light had appeared on the other side of the window. The first firefly that arrived from the world outside. Just after I discovered I couldn't visit that world even if I wanted to, because the kitchen door had always been locked.

It was the first of all the fireflies that had come to die in my jar.

The glass basement to which I'd condemned them.

For the first time I felt lost in that darkness that had always been my world. Unused to it. A stranger in the basement.

The unknown spark that had caught light inside me became a little flame. A flame that burned.

"I want to get out of here," I said into the dark. I breathed deeply, accepting the truth. Giving in to the desire for a new life.

"I want to get out of here," I said again so I could listen to myself.

The heap of clothes that was my sister moved. The different materials brushed against each other. Some of her bones clicked.

"Do you really want to get out?" Her tired voice floated in the room's darkness.

I stroked the cold glass of the jar that would never glow again.

"I want to get out."

"I can help you do it," she then said. The mask rose up among a tangle of hair. The voice reverberated against the orthopedic material, which had been knocked out of place in the last struggle. "If I don't die first."

"You're not going to die. They made you throw it all up. Like the baby."

She groaned.

"Why don't you want the baby to live in the basement?" I asked. "Why don't you like us living here?"

"I don't care where that boy lives. I just don't want to have to look after him. And I want to make your father suffer. Do you not see?" She adjusted her mask, and I covered my face just in case.

"Don't be silly, you can look."

I took away my hands. She finished putting her blouse back on. As she sat up, her hand went to the mask. She stroked that barrier that stopped her from reaching her real skin.

"It hurts," she said.

"What did Dad do to you?"

"It really hurts. I have to loosen it."

She swayed under the lightbulb. She pulled at the mask's strap, and then laid a hand on her artificial face, inserting three fingers in the three holes. I heard an elastic slap when the strap was freed behind her head.

"You can't do that," I said.

My sister pulled the mask forward. "Didn't you see what your father did to me? I just want to stop this plastic pressing against the cuts. You don't have to shut your eyes. I just need to loosen the strap."

She groaned when the orthopedic material came away from her face. From where I was, it looked like the mask was still in the same place. She was holding its chin with one hand, and with the other she was playing with the elastic strap to loosen it.

She let her shoulders drop, breathing all the way out.

"Do you really want to get out of the basement?" she said. "At last?"

I looked at the unlit firefly jar.

"Yeah," I answered. "Do you know how?"

"Course I know. But first you have to make me a promise."

"What?"

"That you'll only listen to me. And you'll open your eyes from now on." She made the vowels long when she spoke. Her waist made a circle, as if dancing with an imaginary hoop. "Do you promise me?"

I said yes with a sound in my throat.

"If you don't open them, you'll never find out what really happens in this basement," she added. "You don't know anything yet, and—"

She let the mask fall before she finished the sentence.

I saw her face for an instant before I could react.

And after that instant, my eyes refused to close.

Because the face that appeared behind the mask changed everything.

My sister blinked. She was as overwhelmed as I was that we could look at each other without the barrier of white plastic that'd always been there. On her face there was no disgusting hole instead of a nose. There wasn't a single burn. Apart from the marks from Dad's recent slaps, my sister's face was as smooth and pink as mine. Under one of her eyes I could even make out two moles identical to the ones I had.

"See?" she said.

At that moment, the fireflies in the jar came back to life to glow brighter than ever.

ELEVEN YEARS
EARLIER

22

A gust of wind banged the window against the frame. It interrupted the woman's concentration. She had been staring at the television. The town was on the news. Until now it had never taken up so much as a minute's airtime, but for the last ten days every channel's news program had been linking up with its correspondent on the island. Sitting at the kitchen table, the woman resisted the urge to look away from the screen. The spokesperson for the missing girl's family was about to make another statement.

"Oh, she must've fallen on the rocks," the woman murmured to the screen. The window banged against the frame again.

The woman continued to chop carrots with her eyes still glued to the television. On the third bang, she wiped her fingers on the dishtowel that lay on her lap and went over to the sink. She closed the window. Through the glass she discovered the dark clouds of an inevitable storm on the horizon. The approach of nightfall and the threat of bad weather had made the landscape so dark that the gravel path crossing the plot had turned the same gray as the surface of the road that went down to the town. On one of the bends in the path, near the old septic tank, the laundry flapped at the mercy of the wind. A peg came loose with a gust, and the white shirt it held in place flew off. It rolled along the ground in a curl of fabric. The sheet of corrugated iron that covered the septic tank took flight as well.

The woman pushed open the kitchen's swinging door, crossed the living room in the direction of the front door, and ran out in search of the shirt. She couldn't find it on the dirt track or the ground that stretched out on either side. Nor had it rolled to the front of the house. She turned toward the cliff and there she saw it. The shirt was fluttering like a flag at half-mast, caught in some weeds. The woman crossed the plot. Her vertigo wasn't so bad if she kept four limbs on the ground. Rather than look down, she fixed her eyes on the heavy gray horizon where the sea ended. She snatched the shirt by the neck. As she pulled on it, the thistle it was caught on tore one side of the pocket.

Wind filled the woman's skirt. The braid of her dark hair, which she had knotted that morning, just like every morning before that, traveled up her back. It fell in front of her face like a rope. Still on her knees, she crawled backward to move away from the cliff's edge. She didn't get up until the rocks were more than five handbreadths away. She brushed the dust and earth from her clothes with an open hand. On the clothesline, the rest of the laundry was threatening to take flight. The woman ran back to the house.

On the TV in the kitchen they'd stopped talking about the town and the missing girl. The news program was covering another story. The woman left the shirt she'd rescued on the table, picked up a Danish cookie tin she used as a sewing box, and placed it on the material so she wouldn't forget she had to mend the pocket. She looked around for the big maroon-colored washbowl. The one she'd bathed her eldest daughter in those first summers when she was a baby. She found it under the sink. The windowpane shook with the wind outside. The laundry flapped, about to come loose.

She reached it with the washbowl resting on her hip. Some pegs leapt off when she pulled at the clothes hanging on the line. Another

white shirt of her husband's. Grandma's petticoat. Grandpa's cordu-
roy pants. Her daughter's bras. The dozen pairs of underpants that
her youngest son dirtied every week. And his sheets, which had to be
changed every day. A single odd sock was left pegged at one end. The
woman's eyes ran the length of the clothesline. She checked the ground.
She turned on the spot searching for the missing sock in the vicinity of
the house. Then her gaze fell on a human figure that was observing her
from the gravel path. A faceless silhouette. It took her a few seconds to
recover from the fright. Then she shouted to her daughter, "You scared
me with your hair like that."

"Hoped I might," she replied. With a head movement she'd repeated
for years, the daughter flicked the hair away from her face. She caught
it behind her neck with both hands, revealing her face.

"We had to stop," she explained. She raised her arm to show her
mother the rolled-up stack of posters. "We couldn't put them up anymore," the daughter continued. "It's going to rain."

"You don't say." The woman pulled on the solitary sock that hung
in front of her nose. The peg twisted rather than come away. The spring
bent out of shape, pinching the material with more force. She heard her
daughter laughing behind her as she ran toward the house.

"Don't shut the door on me," she yelled to her daughter.

The door slammed. The woman pulled at the sock with such anger
that it tore. Part of the material stayed caught in the peg. The woman
examined the frayed remains she held in her hand. She threw them into
the air. The sock flew, lifted by the wind, in the direction of the rocks.
It continued its upward trajectory, passing in front of the lighthouse
tower, before disappearing into the void over the cliff.

A current of air soaked the woman with a sudden spray of water.
Bent over, she fled the rain, carrying the washbowl full of clothes.
Unable to ring the bell, she turned her back to the door and knocked
with her heel. She could forget about her daughter paying her any attention. Her husband, at the top of the tower, no doubt reading another of

those medical books he didn't understand, wouldn't hear the banging, either. And since the incident on the stairs, she couldn't count on her son for much. She felt a pang of guilt in her stomach when she thought about that.

She heeled the door again. The gusts of wind spat the water under the porch roof. The sky lit up with a flash of lighting. Thunder rumbled above her and under her feet at almost the same time. She could hear the raging waves crash against the rocks. The sheet metal that had been ripped from the septic tank resisted the onslaught, trapped against the trunk of a tree. The woman leaned back against the door to rest her shoulders, the washbowl supported on her thighs. She was about to lose balance when the door opened.

"Was no one going to open up for me, or what?"

"I'm here," Grandma answered.

"That granddaughter of yours is insufferable. She closed the door on me on purpose."

"Your daughter, you mean."

"You wouldn't believe she was eighteen years old," the woman went on. "She still behaves like a little girl."

Grandma snatched the washbowl from her daughter-in-law, who made no complaint. The woman shook off some drops of rainwater that had pearled on her fleece jacket. She also dried her forehead and her smooth cheeks, before going over the knots of her braid.

Grandma rammed the kitchen door with her side.

"Everything's wet again," the woman announced. "Where're you going to hang it?"

"In the basement," Grandma answered. "All that space may as well be some use." She passed through the swinging door.

The woman took off her jacket. She hung it on the banister of the stairs that led to the first floor. Her daughter had also left a black raincoat there. And on the floor, resting against the wall, the roll of posters held together with an elastic band, the corners curling from the moisture. A partial image inside that cylinder showed the blue eyes of the girl who was missing on the island. Like almost the entire town, the daughter had been helping the family for days. Forming search teams to scour the craggy coast. Rallying in front of the town hall to call the authorities to account. Helping to monitor the boats coming and going at the main port. Or putting up posters on the streets showing a photograph of the girl. The one that showed her on a bicycle, wearing a pink cardigan, smiling at the camera that captured that image without ever suspecting what it would finally be used for.

The woman looked away from the posters. Gripping the banister, she yelled at her daughter for closing the door on her. Her daughter replied with another slammed door, this time taking refuge in the bathroom. In addition to that bathroom, there were four bedrooms on the first floor of the house. A gate prevented access to another staircase: the spiral one that rose to the top of the lighthouse. The stairway she hadn't climbed since what happened to the boy. That was the stairway her husband went up every afternoon to hide away in the lantern. He'd lived in the lighthouse in the days when the light was still in service. And although they'd managed to maintain the building as a family home when the lighthouse keeper's trade became unnecessary, he'd never been able to devote himself to making the light turn like his father.

The woman climbed two steps to project her voice more loudly up toward the stairwell. "The wind's blown the cover off the tank," she shouted to her husband. "It needs to be covered, it's raining already."

The metal stairs squeaked as her husband came down.

"Check on the boy, while you're there," she added.

"Shall I fix the septic tank or watch over the boy?" he complained. "I can't do everything."

A draft penetrated the house through the gap under the front door. And through the poorly insulated window frames. The building's timber creaked. The wind howled outside.

"Fix the tank," the woman decided. "Before the cover ends up in the sea. I'll go up and see the boy."

The man studied the weather from the window beside the front door. The height of the lighthouse had distanced him from the effects of the rainstorm. Little puddles were beginning to form in the dips in the ground. On the clothesline, the remains of a frayed sock hung from a twisted peg. He saw that the septic tank was uncovered. He pressed his face to the glass, blocking out the reflections with a hand around his eyes. He searched the plot of land for the metal cover, finding it anchored to the pine tree's trunk. The wind was shaking it without managing to tear it from the obstacle that blocked its path. A flash of lightning illuminated the landscape like an overexposed photograph.

As soon as he went out, the man slipped on the clayey surface. The rain attacked his eyes. He reached the cover just as an invisible whirlwind managed to snatch it from the tree. He clutched it under one arm. A gust of air pushed at the false wing, unbalancing the man as he stepped forward. He stopped himself from falling with a swivel that would have been comical in a silent movie. On the way to the septic tank, he searched among the white stones that marked the gravel path that led to the road. Lifting up one of the heaviest, he used it to weigh the square piece of corrugated roofing down over the septic tank, positioning it by eye in the common center of the hole and the cover. He checked it would withstand the onslaught of the wind by pulling up one corner.

Someone screamed inside the house.

The edge of the metal opened a cut on his thumb.

A second howl allowed him to recognize his name and the alarmed tone of his wife's voice. The speed with which he set off back to the house made him slip again. He found the front door closed. He rang the bell relentlessly, turning the usual three-note melody into a continuous tremolo.

It was Grandma who opened.

"What's going on?" the man asked.

"I don't know, I just heard the screaming myself. I was in the basement."

A current of air blew the door shut. The woman came down the stairs two at a time.

"The boy's not there," she said. "He's not in his bed."

"So where is he?" asked her husband.

"Do you think I'd be screaming if I knew?" As she reached the bottom of the staircase, her foot hit the roll of posters of the missing girl. The blue eyes rolled along the floor. "Let's get out and look for him."

"How can he be outside in that monsoon?" he asked.

"I don't know," the woman replied, "but he's not in the house. And I don't want him to end up on the rocks like that girl," she added, now regretting what she'd said to the television.

"Don't say that," her daughter cut in. She was speaking from the floor above, her hands clutching the towel she'd used to dry her hair that was hanging around her neck. "Half the town is still hoping to find her alive."

"Right now it's your brother I want to find." The woman slung her braid over the neck of her raincoat. "Because if something has happened to him—I won't say it. But if something's happened to him, it'll be your fault, too."

"Mine? This? How can this be my fault?"

"We shouldn't have to watch a thirteen-year-old boy like he's six. And we all know whose fault it is he's like that."

Grandma kneaded her rosary when she heard the attack. Another reprimand in the endless string of them that had been flung at the girl since the incident on the stairs. Since an afternoon four years ago when the daughter was left to look after her younger brother. To make sure, most of all, that he didn't try to climb to the top of the lighthouse, because as their mother always said, every step that led up to the lantern was a death trap, especially for a boy not yet ten years old.

As soon as her parents had gone, their daughter did the exact opposite, and coaxed her brother to climb to the top of the tower alone. To the place full of the mysteries and family myths of which Grandpa always spoke, a place where the boy had seldom been allowed to go, and then only when supervised. Up there his mouth fell open when he discovered a sun that, at that time of day, bled red over a dark sea. In awe he ran his hand over the glass screens that covered the giant spotlight. He imagined himself sailing on one of the ships that the light once guided. Slowly, so he'd remember it forever, he breathed in the magical air that seemed to float about in that enchanted place. But when his sister shouted at him to come down to celebrate the adrenaline rush they'd received from rebelling against their parents, the boy slipped and plunged into the stairwell, his fingers searching for something to grip onto on the tower's brick walls.

They didn't find anything. He landed at his sister's feet, and still she kicked him gently in the side, telling him to stop playacting. She knelt to check that he was breathing, holding a hand to his chest and feeling his heart beating. She could've asked for help then. Could've picked up the cream-colored telephone on the side table in the living room to call an ambulance. But that would've forced her to accept her guilt, to admit her disobedience. And she didn't want to imagine Dad's face if he returned home to find the flashing sirens of an ambulance howling at the front door. And anyway, the boy was breathing normally. His heart was beating at the right speed. The fall couldn't have been all that serious. That was why she decided to move her brother's injured body, persuading herself that the boy's silence, the absence of groans, must be a good sign. It couldn't be so bad if he wasn't even complaining.

When he started trembling, she wrapped him in his sheets, blaming the cold for spasms that really required much more attention. She even spoke into her brother's ear, begging him not to tell on her. She'd think of some excuse she could tell their parents, and their prank that afternoon would be their secret. She left the boy in the bedroom, blocking out the voices that screamed in her head. When their parents returned home, she just told them that the boy had felt unwell and she'd put him to bed. But her mother's scream when she went up to see him made the reality clear. The ambulances, and their flashing sirens, finally arrived at the house. Much later than would've been advisable. The child they stretchered away was no longer the boy who a few hours earlier had enjoyed, openmouthed, a sunset that would mark the end both of that day and of his life as it had been. Nor was he the same boy who, to remember it forever, had breathed in the magical air of that enchanted place at the top of the lighthouse. A feeling he never remembered because it disappeared into the tangle of brain connections that were knocked loose by the impact against the edge of the step that cracked open his head. The skull was left as fractured as the daughter's relationship with her parents and grandparents, who from then on made her the gangrenous limb of the body formed by the six members of the family.

The daughter threw the towel down from above. It hit the woman's face.

"You don't have to remind her of the accident every day," Grandma broke in.

"You bet I don't have to." The woman handed the damp towel to her mother-in-law. "All she has to do is look at her brother's face to remember it." She zipped up the raincoat with an energetic tug.

"Let's go," her husband said, grabbing her by the wrist. "Before it gets dark."

He pulled on her just as the doorbell rang.

"That'll be the boy," the daughter shouted from upstairs. "Go give your favorite child a hug."

In a bathrobe, she fled to her bedroom and slammed shut the door.

The bell rang again.

"At least he came back on his own two feet today," the woman said.

"What did I say? Our boy's going to get better and better," noted the man with optimism.

During the first year after the fall, the boy screamed whenever they tried to take him out of his room, but in recent weeks he'd made progress, to the point that he wanted to go out whenever possible. He'd already gotten lost twice. Both times, he was found on the road to town. To his mother's despair he'd been soaked in seawater. She felt breathless every time she thought of her son near the rocks. When they told him off, the boy would run away to some corner of the plot, his hands twisting at chest height, crying with his mouth wide open and hitting his ears to block out his own tantrum. And in the guttural voice that resulted from the fall, he pleaded for someone to make the sea be quiet.

The doorbell rang again.

A shiver ran down the woman's back when she heard the way the last of the three notes trilled. There was something wrong with that sound. An eerie quality that floated in the living room air until the note fell silent.

"I'll go," her husband said.

A plea came from the woman's throat. "Don't open it." Flanked by her husband and by Grandma, she was almost as surprised as they were to hear her own request.

"What're you talking about?" the man replied. "The kid must be soaked through by now."

And when the man took his first step toward the entrance, the woman was certain that two policemen would appear behind the door, standing on the doormat. Lowering their heads in a gesture of respect before giving them the news that those damned cliffs seemed to make inevitable. The woman remembered how she'd murmured her fateful verdict to the television while she chopped carrots.

"My son!" she yelled.

She overtook her husband with a sudden dash across the living room. Without intending it, she kicked the posters of the girl. They rolled to the front door. The woman bent to pick them up. Tiny drops of rain had reached the glossy paper through the crack under the door.

A somber harmony tinged the notes of the doorbell when it rang for a fourth time.

"My son," the woman murmured.

With a chill on the back of her neck, she turned the handle. The door opened in front of her, fanned by a current of air from outside. Before she could register what she was seeing, Grandma screamed behind her.

"What the—?" was all the man could vocalize.

The woman didn't find enough air in her lungs to scream. She just stood there, feeling the raindrops on her contorted face. Hearing them hit the waterproof material of her raincoat. She felt a growing tingling in the hand that held the rolled-up posters. When her fingers were totally numb, the roll fell to the floor. The wind pushed them inside the house as if wanting to tear them away from the scene at the threshold. So that the eyes of the girl in the photograph wouldn't have to see what had appeared in the door.

23

The woman didn't resist when her son pushed her aside. She just closed her eyes. Something soft brushed past her ankles. The hiss from that contact turned her stomach. The boy went into the living room, taking with him the smell of damp earth with which the storm imbued the air.

Her eyes still shut, the woman felt for the edge of the door that the wind had torn from her hands. She closed it. A sudden hot flush made the moisture on her face evaporate. The raincoat's neck choked her. She unzipped it with a trembling hand. She could smell salt residue and a child's sweat.

"Help me," the boy said. He drew out the vowels and got stuck on some consonants. "I don't know what's wrong with her. She's stopped talking."

The man kept his mouth clamped shut, his throat tight.

Grandma felt for the chain of her rosary before fleeing upstairs. She went to yell Grandpa's name, but just babbled a few meaning-less words. She tripped on the last step before crashing through her bedroom door. She let herself fall onto the bed. Her choking sobs and her body's uncontrollable shaking woke Grandpa, whose afternoon nap had prevailed over the storm, the yelling, and the doorbell. Unable to decipher a coherent sentence among his wife's stammering, Grandpa got up. He found his glasses on the bedside table and slotted the arms among the last two clumps of gray hair he still had, the ones that grew over his ears until they ended a little higher than the temples. A crease from his pillow was engraved on his face.

Holding each other, the grandparents went out onto the landing. The next door along opened as well.

"Has the kid shown up?" their granddaughter asked, still in her bathrobe.

Her father yelled from downstairs, "Stay in your room!"

The daughter closed her door with contempt. Her stomach burned with rage every time they spoke to her like that. She hoped her brother had gotten himself in serious trouble.

Grandpa looked at his wife in search of an explanation. She seemed to be staring into nothing. He pushed her so she'd let go of the doorframe. Then he guided her to the top of the stairs leading down to the living room. They heard their grandson speak.

"Mom, open your eyes," he said in guttural gulps. "You have to help me, she's stopped talking."

The woman screamed in the living room.

The boy's words made Grandma cry.

A sudden tension attacked Grandpa's belly.

"Are you going to tell me what's going on?" he growled.

He set off down the stairs, pulling his wife. When he reached the last step, he stopped there and stood, trying to understand the scene he found in front of him. He pressed Grandma's face against his chest to shield her from the image.

The first thing he saw was the lock of blond hair emerging from inside the boy's fist. The son was trying to get his mother's attention by waving the clump of hair. A moist, fleshy sound accompanied each movement. The sound that the girl's neck made when it twisted freely, dislocated from the rest of the body to which it remained connected by a viscous, yellowy-purple skin.

"She's stopped talking," the boy said again. He pulled on the false blond ponytail to show Mom the face of the toy that had stopped working. Two blue eyes looked up at the woman. As they'd looked at her that very afternoon from the edge of some rolled-up posters. The girl's mouth was twisted into a silent scream. Her son carried the body by the armpits, the back resting on his chest.

"Tell her to talk!" he yelled. He shook the body. The girl's head danced on the broken neck until it fell backward with a crunch. It was left resting on the boy's shoulder.

Reality clouded over when the woman's eyes filled with tears. Her son was reduced to a foggy blob pulsating in front of her. The guttural voice of that out-of-focus creature continued to ask for help. He tugged on the waist of his mother's raincoat.

"We're going to have a baby," he explained.

From his position beside the grandparents, the man saw his wife cover her face. He also saw a drop of water run down the girl's hand, which hung from the end of a pink sleeve. And he remembered: that was the color of the cardigan worn by the girl sitting on a bike and looking out at the people of the town from her photograph on every street corner. When the drop hit the floor the man reacted.

The mud on his shoes left wet prints on the living room's timber floor. His paternal instinct manifested itself in an unexpected way when, ignoring his son's ravings, he decided to tear the swollen girl from his arms. He laid her face-up, and without stopping to consider what he was doing, how useful it would be, he covered her mouth with his lips. A salty, sludgy, vegetal flavor raked his throat. He blew hard. He pressed the cold flesh of her cheeks so the lips would give way, then blew again into the opening. He could feel the girl's chest inflating, but the air escaped from her soft anatomy as soon as he separated himself to look for a response in her face. The smell that came from that mouth made him nauseous. It penetrated his body like a toxic gas poisoning his blood.

"She's dead," said the woman, her voice trembling.

But still he tried to revive her. This time he breathed into the girl's mouth while pressing her chest. The taste of sea made his stomach turn, but it was the feel of her tongue, slimy like the soft part of a bivalve, that was too much to bear. The man moved his face away with a convulsion. He pressed his belly as if he could control it. Covered his mouth with both hands.

"She's dead," the woman repeated. The air had dried her eyes. She turned to the boy, who was looking at his parents without fully understanding their reaction. The man, kneeling, was fighting his nausea with deep breaths. He swallowed thick, sour saliva.

"It's the girl," his wife added. She rubbed her eyes with the back of a hand. "It's the missing girl."

Grandma kissed the crucifix on her rosary.

The boy crouched down by the girl and shook the blond ponytail. "Don't tell me she's dead," he sobbed. "She can't be d—dead. We're going to have a baby!"

The boy's face lit up in an expression of euphoria. It gradually twisted out of shape when he grasped that his family was looking at him with horror. When he let go of the ponytail, the girl's head dropped to the floor like an old gourd. The boy's confused face moved his mother despite the bloodstains she saw on his clothes. Despite the mud that was all over his face. Despite the solitary blond hair that shined like a golden filament tangled between his fingers.

The woman hugged her son. Seaweed hung from the shoulder where she rested her chin. The boy cried loudly. She held him to stop him from hitting himself, soothing him with words in his ear. She stroked the back of his head, squeezing seawater from his hair. Sand from the beach came away as well. When the boy was calmer, she positioned her face in front of her son's.

"What have you done, sweetheart?" She brushed aside the boy's wet bangs with her fingers.

"I've looked after her."

"Who have you looked after?"

"The girl I found on the rocks," he said, pointing at the body lying on the floor.

"You found a girl on the rocks?"

The boy nodded.

"When?"

"A—ages ago."

"How long? A few hours?" she asked hopefully.

The boy held up a hand, the wrist folded inward. He moved his fingers, counting in his strange way. "Five," he concluded. "Five days."

"Was she—?" A faltering sigh made her lose her voice. "When you found her. Was she—?" The pressure on her chest stopped her speaking.

Her husband skirted the girl's body. When he stepped on a clump of hair stuck to the timber, the girl's bluish face shuddered in a spasm of artificial life. The man looked away. He knelt beside the boy.

"Listen to me." He gripped him by the chin. "The girl, was she alive?"

The boy frowned, concentrating. His parents studied the wrinkles on his forehead, trying to guess their son's thought process. Grandpa held his breath. Grandma looked at her grandson.

The boy's forehead unwrinkled. He smiled.

"She was alive," he said, as if it were good news. "She's stopped talking . . ." His tongue pressed against the roof of his mouth a moment too long. "She stopped talking today."

After a few seconds of horrified disbelief, the man exploded.

"Christ!"

Upstairs, the scream made his daughter's shoulders flinch. She was lying in bed reading. A corner of her mouth turned upward. Her brother had gotten himself into trouble. Big trouble. Big enough, perhaps, to get him down from the hero's pedestal on which they'd put him since the accident. The smile finished forming on her face, narrowing her eyes. She turned a page.

Downstairs, her father yelled with enraged burbles of saliva.

"Christ! Christ! Christ!"

He pressed against his temples with his fists, unable to bear the pressure he felt in his head. He stood up, shaken by a jolt of panic. He paced around the living room, digging his heels into the flooring and rugs. Bits of mud stuck to the material. He dodged the sofa, where the family gathered in the evenings to watch movies, and avoided the trunk, the cuckoo clock, and two standing lamps that lit the living room. When a chair got in the way of his erratic route, he grabbed its back and threw it against the wall. The windowpanes shook with the impact more than they'd vibrated with the last clap of thunder. The cream-colored telephone fell to the floor from the little table. The receiver stayed on its base thanks to the curly cable that the women of the house twisted between their fingers as they chatted.

The boy started crying.

"Christ!" his father repeated.

"You're going to have to calm down," Grandpa said. "Look at the state of us all."

The man let out a final cry. He released some of the tension that numbed his muscles. Then he was able to look more calmly at the rest of the family. His wife had sat the boy on the floor, hugging him as if nursing a giant baby. Grandma, shrunk back in fear, looked at them while clutching Grandpa, who was fighting to keep his composure. The missing girl lay on the floor where she'd been left. Judging by her appearance, the boy had told the truth: the girl had not been dead long. Certainly not the six days that had gone by since her disappearance. The skin was bruised and had a viscous texture, but did not smell decomposed, and there weren't any obvious signs of putrefaction. The man guessed that she had been exposed to the seawater for a long time, to the crashing of the waves and to . . . When he thought about the other blows, the ones he imagined his son might have dealt her, he felt an urge to throw another chair against the wall.

"What have you done to her?!" he screamed at the boy. He swooped on him, unable to contain his rage.

The woman blocked her husband's path with her back. Grandpa freed himself from Grandma, who was left standing with her arms hanging. He grabbed the man by the neck, pulling him away from the boy, who trembled in his mother's arms.

When the man saw his son's frightened face, the fit of rage vanished. He managed to get away from Grandpa. He hugged his wife through the raincoat. The boy was encased between them. The man said sorry several times.

"What have you done to her?" he whispered. His breath warmed the damp space the three of them faced, the parents' heads brow-to-brow.

"I looked after her," said the boy. "She was on the rocks." The last consonant whistled between his teeth. "She wasn't moving. But she spoke. To the rocks. To me."

"Why didn't you say anything?"

The boy blinked in silence. As if waiting for a question that was worth answering. A bitter smell filled the inside of that embrace when the boy breathed out.

"We're going to have a baby," he said.

"A baby?" asked the woman.

"A baby," he said again.

"Why?"

"Because I did this to her. Like this . . ." The boy moved his body in thrusts to explain himself. He moved his pelvis back and forward, back and forward, back and forward.

"I put a baby in her tummy," he whispered.

The woman grabbed the boy's neck. She squeezed it to stop that repugnant display. He shrank back, twisting his body and making a mewing sound, as his mother remembered what some medical prognoses had predicted.

The boy's mewing stopped.

The parental hug dissolved.

Standing, the four adults exchanged profound looks as impenetrable as the mysteries of the boy's brain. A deathlike silence overcame the room, broken only by the sound of the rain beating against the roof. Drops of fresh- and saltwater slid down the girl's face before falling into the puddle that framed her body on the floor.

The woman finished unzipping her raincoat. She took it off and shook it, splashing her son.

"Get off," she said when he tried to hug her legs.

Watched closely by the rest of the family, the woman approached the dead body. She dropped the coat onto the corpse, covering it from forehead to waist. The hands poked out from each side of the improvised shroud. She pushed them under the raincoat with her feet.

"What are we going to do?"

"What're our options?" her husband asked.

Grandpa cut in. "We have options?"

After thinking about it for a few seconds, the man persisted, "Well, what can we do?"

Total silence was the only response.

"How're we going to explain this?" The woman pointed at the shape on the floor.

Grandma had to grip the banister to stay on her feet. "My grandson's killed her," she said, and immediately went on. "My grandson's killed that girl."

"We don't know he killed her," the man said.

"He didn't do anything to save her," his wife argued, and she pressed the boy again. "How many days ago did you find her?"

He counted with his hand, twisted at chest height. "Five."

His mother used the answer as proof.

"And he says she was talking," she went on. "In other words, she was alive. The girl must've fallen on the rocks when she went missing. Onto one of those ledges. And our son found her . . ." Her voice failed when she remembered the two times the boy had run off in the last few days. And how he'd shown up soaked on the road to town. The woman closed her eyes. The darkness showed her an image of her son thrusting his pelvis over the girl's battered body.

"Oh God, what're we going to do?" She sucked in saliva loudly and massaged the back of her neck with both hands. She groaned a mixture of pain, despair, and disgust. When she felt her husband grasp her by the waist, she opened her eyes. "What're we going to do?" she said again.

As if they didn't know, she explained to the others that the girl was all over the news. That she'd seen her on the television that very afternoon, while she chopped carrots, before it started raining. That the police, the fire department, everyone was searching for her. That the town had organized teams of volunteers to comb the island.

"Even our daughter has just been putting up posters with a photo of her," she said, pointing at the roll that the wind had blown to the other end of the living room.

The man held a finger to his mouth to stop her from raising her voice. "The last thing we need is for his sister to find out as well."

"We have to decide," the woman blurted out.

"Our son's a minor," the man suggested. "And he's not well. What can they do to him?"

"That girl has everyone moved to tears. Imagine what'll happen when they discover what our son did to her." She shook her head to free her mind of the image it insisted on projecting. "His life will be over. For the second time."

Her eyes welled up, full of sadness and guilt, as she remembered with nostalgia the boy who had said good-bye to her the afternoon of the accident.

"And this time it will be forever. He'll never be forgiven for this."
The woman bit the inside of her lips to stop herself from crying. "It's
not fair . . . Not again."

The man hardly thought of the legal process. It was enough for
him to imagine what the boy's future would be like, forever rejected by
society. A future that had been uncertain since the fall and that would
be marred for the rest of his life. He looked at his son, who was stroking
the dead body's hair, and remembered the little boy full of imagination,
who played with the toy scarecrow that Grandma had made from two
handfuls of straw and tiny hand-sewn clothes, making it walk over his
cereal bowl at breakfast. A perverse twist of fate had turned him into
his favorite character from *The Wonderful Wizard of Oz*. The memory
of the boy's childhood moved the man. His son didn't deserve the dark
future that destiny was intent on offering him.

"It's not fair," the woman repeated.

"And what happened to that girl's not fair, either," Grandpa said
then. "She had a family, too."

He took a step forward. Some of the sand the woman had brushed
from the boy's hair crunched under his shoes. He walked around the
living room, over the muddied rugs, until he reached the telephone that
was lying on the floor. Grandpa crouched down, his knees clicking as
they bent. He pushed up the glasses that had slid down his nose. First
he took the base of the telephone, and then he pulled the wire until he
could reach the receiver and hold it to his ear. There was a tone. His
knees clicked again as he stood up.

"What're you going to do?" the boy's mother asked.

Grandpa put the telephone down on the side table. He picked up
the receiver and held it between his cheek and shoulder.

"The only thing we can do," he answered. "The right thing." He
inserted his finger in one of the holes in the telephone's rotary dial. He
turned it.

"Don't call," she pleaded. "Think of your grandson." The dial returned to its initial position with a crackle.

"What will happen to your grandson?" she persisted. Without answering, Grandpa began to turn it again. "He's not even responsible for his actions."

The disk repeated its return journey. Grandpa felt for the hole to dial the third digit before his daughter-in-law could say anything else. He moved his face closer to the telephone, pushing up his glasses to restore his vision.

"This girl's dead already," she continued. Grandpa found the hole he was looking for. He inserted his finger. "But your grandson has his whole life ahead of him."

The finger trembled. The fingernail scratched against the telephone's plastic cover. When he'd regained his composure, he turned the dial. Then Grandma spoke.

"He's our grandchild," she said. She swallowed when she finished the sentence. "We came back to live in the lighthouse for him. We came to look after him."

With his finger still in the dial, the receiver pressed against his face, Grandpa looked at his wife. He questioned her without the need for words. With just a crease in his forehead, he asked whether she was sure of what she was saying. Sure she knew what it meant. Grandma squeezed the banister's ball top as if wanting to strangle it.

"I'm sure," she answered.

His eyes then traveled to the crucifix that hung from her neck. Grandma squeezed it in her fist. She moved her other hand to the back of her neck. The chain came undone, the two ends hanging on each side of her closed hand. She kissed her tensed fingers before hiding the jumble of beads in the pocket of the cardigan that she had knitted herself.

"He's my grandson," she whispered as an apology to the ceiling, her sky.

Grandpa understood what his wife's gesture meant. He accepted her decision. He took his finger from the dial, but didn't notice it returning to its position and completing the call to emergency services. The woman jumped over the girl's body in the direction of the side table. She pushed down the tabs to cut off the line just as a female voice took the call. She took the receiver from Grandpa's shoulder and deposited it on the telephone. Then she turned to address the family.

"I'm not going to hand my son over," she said in a deep voice. The boy applauded when he heard himself mentioned. On the third clap, with nobody joining in, he gave up the celebration.

"So, what are we going to do with the girl?" Ashamed by his question, the man looked away. He scratched his forehead despite it not itching.

"They still haven't come to search the north of the island," explained the woman. "They started from her house, but headed south. They didn't come up this way."

"And what're we supposed to do?" The man fell silent to give someone else the opportunity to voice the idea. He didn't want to be the one to spell out what they were all thinking.

"Hide her?" he finally said.

A high-pitched whimper escaped from Grandma's throat. She approached her grandson with a hand over her eyes, so she wouldn't see the body. The boy's drool wet her blouse when she hugged him.

"Bury her?" the man asked, pronouncing the words as if they were foreign to his language. The taste of the salty lips returned to his palate. Along with the stench exhaled by the swollen body. And the slimy feel of her shellfish tongue. "Are we really going to bury this girl?"

Nobody answered the question.

Lightning flashed in the sky. For an instant it accentuated the shadows on the faces in the living room. The clap of thunder that followed rumbled under their feet. The windowpanes reproduced the vibration.

The cuckoo popped out of the clock.

It cuckooed once. Twice. Three times.

Four. Five. Six. Seven. Eight.

Nine times.

"Tell me if that's what we're going to do!" the man yelled.

Upstairs, his daughter, alarmed by the intensity of the lightning and her father's voice, jumped out of bed. Her book fell to the floor on the way to the window, which looked out of the front of the house, illuminated by the porch light. A violent gust of wind picked up just then. The metal fence that demarcated the plot shook wildly from post to post. Invisible hands pulled on the tree branches as if wanting to uproot them. The air whistled through their leaves. The corrugated iron that covered the septic tank fought against the weight of the stone the man had used to pin it down. A corner lifted up. The rock rolled off onto the ground. The metal cover flew into the air like a kite with nobody holding its string. It floated for a few seconds, before a second rush of wind propelled it against the house like a projectile. The daughter's hands went to her face.

The living room window smashed into a shower of glass when a corner of the metal sheet went through it. Grandma hugged her grandson more tightly. The man had just asked what the hell they were going to do with the girl. The corrugated iron fell inside the living room. It slid along the timber floor until the corpse itself stopped it in its tracks.

It took the man a while to identify the object. Discovering what it was, he looked at his wife, his eyes wide open. His heartbeat quickened. She nodded in response to the arrival of a solution.

"The septic tank," the man whispered.

Grandpa read the words on his son's lips. He, too, glimpsed the idea that had formed in his mind. He pushed the bridge of his glasses up his nose and adjusted the arms. Then he began to roll the cuffs of his sweater up his arms, to the elbow.

A door opened upstairs.

"Has the window smashed?" the daughter asked from there.

And she started coming down the stairs.

24

The sudden intrusion of his granddaughter's voice made Grandpa initiate a series of movements that he did not complete, unable to decide what the best reaction would be. Grandma closed her eyes, hugging the boy, preparing for the worst. The woman looked at the roll of posters that her daughter had been putting up that afternoon. She sighed, accepting what would happen if she discovered what her brother had done.

The man rushed to the girl's body.

"Don't come down if you're barefoot," he shouted to his daughter. "There's glass everywhere down here."

The wood of the staircase creaked under her weight. A foot stopped on the second step. She hadn't put her shoes on after drying herself with the bathrobe. A cold breeze climbed her legs to her groin. The elastic on her pajama bottoms, the worn, gray ones that were so comfortable and warm, danced on her bare ankles.

"So the window *has* been smashed," she assumed.

"I've already cut myself," her father lied. He trod on the floor to make the glass crunch. "Don't come down."

"It's dangerous," added the woman.

There were a few seconds of silence. Looks were exchanged in the room. Then the boy yelled, "We're going to have a baby!"

Grandma shushed him in his ear. The man grabbed the girl's wet arms through the raincoat, ready to escape outside.

"What nonsense is he spouting now?"

"It's nothing. Go back to your room."

"You're fine now that the boy's home, huh? And you don't want me around. Makes a change."

"It's because of the glass," the woman said.

"It's always because of something."

She moved down to the third step. The wood creaked again. Grandma, who was rocking the boy in her arms, couldn't keep the words in.

"Please, don't come down." She waited for her granddaughter's reaction, allowing herself to be hypnotized by the curtain fluttering in the living room, lifted by the wind that came through the broken window. In the random curves in the fabric she saw the same randomness that the future of the boy in her arms depended on. A whole life staked on the effect those four words would have on her granddaughter. Please. Don't. Come. Down. When the ceiling shook under her angry footsteps, returning to her room with energetic strides, Grandma sobbed with silent relief on the boy's shoulder.

The whole house shook when the door slammed.

"Come on," the man whispered. "We have to do it now."

He lifted the girl by the torso. The raincoat slid down, revealing her bluish face. His wife put it back, tying the sleeves behind the broken neck. The man gestured to Grandpa to take her by the legs.

"Hurry up," he insisted. "Before the tank gets flooded. If it fills up with rain we won't be able to—"

"Shut up," Grandpa cut him off. "Don't say another word." His knees clicked when he crouched down. His hands were trembling. "God forgive me," he murmured.

As he wrapped his fingers around the girl's ankles, so slender it seemed as if he would be able to close his fist entirely, he felt dizzy. And when he lifted the little body, as light as his granddaughter's had been years ago when he'd held her up by the belly to make her fly like an airplane through the air of that very living room, the dizziness became a feeling of repulsion toward himself. He opened his hands. The heel of the one shoe the girl still wore hit the floor in a sad and incomplete tap-dancing step.

"I can't," he said, showing the palms of his hands as if those very words were written on them. "I can't."

The boy escaped his grandmother's arms. He took Grandpa's place. "Let's go to the rocks, Dad," he said. "She lives on the rocks."

His father tried to speak, but the anguish swallowed his words. The woman approached the boy, and, one by one, she unpicked the fingers that squeezed the girl's legs.

"Are you going to help him or not?" she asked her father-in-law.

Grandpa shook his head. He showed his palms again.

The man clenched his jaw, chewing on the cry he didn't let out. "I'll do it by myself if I have to," he said. He picked up the girl in his arms to illustrate his words. He turned toward the door. The air that came in through the window dried the sweat from his forehead.

"I'll help you," the woman said. She signaled to Grandma to take care of the boy, pointing at the crown of his head. "You give him a bath. He can't stay like that, he'll get sick."

The woman picked up the corrugated iron. She approached her husband and grabbed his tensed arm, the bicep swollen with the effort. She stood on tiptoes to speak into his ear.

"I won't hand my son over," she whispered. And it was her who took the first step toward the septic tank.

The boy spoke behind her. "Don't take her. I want her."

The woman turned around and noticed the same confused expression she'd seen the day the hamster had stopped moving between his twisted hands. The pet they'd given him after the accident, when the boy still screamed if he was left alone in his bedroom, was crushed to death between the fingers of its owner, who squeezed it until it died, showing it how much he loved it.

"I really want her," the boy added, pointing at the body his father carried.

The woman contained a sob as she remembered the lethal consequences of her son's love, which turned the rodent into a purée of hair and blood that she cleaned from his fingers with an ammonia-soaked rag. And it occurred to her that it was the same thing they were doing now: cleaning away the girl's remains by hiding her in a septic tank.

"Get the door for me," the man said.

The woman peeled her eyes away from her son, who was folding his bottom lip into an endearing pout. She opened the door. Lightning flashed in the sky. It allowed them to make out the silhouette of the septic tank. A gust of wind from the night's storm unsteadied them both. The woman swallowed as if she could ingest her guilt, and said again, "I'm not going to hand my son over."

Grandma pushed the boy toward the stairs. "Let's go get you showered and dried," she said as they went up. Before reaching the bathroom, they heard the front door slam shut.

"So we really are going to do it," Grandpa said from somewhere.

Grandma closed another door behind her and sat her grandson on the bath's edge. "Arms up."

The boy obeyed. He laughed when the T-shirt tickled his armpits as it rose up his body. She used the damp piece of clothing to wipe her grandson's face, then put him in the bathtub and stripped him naked. It still surprised her to find hair in some places.

"Why am I so dirty?"

Grandma heard the question, but preferred to ignore it. She unhooked the showerhead before turning on the hot water. She untangled the hose and directed the jet onto her wrinkled hand to check the temperature. The boy extracted remains of sand from under his fingernails.

"I'm really dirty," he whined. "Why am I so dirty?"

Grandma watched the swirl of water, which was beginning to steam. She turned down the temperature.

"You're dirty because you've come from the rocks."

The boy frowned so much his eyes closed. As if straining to remember something that eluded him.

"Why didn't you tell us you'd found the girl?" Grandma asked.

The boy twisted his fingers. Ashamed, he lowered his head and covered his face to hide it. Accepting his guilt.

She grabbed him by the shoulders. "Do you realize what has happened to that girl?"

The boy mewed.

"Tell me, do you realize?"

After a silence, the boy broke into laughter hidden behind his hands, which shot open, revealing his grubby face.

"She's going to have a baby!" he yelled. The boy began thrusting his pelvis arrhythmically.

"Stop," said Grandma. She looked at the shower, which was flowing directly to the plughole. "Stop!"

The boy stopped. He opened his mouth in an exaggerated way as he did when he was about to cry. Or to pretend to cry.

"Don't cry," Grandma said. "I'm sorry. Don't cry."

The enormous mouth closed.

"You're going to have to promise me something," she added. The boy opened his eyes with the same curiosity he'd shown when she gave him the toy scarecrow.

"That you won't tell anyone about this," Grandma went on. "You must do as I say."

Her grandson covered his mouth with both hands.

"Not anyone," she repeated. "Do you swear?"

The boy pinched an imaginary zipper that hung from a corner of his mouth. He ran it from one side of his lips to the other. He rotated his wrist to padlock it shut. Then, despite having sealed his mouth, he opened it to swallow the invisible key that he threw down his throat.

"There's a good boy," said Grandma. "Lips locked and the key in your tummy. You can't tell anyone. Not even your sister. Especially not your sister."

Earnest gravity darkened the boy's face. "She doesn't love me," he said. Then he repeated something he'd heard many times in that house. "It was her fault I fell down the stairs."

Moved, Grandma hugged her grandson, naked in the bathtub.

"My sister doesn't love me. But I love her very much."

If his mother had heard that sentence, she would have remembered the remains, the blood and hair that came from the boy's love for the hamster. But Grandma just kissed her grandson's head. She smelled the salt in the child's hair.

"Shower time now, you stink," she said. "And afterward we'll put some talc on you, so you smell as nice as I do."

When he'd finished his shower, the boy laughed when he saw his face covered in white powder. Grandma kissed the cowlick of dry hair that formed in the middle of his head. An image of his fractured skull flashed somewhere in her mind.

"And now to bed," she said.

They went out onto the first-floor landing. Grandma pricked her ears. The silence told her that neither her son nor her daughter-in-law had yet returned from the septic tank. Seeing the gate at the bottom of the spiral staircase open, she clicked her tongue, incredulous that her son still sometimes forgot to lock it. She went across to the painting of a naval battle on a stormy night. On tiptoes, she ran her fingers along the top of the golden picture frame, making channels in the accumulated dust. She found the mermaid figure that acted as a key ring and locked the gate they'd fitted after the accident to stop the boy going back up to the top of the lighthouse. Lamenting as she always did that they hadn't installed it before, even if just a day earlier. She returned the keys to their hiding place.

They went past the daughter's bedroom without stopping. Without suspecting what was happening inside. When Grandma went to close the shutter and leaned out of the boy's window, which was just along the wall from his sister's, she stopped breathing.

"What's wrong?" the boy asked. Grandma didn't respond. Her hands went white squeezing the shutter's cord. Outside, in the rain, two silhouettes lingered around the septic tank. And she sensed what was happening in the bedroom next door.

Sure enough, her granddaughter had watched the man and woman's every movement through the glass. A circle of condensation grew with each breath from her mouth, her nose pressed against the window, unable to believe what was happening in front of her house. The daughter had seen her father carrying something. A bolt of lightning showed her the blond hair that hung from his arm. She held her hand to her heart. A second bolt allowed her to make out a fleeting, pinkish flash over the septic tank as her father let the bundle drop. It was enough for her to recognize the piece of clothing. An unusual movement of muscles contorted her features. She covered her face, but kept watching through the cracks between her fingers. Her father and mother made a dozen or so trips to the path that crossed the plot. They picked up the rocks that marked it out and threw them to the bottom of the tank. Until they'd filled it. They kept the biggest one to weigh down the sheet of metal that had come through the window.

Then she saw them go back to the house, which was when she sprinted down to the living room.

From the boy's room, Grandma glimpsed her granddaughter crossing the landing. She let the shutter fall like a guillotine of gray plastic that blocked out the window. She rescued the rosary she'd earlier forsworn from her pocket and hung it on her neck, welcoming the weight of the crucifix.

"By the sign of the holy cross," she recited, plotting three crosses, on her forehead, mouth, and chest. "Amen."

"What is it?" asked the boy from under the sheets.

Grandma went to the door. She softly closed it to protect her grandson from what he might hear.

"It's nothing," she answered.

She sat on the bed's edge, adjusting the bedspread. Thinking it could be the last time she'd do so, a tear appeared in each eye. She dried them before the boy could see.

"Show me that thing you can do with your mouth," she said to distract his attention. "The cricket thing."

The grimace he had for a smile lit up the boy's face. Then he positioned his lips in a certain way, whistling through them while the air that he pushed out made them vibrate. A perfect imitation of the chirping sound made by the crickets on the plot. Grandma listened to her grandson, trying to detach herself from what was happening in the living room.

Outside, the daughter found her parents soaked through in the middle of the room. She held the banister to stop the trembling in her hands. She spoke from the second-to-last step on the stairway.

"What have you done?" she asked.

"What is it you've seen?" her father asked back.

"I saw everything."

"Then you know," said the man.

Their words were serious. Heavy. Thrown between them like the rocks had been thrown onto the girl's body.

"Was it her?" She gestured with her chin at the roll of posters in the middle of the living room. Her parents exchanged a look, not knowing how to respond.

"Was it my brother?"

The air that came in through the window made the gray pajamas hug her body.

"Kind of," answered the woman. "He's not responsible for his actions."

"What did he do to her?"

"You don't want to know," the father said.

"And you haven't called anyone?" she asked.

"What do you think?" The woman wrung out her braid as if it were a dishcloth. "You know why we're so wet."

"Dad?"

"The girl was already dead," he explained. "We're protecting the life that's still alive. Your brother's life."

"That girl has a family, too. If my brother has done something to her, I don't care what happens to him."

"We've known for a long time how much you care about your brother," her mother cut in.

The daughter clenched her fists, setting off an intense pain in the palms of her hands. "The entire town's looking for her," she said.

"But people are already guessing what could've happened," her father replied. "And it's what actually happened. The girl fell on the rocks."

"So why are you hiding the body? What has my brother done to her?"

"You don't want to know," the father said again. "In a few days' time they'll start to give her up for dead. She's not the first child on this island to get herself killed on the cliffs."

"Her family won't give her up for dead."

"Well . . ." Her father paused. "But she is."

"Because of my brother."

"That's not true," her mother corrected her.

"Oh, no?" She eased the tension in her fists. "Let's leave that decision to the people who are meant to decide."

She came down the last step. Pieces of glass crunched under the rubber soles of the slippers she'd just put on. Her father guessed her intentions and reached the telephone before her. He held the device behind his back.

"You're not going to do it," he said.

"Give it to me." His daughter grabbed at the air.

"Do you really want to destroy this entire family?" her mother asked.

"It was my brother. Not the rest of you."

"And how're we going to explain the fact that the girl's in the septic tank? Under a pile of rocks." The woman's soggy shoes squelched with each step she took toward her daughter.

The girl opened her mouth to respond. She found no words.

"What will happen to you when they find out what we've done?" her mother added. "You'll be left alone."

"I'm already alone."

"I mean really alone."

"I've been alone since what happened on the stairs," she clarified. "Ever since everything that happens in this house has been my fault."

"Look at yourself." Her mother gestured at her with an open hand. "It's you who wants to call to give us all away. If this family's destroyed because of this, it'll be your fault again. What a coincidence."

The daughter pulled her hair away from her face, holding it with both hands in two ponytails. "Are Grandma and Grandpa in on this as well?"

"We're all together in this. Like we always are." She paused to emphasize what she said next. "All of us, except you."

"Tell me you want to rob your grandparents of the last years of their lives," the father added.

The daughter pulled on her ponytails so that the pain would override her thoughts. It was something that had worked before. She was comforted by the pinpricks on her scalp. And in her mind, she repeated every word of the conversation they'd just had, one by one. She thought of Grandma. Of Grandpa. Life without her family seemed appealing for a few moments. Then she imagined the house empty. Tears sprang from her eyes, but they had nothing to do with the roots of her hair. A heartbroken sigh issued from her belly. She felt as if she could have vomited her soul. She eased the tension in her hair. The tears blurred the image of her parents in a perfect symbol of what they meant to her.

"I hate you," she said to them. "I hate you for doing this to me."

"We're grateful to you," said the father.

"I can still talk whenever I want."

"But you won't."

"Don't test me."

"You're doing the right thing," her mother cut in. "Standing by your family."

"I'm doing it for myself."

"You know that's not true." When she went to squeeze her daughter's arm, the girl snatched it away.

"Don't even think about it!" she yelled. "I don't want any of you to touch me."

For a few seconds she took deep, painful breaths. When she was calmer, her father asked, "So can I leave the telephone on the table?"

The daughter didn't answer. She just turned around to escape as quickly as possible. On the way to the stairs, something crackled underfoot. She knew what it was before she looked down. The missing girl's blue eyes, printed on the stack of posters, crumpled under her slipper. Damp after rolling through the puddles that flooded the living room. Torn by the broken glass scattered across the floor. She looked away, ashamed. Full of guilt.

"I hate you!" she screamed at her parents. She set off up the stairs. A hand stopped her when she reached the landing.

"Take back what you just said," Grandma told her. "You don't hate your parents."

"Let go of me."

"Say sorry to them."

"Let me go."

"Say sorry to your father," Grandma insisted.

The girl grabbed the crucifix that hung from her grandmother's neck. She held it in front of the old woman's face. She turned it so that the Christ looked at her head-on.

"You say sorry to your father for what you've done to that little girl," she said. The force with which she threw down the chain unbalanced Grandma, who had to support herself on the wall to stop herself from falling.

25

The light from the evening's orange sun accentuated every curve in the
metal sheet that covered the septic tank. They had left it there despite
having filled the tank with concrete. No measure seemed sufficient to
block off that memory. From the living room, peering through the
window that the same metal sheet had broken two months earlier,
the woman watched night fall. Nervous from the waiting, she twisted
the end of her braid in front of her chest. She untied some of the knots.
She braided them again. A blanket of purple light covered the plot at
that moment. She had to look away when the tone taken on by the
corrugated iron reminded her of the girl's body. The landscape blurred
in the background as she focused on the remnants of silicone around
the edges of the glass, Grandpa's imperfect repair work on the shattered
window.

The kitchen's swing door opened behind her.

"Come on," her husband said. "It's done."

She turned around and slung the braid onto her shoulders. "How
does it look?" she asked.

"You'll see."

A voice came from among the shadows that the banister cast onto the staircase.

"You make me sick." The daughter spoke sitting on the same step from which she'd discovered her parents soaked through in the middle of the living room the night of the storm. She was wearing a brown ankle-length skirt. The neck of her blouse buttoned up to the top. The sleeves covered her arms to the wrists. Her hair covered her face, forming a dark curtain in front of it. With her usual movement of the head, she sent it to one side.

"Anyone would've thought you were enjoying yourselves," she added.

The man, lifting a finger, signaled to his wife not to respond. "Don't give her the satisfaction," he said. "She's just trying to provoke us."

She gave her father a false smile. "You don't say!" she replied. "What a bad girl I am."

The man beckoned to his wife.

"So, are you really going to do it?" the daughter asked.

"You know we have no other option," her mother answered on her way to the kitchen.

"Poor things, you never have any options but your own. Tell me at least that my brother knows about it."

"Not yet."

The daughter feigned a laughing fit. "And when do you plan to tell him? After he's down there?"

The man shushed his wife to stop her answering more questions. The swinging door hit the frame several times as a final reply. The daughter snorted, alone in the shadows.

In the kitchen, two pots bubbled on the stove. The smell of carrot soup filled the room. Grandma stirred the contents of both with the same wooden spoon. She stepped back to adjust the heat, bending over to see the controls. As she straightened her back she held a hand against her kidneys. With a finger she rubbed the windowpane, which had misted up with the steam from the pots.

"The sun's nearly gone," she said as she discovered the dusk outside. "Are you going down now?"

"You should come down, too," the man broke in.

Instead of answering, Grandma made an unnecessary knot in her apron strings. She set to work with the spoon, remarking how thick the soup had gotten.

"It's going to be your grandson's home," the man said to cut through her feigned indifference.

Grandma sighed. She leaned with both hands on the edge of the counter. She looked outside through the streak she'd drawn in the condensation.

"My grandson's home is still this one," she said. Her voice faltered as she said the last word.

"But you know we're going to have to keep him down there."

"Of course I know. I'm not senile. And I also know that it makes no difference what I think."

"Don't say—"

"Sometimes I think only God listens to me," Grandma interrupted him, stroking her rosary. "And I don't know if He still will after this. Any punishment He has ready for me will be deserved."

The steam from the pots completely covered the glass she was looking through, clouding her view. She turned around. "Do we really have to send him down there?"

"I'm not going over this again," the man answered with his hands in the air. "We're doing it to protect his life. And ours."

"And what life are we going to give him?" asked Grandma. "A life of darkness, locked away underground? Visited by us once a day?"

The man puffed his cheeks and blew out a large quantity of air. He looked down at the floor. Then at his mother. "And what do you suggest?"

Grandma opened her mouth but didn't know what to say.

"We're risking everything every time the boy leaves this house," the man went on. "And every time someone comes here. He doesn't understand that he can't talk about the girl. Do we keep sending him to school until he blabbers everything? Shall we do that? Until he gives us a fright like he did the other day with his teacher?"

The woman gauged her husband's growing anger from the speed at which his ears reddened. She tried to calm him down by stroking his shoulder.

"And this family can just go to hell like it should have two months ago?" he added. "Shall we do that?"

Grandma barely dared to blink.

"Or we could wait for the boy to run off, do the same thing again, and show up with another dead girl in the living room."

"That's enough!" cried the woman. She pressed her hands against her husband's mouth so he wouldn't say another word to Grandma. "We don't need this."

The man spat away the mass of fingers that were meant to silence him. "It's the only way we can give the boy a future," he added. "And give ourselves one. Don't forget that."

Grandma finally blinked. She breathed before speaking again. "I'm not sure this is a future I want to have."

"Then think of it as the future of some girl who won't show up broken on our rug."

"My grandson won't do anything like that again."

"Did you think he could've done it the first time?"

Grandma didn't say another word. She turned off the stove. The kitchen door then opened.

"I can hear you from upstairs," said Grandpa.

"Take her away," the man suggested. "And explain everything to her again. She doesn't seem to want to understand us."

Grandma untied her apron, threw it on the floor, and left the kitchen, sobbing.

The man led his wife to the stairs that went down from the kitchen to the basement. He positioned himself behind her and covered her eyes with both hands. Just as he'd done the first time he showed her the lighthouse, so long ago. The memory made a tiny smile appear on her face. *Anyone would've thought you were enjoying yourselves.* The words her daughter had just uttered resounded in her head. She pulled off the blindfold made by her husband's hands. The boards that formed the stairway creaked underfoot.

"And this wall?" she asked, discovering the new partition that had appeared in the basement, three paces from the bottom of the stairs. It divided the gigantic space in such a way that it was reduced to one-eighth of the size it was before.

"It's one of the walls we built."

She rested the palm of her hand on it as if she could feel the freshness of the concrete that her husband and father-in-law had used.

"So much work," she replied.

The man used a key to unlock a door in the middle of the wall. He held out a hand to invite her to go in.

"And you haven't seen anything yet," he said. From the door, together they looked into the new home, arm in arm like they'd been when they peered into the hospital crib to see their son for the first time. "He'll be fine here," the man said.

His wife shivered. He tried to warm her by rubbing her back through her cardigan. The friction charged the material with static electricity, and two sparks went off in the air. It reminded them of the ones given off by the rocks they threw into the septic tank, on top of the girl. The woman tossed her braid forward. She stroked its knots and took a deep breath.

"I can barely smell the damp," she said.

"Because it's a proper home." The man walked into the new basement's main room, skirting a large table. "It even has a kitchen. And a TV." He pointed at the device. "And look at all those shelves. He can start filling them with books and movies. I've already brought some down for the first few months. There's a video recorder there."

She stood looking at the many empty shelves. Just one section was full of Betamax tapes of movies recorded from the television. A year of recordings contained in a single section of a bookcase that had another twenty sections. She thought about how much the boy would have grown when that whole bookcase was filled. An image was projected in her mind: her son sinking into the sofa after years of isolation.

"I don't want to lose my son," she said.

"You won't."

The man felt the soft pink flesh of the woman with whom he'd fallen in love twenty winters ago. When a surprise wave had soaked her while she was posing near the rocks for a photo that ended up being taken at that precise moment. Afterward he had invited her up to dry her clothes. He covered her eyes as they climbed to the top of the tower up the same spiral staircase that would make them so unhappy years later. From there, they observed the night sea. Naked, wrapped in two towels, she had asked from how far away the ships would have seen the lighthouse beam when it still worked.

"Come on," he said in the basement, "look at this."

They reached an arch that opened into a hallway.

"What about that?" the woman asked. She was looking at a circle of light that was projected onto the floor from the ceiling. A beam of sparkling powder was flowing into the room. "Where's it coming from?"

"There must be a crack up top," he explained. "The sun comes in through that hole in the ceiling." He stepped on the light spot as if he could kill it that way. "I'll have to fill it in so that—"

"Don't do that," she broke in. "Don't fill it. Let him see the sun."

The man withdrew his foot. The sunlight slithered off his shoe and clung to the floor again. "Come on, I want you to see the bathroom." He pushed the door open.

She went inside. The skin on her arms tightened. When she opened the drawers that were behind the door, the movement knocked the tubes of toothpaste and bars of soap they contained out of place. Then she turned one of the faucets on the sink, expecting remnants of plaster to fall out of it, or the air in the empty pipes to whistle. But what came out was a firm stream of pressurized water. She turned it off and turned the left one on, holding two fingers under the jet.

"There's no hot," her husband explained. "I couldn't get it to work." She looked at him in the mirror. He saw that her chin was trembling, that she was about to cry, as if the absence of hot water had reminded her that it wouldn't be a normal life that the boy would lead in the basement. He went up to her and hugged her from behind.

"Don't be upset," he said. "I'll keep trying. It's got something to do with a pipe. I'm not sure where it goes."

They looked at each other's reflections in the glass. The woman squeezed her husband's arms, which held her at waist height. "Are we doing the right thing?" she asked.

"He can't stay up there. It's dangerous for everyone."

"What your mother said earlier . . . Do you think it's a life, what we're offering him?"

Her husband shook her gently to make her turn around.

"Right now it's the best life we can give him."

Her chest rose.

"Let's go," he said. "You haven't seen the bedroom yet."

The hinges creaked when they opened another door and walked into a room.

"The bunk bed?" said the woman.

"He loved sleeping up there."

She remembered the afternoon in the mattress store. And how, after her husband had chosen a new bed for the boy who was too big for his crib, she'd approached the bunk bed that was at the back of the store. She pointed at it timidly with a smile. An invitation to have a third child that he accepted without a second thought. The boy celebrated the decision to buy the bed by clambering right then onto the top bunk, and to the salesclerk's despair, messing up the display sheets. In the end, the bunk bed's second occupant never arrived. And the bottom bunk was still empty when the accident on the stairs upset all of their plans for the future.

"Do you remember?" she asked, without needing a response. She approached the bed for two and gripped the red metal frame. She shook it. She examined every part of the structure, her eyes resting on each corner and joint.

"At the rate the boy's growing, this bed's going to collapse within a few months," she noted.

"We'll be upstairs," he said. "If the bunk bed breaks or if he runs out of food . . ." He positioned himself beside his wife and laid a hand on the frame. "He'll be hidden. But he won't be alone."

The woman recovered her braid. She twisted it in her fingers. She lifted a foot and swiveled on her heel to take in the rest of the room. Something caught her attention on the shelves that covered one of the walls. She hugged her cardigan around her, crossing her arms at belly height instead of buttoning it. She crouched down on her knees to take out one of the dozen books lined up in a row. She pulled on one of the cardigan's sleeves and used the cuff as a handkerchief, wiping the book cover in circles. *The Wonderful Wizard of Oz*. She remembered reading that book to the boy at night, when he was ready to sleep on the top bunk, and the laughter that had exploded in his mouth at the silly things the Scarecrow said. *When I grow up I want to be like him,* the boy had said one night. The woman felt like crying when she thought of that sentence, remembering what had happened to the boy and what the Scarecrow was seeking on his journey to Oz.

"We read such nice things to him . . ."

The man contemplated the book cover, peering over his wife's shoulder.

"Our son's still a lovely boy," he whispered in her ear.

The woman ran her forefinger along the book's edges. When she reached the top-right corner, she opened it on a random page. She heard the moist sound of her husband's lips as they stretched into a smile near her ear.

"See?" he said into her ear. He ran a finger along the sentence printed on the page, the one that said there's no place better than home. "And a home is what he'll have here."

"A home," she repeated. She folded the top corner of page twenty-one to mark it.

The man grabbed the book by the spine, making his wife close it. He put it back on the shelf.

"And look who's going to sleep with him every night." He reached for a photograph frame that stood on the next shelf along.

She smiled when she saw the image. The one her husband had taken of her on the rocks. "What a soaking I got from that wave," she said. "You took too long taking the picture."

"I wanted you to get wet so you'd have to come up with me," he joked.

The woman took the photograph from him. She stroked it through the glass. Remembering better times.

"You'll be here with him every night."

She sighed.

"We still have the other side to see," he said. The woman put the frame back. Before leaving the room, she cast a last glance over the bunk bed. And the shelves. The walls, the corners, and the ceiling. The space that would be her son's bedroom for a long time, perhaps the rest of his life. When her stomach contracted until it hurt, she turned away to stop looking, and went out into the hall behind her husband. His hand was already resting on the handle of the door opposite.

"And this is the guest room." They went into a room slightly smaller than the one they'd just visited. There was another bed. "In case one of us wants to stay and sleep with him," the man explained.

The woman walked around the empty space.

"What if we take turns staying the night here?" She imagined herself sleeping in that room, spending the night there as if visiting a grown-up son who'd moved out. The idea gave her a sudden feeling of peace. Without realizing it she turned to smile at her husband. It was a sincere, proud smile, the smile of a mother who knows for certain that her son is the best son in the world.

"That's what I like to see," he said. But now she had to force her cheeks to maintain the smile, because she knew that in reality her son wasn't moving out. Instead he was being locked in the basement of his own home to become a secret hidden under their feet. One they'd walk over every day. Like a mother walking over the grave of a son dead before his time. She pretended to look at something on the bed frame to give her eyes time to dry, the smile remaining like a cut on her face.

"There's still the storeroom," her husband added from the door.

She blinked several times before turning around, and then rubbed her lips together, tasting the bitterness of her fleeting smile.

"This way," he indicated. At the end of the hallway, a final door appeared on the left, opposite the bathroom. This door was different from the rest, gray in color. The man tapped it with his knuckles as if knocking.

"It's metal," he said. "And it can't be opened from the outside. It doesn't even have a handle." He waved his hand in the air in the place where it should have been.

"Here, it can only be opened with this key," he said, showing it to her between two fingers before inserting it in the lock. "He can't have access to this part, you'll see why in a second."

He pushed the door with his shoulder. The dust crackled under the metal's weight as a room larger than the others appeared in front of them. Once inside, the woman noticed the large wardrobe against one of the walls.

Then there was a bang that made her shoulders flinch. She thought that the renovations that her husband had carried out in the basement over the last two months had undermined the structure of the house.

"It closes on its own," her husband said, indicating the metal door. "And it's heavy."

She opened her eyes, her shoulders still tense. "I thought the lighthouse was coming down on top of us."

"The people in the town won't be so lucky," he answered.

His wife tutted her disapproval. "Nobody wants that."

"They would if they knew the truth."

She pulled her cardigan around her.

"It's colder here," she observed. She attributed it to the room being empty.

"All the better, don't you think?" He opened his palms toward the ceiling to feel the temperature with more accuracy. "The basement keeps the temperature constant. It never gets too hot or too cold," he explained.

"That's good?"

"No need for heating. Or ventilation. The earth regulates the temperature. It's one less thing to worry about. He'll be as comfortable in summer as in winter."

She examined her husband's face, his features rugged now from the weeks of work in the basement. He hadn't shaved.

"The wardrobe's enormous," said the woman.

He smiled, his eyes shining like they always did before he revealed a secret. He approached the four doors that ran along the wall perpendicular to the one they'd come in through. He gripped one of the knobs and looked at his wife. He stayed like that for a few seconds, unmoving.

"What?" she asked.

He remained on pause.

"What is it?" she insisted.

Her husband didn't answer.

"Please . . ."

The man pulled the door open when he guessed his wife was about to leave the room. "Because it's not just a wardrobe," he said.

The latch was released with a metallic sound. The handle hit the wood of the next door along. In front of them a rectangle of total darkness appeared. "It's much more," added the man.

A current of air rushed out of the wardrobe. It made the bottom of the woman's skirt flutter. She rubbed her ankles to fight off that subterranean draft.

"Are you going to explain what it is?"

Her husband positioned himself in the center of the black rectangle, his silhouette blending into the dark background. "It's the other entrance."

"Another entrance?"

"Come here and I'll explain." A curved line of light reflected on her husband's chin betrayed his presence. "Coming?"

The line of light went out as she approached the rectangle of darkness. The current of air began to blow up her body, making the skirt hug her thighs like a second skin.

"What do I do? Go in?"

"Come here."

The hand emerged from the darkness. The woman screamed. Because that was how it came out in her nightmares, from among the rocks, the blue hand at the bottom of the septic tank. She could see it now in front of her. A child's hand made into a claw, sprouting from the ground like a carnivorous plant. When she managed to shake off the image and she recognized her husband's hand inviting her into the wardrobe, the woman gave him a cuff.

"You frightened me," she protested. Then she took the hand and let herself be led.

In one step, she was in the darkness.

The storeroom was left empty.

The inside of the wardrobe smelled of damp earth.

"It's this way." The man's voice resounded in the small space. "Let's go."

"Where?" she asked. "We can barely fit in here."

They began to walk to the left, into a space much bigger than there should have been behind the wardrobe doors. She felt along the wood until her fingers reached an edge. A change in texture as the wood transformed into soil. She took her hand away. They continued through the new corridor that came from nowhere. Behind them, the light from the storeroom was reduced to a distant radiance. They turned right, then left, and then right again, the moisture becoming an invisible shroud. When the man stopped, the woman's momentum carried her into his back. She took the opportunity to hug him from behind.

"What is this place?" she asked into his ear.

"Why are you whispering?"

"Tell me where we are," she whispered again, her chin resting on his shoulder.

"Look," he replied. A circle of orange light was projected against the wall located in front of them. Its contour gently vibrated because of the trembling hand that held the match. The woman felt the wall of dark earth, lingering on the grayish roots that sprouted from it. She wrinkled her nose when she discovered an orange slug slithering along the wall. The man turned to look at his wife. The flame went out with the movement, and the space was flooded with the smell of phosphorous and burned wood. Straightaway a spark spawned another cloud of light between them. It lit up two faces that found themselves looking at each other. Orange-colored faces with deep, dark furrows.

"This is how we'll bring him the supplies he needs." The air he breathed out made the flame dance, distorting their faces' shadows.

"You look scary," she said. "Like you're deformed."

"So do you," he replied. He held the flame nearer his wife's face. The patches of shadow blurred her features until her orangey eyes floated in midair. Hypnotized by the effect, the man miscalculated, and the match touched the woman's cheek. She batted his hand away.

The darkness returned when the flame went out. "You moron!" she yelled. "You burned me."

He lit another match. "You're fine," he concluded after examining his wife's face. He blew gently on the left cheek like he'd blown so many times on his children's grazed knees.

"Well, it hurts." The woman exaggerated her anger until he kissed the place where the burn wasn't. "OK, it doesn't hurt anymore."

They both smiled. There was a surge of attraction between them. A desire that they thought had died in their marriage until a few days ago.

"The supplies?" she said, getting back to the conversation. "You mean the food."

"Food, toilet paper, medicine, lightbulbs . . . whatever he needs. We bring it down to the storeroom through here, and put it in the basement."

"Why don't we just use the other door? The one we used to come in?"

The match burned down.

The man lit another. As he held it to the opposite wall, two metal handles that emerged from the earth reflected the orange light from the flame like worms of fire. He slapped one of them with his free hand.

"They're steps," he explained. "Look up."

Several of the same handles ran up the wall as far as the circle of light reached.

"They lead to the surface," he continued. "There's a trapdoor in the grass. This basement mustn't exist. There can't be an entrance from our house. When we put him down here, it'll be the last time we use that other door. I want to build another wall to hide it. This basement won't exist anymore."

Her sigh blew out the match, erasing everything around them. As if the basement really had ceased to exist. This time he didn't bother to light another. He took his wife's face in his hands and stroked her cheeks with his thumbs.

"We'll be able to come in this way," he whispered. "But if someone comes to search the house, if someone questions our story about our son's disappearance, they'll only find a brick wall in the first basement. There'll be no way to get to this place."

The woman nodded as if accepting what he said, but the man's thumbs spread two tears around her face, two tears that gave away the truth.

"Don't cry," he said in her ear. "It's the best thing we can do."

When he held her, he felt her heart beating against his chest as if it were his own. She sniffed. Then something moved between their feet. A moist tickle nosed the woman's bare ankles. Her every fiber wanted to escape that darkness.

"It's a rat," her husband whispered. "That's something else I have to take care of. Now don't move."

She stood paralyzed. Barely moving her lips, she asked, "Will he be all right?"

"Huh?"

"Our son," she clarified. "Will he be all right?"

In the total darkness of the basement that shouldn't exist, they heard the rat run off in the direction of the wardrobe.

26

After returning from their first visit to the basement, the woman went to look for her son. She found her daughter on the stairway, still standing on the second-to-last step. Her mother tried to move her out of the way, but she wriggled from her grasp. Guessing she was intent on blocking her path, the woman dodged around her daughter as best she could. No words were exchanged.

In his bedroom, the boy spun around in the office chair he'd inherited from his sister's room. He grabbed the desk to propel himself and squealed with excitement with each spin, his legs outstretched, his forehead pressed against the chair to combat the dizziness. The room smelled unpleasantly of feet and another smell, one similar to bleach. She approached the bed knowing what she'd find. She felt the sheets until she found the stains. She pulled them off the mattress, rolling them around her arm.

The boy carried on, floating around the room in circular motions. The genuine delight of his howling made his mother smile, watching him while he completed the space odyssey that must have been taking place in his head. The woman gave him a few minutes to enjoy the total freedom of his childhood, his imagination, and his complex innocence. She dodged his flying feet to open the window and air out the room. The approaching nightfall's breeze brought with it a cricket's chirp. The boy threw a hand onto the table and stopped the journey through space. He rolled to the window in the chair. The dizziness made his eyes plot orbits like the ones he'd just traveled. Gripping the frame, he poked his face outside. He mimicked the cricket sound with his lips. The boy's head still moved in circles.

"Son." She held his shoulder. "Son, listen to me."

The boy carried on his imitation. A third guest, hidden in the grass, or among the pine tree's branches, joined the chirruping conversation.

"We have to talk," his mother insisted. He remained oblivious, absorbed in his dialogue, still rocked by the dizzy hangover. And she felt an urge to grab her son's head. Full of guilt, she thought about how she'd squeeze him in her hands and scream at him until she lost her voice to please stop being like he was. To be a normal boy. The boy he was before the fall.

He stopped his head's swaying. Almost as if he'd heard his mother's terrible thoughts, he looked at her with eyes that had regained their usual angle, equally as uncoordinated.

"I know what you're going to say."

The woman hugged the bundle of sheets. "What?"

"I know what you're going to do with me."

Not knowing how to respond, the woman simply knitted her brow.

"You're going to hide me," he added.

She wondered whether she had heard right.

"What did you say?"

"I've seen Dad and Grandpa. Th . . . they're . . ." His tongue fought to separate from the roof of his mouth. "Working in the basement. They're making a house. You're going to hide me. Underground. Because of what happened with the girl."

The boy looked at his mother, though his eyes seemed not to go much farther than the tip of his nose. She tried to dry her tears with the dirty sheets before her son realized she was crying. He got up from his chair and took the sheets from her. He hugged his mother and played with the knots of her braid while her shoulders shook. Her chest rose with little in-breaths. She sniffed. When his mother had stopped crying, the boy separated from her and dried her face with his hands. He kissed her left eye first and then the right.

"Don't be sad," he whispered. "Crickets live underground. I don't mind living like them."

She held him tight. Over his mother's shoulder, the boy discovered his sister watching them from the door.

"Oh, how sweet. Moments like this make everything you're doing worthwhile, don't they?"

The woman turned around. Her daughter's voice had cut the flow of emotions dead.

"Leave us in peace," she replied.

Behind the girl, on the landing, she saw her husband appear, followed by Grandma and Grandpa. They were returning from saying sorry to each other for the argument in the kitchen. None of them wanted to stay angry on the night they were to take the boy down. It was important that everything was as good-natured as possible.

"Ooh, everyone's together," the daughter noted. "Pretending to be a normal family."

The man pulled her away from the door.

"Come on," he said to his wife. "Let's go."

The boy took the hand his father offered him. Mother and son walked over the creased sheets on their way to the landing.

"Do you know where they're taking you, little brother?"

The woman covered the boy's ears. "Of course he knows," she answered her daughter. "Your brother's much cleverer than you think."

"And you're taking him down in his pajamas so he feels at home, huh?"

Nobody replied. She was left at the end of the line that went down in the direction of the kitchen, led by the boy and his father. Her mother followed them, and her grandparents advanced a few steps behind. Grandma sobbed, her head resting on her husband's shoulder.

"You look like a funeral march!" the daughter yelled from behind.

"Well, you *are* going to bury a son, so it makes sense."

It satisfied her to see Grandma hunch even more under the effect of her words.

The man held open the kitchen door to let his son through. He also waited for his wife to go in. She held it until the grandparents arrived. Once they were through, she let go of it. Still in the living room, the daughter watched the door close.

Then she noticed the cream-colored telephone. The one she'd wanted to use the night she discovered what her parents had done with the girl. She cursed the moment she'd allowed herself to be blackmailed. If only she'd called the police then. Or the girl's family, who she'd met one day when they were putting up posters. She still knew she could do it. She'd wanted to. She'd wanted to every day. And each day that passed, it became harder and harder to justify her silence. At the beginning two days seemed a long time: they would consider her an accomplice to her family for not turning them in as soon as she discovered them. Then five days went by. *I can't do it now.* Eight days. *Now I really can't.* Two weeks. *I have to call.* Three weeks. *Nobody will believe me.* Until two months had gone by, in which time her parents had carried through the plan to hide the boy. To bury him like a criminal buries the evidence of a crime. Like they'd buried the girl's body. Except that her brother was still alive.

While she remembered the two months of inner conflict, her feet had acted by themselves and taken her near the side table. She was surprised to find herself beside the telephone. She heard the murmur of the conversation in the kitchen. She felt repulsion toward that group of people who had turned her into a ghost since the incident on the stairs. Always looking through her as if she were no longer a part of the family. She could make them pay for all of that. She lifted the receiver.

She listened to the tone that invited her to dial.

It remained off the hook until the line went dead with a series of beeps.

She hung up.

Energetically massaging her face, she breathed through her fingers. Wavering. She walked in short steps over the rug, traveling back and forth, again and again, along an imaginary line. The brown skirt moved to the rhythm of her restless legs.

As she completed a lap, she lengthened her next step. Three more took her to the swinging door. With a push she entered the kitchen.

The boy was already going down the stairs to the basement, his mother beside him.

"Would you do something like this for me?" she asked. The five members of her family looked at her.

"What did you say?" asked her father.

"Would you do something like this for me?" she said again. "If I did something as terrible as he's done. Would you protect me like this?"

There was silence. When the man went to speak, his wife raised her voice to talk over his reply.

"You already did something just as terrible," she answered, observing her daughter's questioning expression. "You put your brother in his bed with his head cracked open. And we protected you. We protected you in the hospital by hiding the truth about what happened."

The daughter blinked twice in quick succession. She hadn't known that piece of information.

"This isn't the same," she said back to show she wouldn't budge. "He killed a girl."

"And your brother could've died in that bed."

The daughter examined the faces in front of her. Her eyes came to rest on her brother's.

"Seeing how he's going to end up"—she gestured at him with her chin—"maybe he would've been better off dead."

Grandma held her breath. The woman held a hand to her mouth. "I don't know who you are. I don't recognize you."

The man positioned himself in front of his daughter with his hand held high.

She shielded her face with her arms. She closed her eyes and waited for the slap.

But it never came.

When she reopened them, she discovered her father looking at her, his hand still raised, struggling to control his rage. He breathed with difficulty, overcome with fury. Or sadness. Or disappointment. The man studied his daughter's half-closed eyes. Those eyes that her pale cheeks squeezed almost totally shut when she smiled. And he remembered how she had smiled, years ago, on the night when they looked up at the sky from the cliffs, by the lighthouse, when he had made her believe that the freckles that dotted her nose were fallen stars. She'd celebrated by lifting her arms in victory, and he'd picked her up to hug her while they spun around on the rock, the girl kicking the air with pure joy. Now the freckles had disappeared, leaving just two moles. The man knew the girl had gone, too.

"I'm not surprised the stars wanted to leave your face," he said.

She feigned a smile. "Is that supposed to hurt me?" she asked. "First you threaten to hit me and then you come out with some stupid crap like that?"

The way his daughter spurned one of the memories he treasured rekindled the rage that had gripped his stomach. It spread to his chest, to his shoulder, to his arm, to his hand. He slapped his daughter.

She held her hands to the side of her face. She looked at each member of her family through incipient tears. Grandpa exhaled two breaths onto the lenses of his glasses and wiped them with his shirt. Grandma crossed herself. Her mother shook her head as she stroked the boy's hair, while he deciphered some kind of code in the lines of her hands. In front of her, her father examined his warm, palpitating palm.

"You're going to regret this." She spat the words through her teeth, trying with her numb lips to contain the saliva that overflowed from her mouth. A string of red drool, tinted with blood, was left hanging from her chin. It swung as she uttered each of the words that she repeated. "You're going to regret it."

She left the kitchen.

"What's that supposed to mean?" the man yelled at the door, which closed with its usual to and fro.

Grandma approached him to examine his hand. She felt the reddened areas while he waited for an answer from his daughter.

"What else can you do to us?" he shouted. Then he lowered the volume to speak to Grandma. "Mom, get off, it's nothing." He snatched his hand free like he had as a child. "I'm asking you, what else can you do to us?" He raised his voice even more than before, assuming his daughter had reached the first floor by now.

But then a thought knotted his throat. Another cry died in his mouth before it existed. Almost at the same time, his wife voiced his thoughts.

"There is something she can do," she said.

The grandparents understood what she meant right away. "Not now. I don't think she'd be capable of—"

The man didn't wait for Grandpa to finish the sentence. He launched himself at the swinging door with his hand raised, ignoring the pain in his palm from the impact.

In the living room, he found what he'd feared.

The telephone's curled wire vibrated in time with his daughter's accelerated pulse. She trembled as she held the receiver. Her mouth opened when she knew she'd been caught. The string of drool that still hung from her chin broke. A drop of blood fell to the floor. She had already dialed the number, but nobody was answering the call. She knew straightaway that there wouldn't be time to speak before her father crossed the living room and reached her. And she also knew that if she didn't seize the moment, if she didn't feed off the rage that the slap had provoked in her, she'd never muster the courage she needed to turn in her family. Alarm bells went off in various parts of her brain, trying to warn her about her own future. She didn't listen to them. She acted without thinking. Driven by pure instinct. She hung up and held the telephone in one hand. Crouching down, she searched the bottom of the wall for the socket where the wire was connected. She found it right away. She pulled on the cable before her father had taken two strides. With the telephone unplugged, she made a run for the stairs, knocking over the two lamps that stood in her path. One of them fulfilled its purpose: to trip her father. She heard him fall with a deep groan, an animal snort. She set off up the stairs.

On the landing, she pulled at the gate that led to the lantern. She shook it in its frame. A metallic rattling accompanied the action. Locked. She could hear her father cursing downstairs. It seemed that neither his wife nor the grandparents were succeeding in giving him the help he'd asked for to get to his feet. Another thump on the floor confirmed the uselessness of their assistance. A crystalline detonation signaled a broken bulb. With a single leap she positioned herself in front of the painting of the naval battle on a stormy night. On tiptoes, she searched for the mermaid key ring that they kept out of the boy's reach. She ran her fingers along the top of the picture frame, her hand's frenetic shaking lifting clouds of dust. With one shake she hit the key ring. The mermaid fell to her feet.

The tip of the key clinked around the lock, her fingers' trembling preventing her from inserting it. The telephone she held against her stomach was beginning to slip. She heard a footstep at the bottom of the stairs. And another on the next step. Her father was coming up. A grunt came from her throat, bringing her momentary relief from the tension and steadying her pulse for just an instant. Just enough time to insert the key. She turned it. She saw her father appear on the landing the moment she closed the gate from the other side. She screamed as she inserted the key again. The lock clicked into place with one turn. There was no time for anything else. Her father's hand attacked through two of the bars, as aggressive as a piranha. He managed to catch her by the blouse, but she got loose with a tug that tore the seam of a sleeve.

She climbed the steep staircase in a spiral as twisted as the events that were ruining life in the lighthouse. The man watched his daughter's shoes go up until they disappeared. He gave up trying to catch her. His tensed arms, stretched as far as the top of the gate allowed, fell like dead weight.

"Please," he begged into the darkness of the tower, his face lodged between two bars. "We're your family."

There was no response. She didn't want to hear anything that would make her change her mind. She rounded the lantern room. The chalky glow of a moon blurred by the mist flooded the space, giving it a dreamlike texture, full of shadows that might not have been shadows. She moved along the curved space between the lantern and the dome's windows.

Down below, listening for his daughter's footsteps, the man made a desperate attempt to prevent what seemed inevitable.

"If you're planning to plug the telephone in up there, don't bother. It's never worked properly."

But she knew that wasn't true. And she also knew that her father had always made an effort to keep the lantern workable, because he still held out hope that the lighthouse would one day shine again. Like he hoped that her brother's head would suddenly fix itself. On a desk, she felt along the spines of a row of books. The thick volumes on medicine, psychology, and psychiatry that her father labored to read without really understanding, hoping that on one of their pages he'd find the words that would allow him to work a miracle. She kicked a stool and crouched under the table, treading on her skirt. She searched on her knees for the telephone socket.

The man set off downstairs. He ran to the side table and batted it out of the way while his family members gave each other puzzled looks. He tried to rip out the telephone jack with his fingers, looking for some internal connection that he could interrupt. A fingernail broke in the attempt. "Christ!" he yelled. "We have to rip this thing out!" Grandpa shot off to the kitchen. He returned with a screwdriver. The man snatched it from his hands. He hit the socket with the tip, and chips of plastic flew from it. It was all for nothing. Because of the time it took to break the plastic and because there was nothing there anyway behind that cream-colored square that could cut off the call his daughter made.

At the top of the tower, squatting under the desk, with trembling fingers she turned the dial seven times. After the first ring, a man's voice answered the call.

And she spoke.

She spoke in a voice as deep and as dark as the sea they had looked out on as a family from that tower on so many nights. She spoke without pause. Tears, blood, and saliva fell on the receiver. After identifying herself, she told the man how her brother had found the girl on the rocks. How he'd kept her existence secret in order to live for a few days in a crazed fairy tale in which the two of them made a family together. Until the girl's body faded forever. She told him how her brother had then brought the corpse to the old lighthouse. The decision her family had made to hide the body. And she told him also that the girl lay in the septic tank. Under a pile of stones that they later sealed off with concrete.

"Hello?" She looked at the telephone with an anxious expression. She'd heard a bang. "Are you there? I have more to tell you. They're going to hide my brother now . . ."

But nobody was listening at the other end of the line. Her last words were reduced to an electrostatic crackle emanating from the receiver of a telephone left lying on the floor. Because the man who'd answered, and who had dropped the receiver when the voice mentioned the concrete that they used to cover the body of his daughter—the girl he'd dressed in pink one spring morning to teach her to ride a bicycle—that man was now moving frenetically around his garage. Searching among empty cans. Praying to the God he no longer believed in that he wouldn't find a full one. When he found one, he changed his plea. Now he prayed for the strength he would need to stop himself. To prevent himself from going through with the idea that had germinated in his mind.

"Have you done it?"

Her father's voice, reverberating around the dome's glass, startled her. She hit her head as she came out from her hiding place under the table. She brushed her damp hair away from her face and hooked it behind her ears. She wiped her mouth with the torn sleeve of her blouse, then dried her eyes with her fist. Until now she hadn't noticed the intense throb in one of her back teeth caused by the slap. She returned the receiver to its base. She even went to untangle the curled wire, but her father shouted again, interrupting the task.

"Tell me whether you've done it!" The gate rattled, shaking in its frame.

"I did it."

"The police?"

"Her father."

The reply filled the man's chest with air contaminated with guilt, with remorse. He let it out in an agonizing sigh, a wretched, high-pitched wail that rose up the staircase. His daughter heard him from upstairs. Never in her eighteen years of life had she heard her father cry.

And she smiled.

The blood that soured her tongue took on a sudden taste of victory.

27

"He's going to come for us," the man said in the living room. "Do something."

Grandma, who was repositioning one of the fallen lamps beside the cuckoo clock, whimpered. The boy, by his mother's legs, let out a misguided guffaw. The woman covered her mouth with the flaps of her cardigan, as if she felt cold. She wanted to cower behind them and disappear. She knew what her husband's words meant.

"She's told them," she whispered. She said it for herself, bringing a deep trail of thought to its conclusion. Then her mouth appeared over the woolen neck.

"She's told them."

Her husband acknowledged it with a long blink. She cursed her daughter with murmured words that were unintelligible.

Grandma ran to the front door. She turned the keys that hung from the lock. Spinning around, she pressed her hands against the door, as if keeping at bay an onslaught from outside. "What do we do?" she asked.

Grandpa improvised. He drew the curtains in the adjacent windows, including the one that the corrugated iron from the septic tank had smashed two months earlier, and which he himself had mended.

He crossed the living room and closed the curtains on the other side. Then he headed for the kitchen.

"I've drawn the curtains in the kitchen, too." He took a deep breath. "Nobody can see us from outside." He said it as if it were a solution to the problem. As if the sections of curtain that hid them could separate them from the outside world. Insulate them from the truth.

Grandma heard her husband's labored breathing. She saw him bent over, his hands on his knees, his glasses out of place on his nose. She noticed how weary he looked, the result of an absurd idea that she herself had initiated when she blocked the door. As if two turns of the lock were enough to keep them captive in the alternate reality they'd invented. The one in which there was no girl who'd appeared dead in the living room. In her actions, and Grandpa's, she recognized a final desperate attempt to prolong the lie they had kept up for two months. To keep the secret covered up any way possible. This time with curtains. Just looking at her husband made her feel exhausted. The two months of guilt, fear, and bad decisions fell on top of her like the pile of stones they'd used to cover the body. A sigh escaped from the depths of her chest.

And then, almost at the same time, the rest of them also realized the uselessness of their improvised solution. Several looks were exchanged in a silence broken only by a cricket's chirp.

"Not now," the woman whispered to her son to get him to stop his mimicking. But she discovered that the boy had his mouth shut. The cricket continued to chirp outside the house. A cyclic chirp that seemed to measure the time that was running out on them. Time spent among secrets and lies.

Grandma was the first to accept it. "We won't be able to hide forever," she said.

"We have the boat at the jetty," the man suggested. "We can make a run for it."

"And then what?" Grandma asked.

Grandpa hugged his wife. He grasped the ultimate meaning of her words. And he seconded her decision. "You know how long we'd take to get to the mainland," he said to dissuade his son. "They'll be waiting for us there."

"There are other islands," the man insisted. "We can get away."

The grandparents didn't listen. They just looked each other in the eye and accepted the end of the time of secrets. The cricket outside gave a final chirp. It, too, confirming the end of an era.

Grandpa repeated his wife's sentence. "We won't be able to hide forever."

"That's what you were going to do with me!" yelled the boy, who began to laugh compulsively. "Hide me forever! There's a house in the basement!"

"The basement," said the woman.

"Could we go down?" Grandpa asked, wrapping his hand around the fist in which Grandma squeezed the rosary.

"It's not designed for all of us," said the man. "But we could."

The woman swallowed a large quantity of saliva. "Forever?" she said in barely a whisper. "Would we be going down forever?"

"Of course not," her husband answered without knowing whether he lied. "Just until we think of something else."

"And what would that be?"

"I don't know," he said, shaking his head. "I really don't know. But what other options do we have? Are we going to wait for them to come for us? Give up like that? Now?"

Grandma burst into tears.

"What will they do if they find us?" the man went on. "What can they do to us?"

"Lock us up," Grandpa replied.

"So either way we end up imprisoned," his daughter-in-law concluded. "The outcome's the same."

"It's not the same," the man corrected her. He used a pause to reorganize his thoughts. "Out here they'd lock us up separately. Down there we'd be together."

"You're going to live with me!" cried the boy. His feet began an arrhythmic dance that he accompanied with spasmodic movements of his waist. He also waved his arms with pure joy, launching his elbows at the ceiling, until his mother halted him with an arm that was really a straitjacket.

"Stop. Please, don't dance." But the boy kept wiggling his body in her arms, humming a tuneless melody. The murmuring continued while his mother, father, and grandparents observed the unexpected outbreak of happiness and optimism with confusion. At the end of the song, the boy managed to free an arm from the straitjacket that had now loosened, and he stuck a finger in his mouth, his cheeks inflated. The slobbery plop that detonated on his lips when he took out his finger made his mother expel air through her nose in a timid chuckle. And when the grimace that the boy had for a smile lit up his face, the decision suddenly became simpler.

"I want to go down," the woman said.

Grandma rested her forehead on Grandpa's face. "So do we."

Grandpa confirmed it with a nod. Then he moved his wife's head so it rested on his chest. Almost identical smiles spread across their faces. The man then realized something. He looked at his parents, who were talking to each other without words, in a conversation of caresses. He observed the tender way they rubbed their heads together, a loving gesture achieved only after decades of coexistence.

With the words still forming hastily on his tongue, the man granted his parents a final few seconds of peace before speaking. "We can't all go down," he said. "Someone has to stay up top."

"Our daughter's going to stay," the woman reminded him.

"We have a daughter?" was the question the man offered as a response.

The woman lowered her head.

Grandma rubbed her forehead against Grandpa's wrinkled cheek. She wanted to cover his mouth to stop him from saying what she knew he was going to say.

"It has to be me," said Grandpa. First he spoke to his daughter-in-law. "You have to look after your son."

She confirmed she would by kissing the crown of the boy's head. He was still listening to music in some corner of his mind.

"And you." Grandpa now addressed his own son. "You have to look after her," he said, indicating his daughter-in-law with his chin. She smiled back at him. Grandpa hugged his wife with such force that he felt the beads of her rosary dig into his chest. "And you have to look after all of them," he said into her ear. "Please, don't cry," he added when she began to tremble.

He repeatedly kissed his wife's white hair to give himself time to think. Concentrating, he pinched the right arm of his glasses.

"You need someone up here," he went on. "I'll go down to the jetty. I'll get the boat started and let it go."

He dried his lips with his fingers.

"When they arrive, I'll tell them you've fled." Grandpa delivered his speech with his eyes on his son and daughter-in-law, inviting them to get involved in the plan that he was improvising. "I'll say that I didn't know anything. That my granddaughter's lying."

"Will they believe you?" the woman asked.

"They'd better."

"And if they don't?"

"They'll have to." They all acquiesced in silence. Accepting the risk like they'd accepted others that they hadn't even thought of. Taking on in their hurried decision all of the pitfalls, all of the failures, cracks, errors, mishaps, and unforeseeable events that might arise in their escape plan.

"I'll tell them I feel hurt," Grandpa continued. "Betrayed by all of you. And by my wife. I'll say that was why I didn't go with you."

Again he observed his family's faces. They nodded, seeing the logic of the plan.

"They'll find the boat floating somewhere. Or dashed against some rocks. They'll assume you've gone overboard. With a bit of luck this island will want to erase you from its memory after finding out what you did with the girl."

"And you?" his daughter-in-law asked him. "If they believe you, if everything goes OK . . ."

"I can go back to the mainland," he said. "To our house. We've got money, and it'll be easier to go unnoticed there. To get ahold of everything you're going to need."

"You won't be able to come much," his son said. "The town mustn't see you near the lighthouse. They'll wonder what you're doing here."

"I worked in this lighthouse all my life," he replied. "And now it's yours. This lighthouse belongs to us. I have every right to come to remember my missing family." He curved one side of his mouth in something like a smile.

"But for that we have to disappear." Grandma sobbed.

"Come on," Grandpa encouraged her, "we need to be quick. If they find us here it'll be worse."

"I don't want to—" A crying spasm interrupted Grandma's sentence.

Her husband looked at her with raised eyebrows, as if looking at a child exaggerating a tantrum more than was believable. "You just said you wanted to go down."

"But with you," she spluttered.

Grandpa spoke to his wife from very close to her face.

"We gave up everything to come back here, to help our grandson." He swallowed. "We've done unforgivable things to protect him." A slight tipping of the head was enough to relive the last two months. "Are you going to abandon him now, when he needs you most?"

He forced a smile to hide the trembling that surfaced on his chin. Then he inserted a hand between their bodies. He squeezed the fist in which his wife held the crucifix.

"Has He ever abandoned you?" An imminent sob was reduced to a change in intensity in the brightness of her eyes. "It's what we have to do," he whispered.

"It's what we have to do," she repeated.

And that was when the four adults synchronized a deep, spontaneous breath, as if an epiphany had been reached, as terrible as it may be. "We have to do it right now," said the man. "You get to the jetty and let the boat go."

Grandpa broke away from the embrace with his wife. She didn't fight against it. She stood there with her arms hanging, her eyes moving from point to point on the floor without coming to rest on any of them. As if her gaze were nothing more than a ball of fluff. Grandpa ran to the kitchen. Before reaching the door, he went back to his daughter-in-law.

"Give me your jacket," he said.

"What for?"

"Come on, give it to me," he insisted.

She took off the jacket. Grandpa snatched it from her hands. His joints clicked when he knelt beside the boy. He pulled down his pajama bottoms, guiding the boy's feet to take them off him.

"Good idea," said the man. "Here, my watch." He undid it in a second. Grandpa added it to the collection.

"What do I have to do?" Grandma asked.

"Give me something of yours. Anything. I'll put it all in the boat. In case they find it." Before she could decide, Grandpa tore a brooch from her blouse.

"Not that. That's from when—"

He silenced her with a kiss. "Nothing matters anymore," he whispered. "Nothing's worth more than your family." Without giving her a chance to respond, Grandpa escaped to the kitchen.

"So we're really going to do it?" Grandma said.

"We're going to do it," replied the man.

Grandma consulted her daughter-in-law.

"We're going to do it," she confirmed. Beside her, in his underpants, the boy shivered. His mother hugged him. Grandma joined them. She pressed her cheek against her daughter-in-law's. They were both enveloped in a new warmth when the father joined the hug.

"We're going to stay together," he said.

And they stayed like that for over a minute.

Enjoying a final moment of total calm.

Until the window, the one that had been smashed two months ago, shattered again.

A shower of glass rained on them. They separated from each other, confused. One shard found its way down the neck of the man's shirt. Grandma looked down at her feet to discover what it was that crunched under every step she took. She saw glass lodged in the cracks in the timber floor. Some pieces still rolled along under the momentum of their fall. The man felt for the shard that danced around inside his shirt. He shook the garment until the fragment fell out. The woman covered her son's ears.

At the top of the tower, the daughter heard the racket. She walked uneasily down the stairs, peering through two of the gate's bars without opening it. She pricked her ears to listen to what was happening on the ground floor.

A sudden draft penetrated the living room through the new opening. Its occupants felt it on their skin like the caress of a ghost from the past, the one that had visited them in the same way one stormy night two months ago.

"What's going on?" Grandma asked.

The man shushed her. He tapped his lips with a finger. Then he leapt to the front door. Glass crunched when he landed. He flicked the switches that were beside the doorframe.

"Turn off that lamp!" he yelled in a whisper.

The woman ran to the sideboard in the middle of the living room wall. The switch, a protrusion halfway down the wire, danced between her fingers until she was able to get her nerves under control. She slid the notch along in its groove with her fingernail. When the light went off, an unidentified orange glow came from behind the armchair near the cuckoo clock, at the bottom of the stairs. Projected against the wall, the ring of light expanded and contracted, as if its source palpitated. The man thought of fire, of the matches he'd lit to illuminate the secret passage in the basement that very afternoon.

That was when another man's voice came in through the open hole where the window had been.

"She was my daughter!" the voice screamed. "I know you're in there!"

The yelling reached the living room with another current of air. The man scanned the darkness of the room, guided by the flashes of silvery light that seeped in with every movement of the curtain. When he arrived at the armchair, he found what he expected. The orange glow came from a piece of material that burned on the floor. Near it, a green glass bottle dripped gasoline.

"It's a Molotov cocktail," the man explained in a low voice. "But it didn't smash when it dropped. And the cloth's come away."

Before Grandma could react, a second window shattered. Another volley of glass surprised them as a second firebomb fell into the room. It was thrown in too much haste. The flame on the fabric had almost gone out before it fell to the floor, and it burned down even more with every turn of the bottle, which, like the other, remained intact. It was reduced to a band of incandescent pores on the edge of the material.

The second smash made the daughter of the family even more anxious, and she used the key on the mermaid ring to open the gate. Squatting at the top of the stairs that led to the living room, she listened in on what was happening down below. Suddenly the windows on the second floor shattered. In her bedroom and in her brother's. Both bottles smashed when they hit the floor. The daughter felt heat on the back of her neck. Turning around, she saw a tongue of fire lick from inside her bedroom to the middle of the landing. The fright made her stagger backward to halfway down the stairs.

"Look where she was," her father said, seeing her appear. "A front-row seat to watch the result of her handiwork."

His daughter turned around.

"I didn't want this to happen," she stammered. "They're burning the house down!"

"And it's all your fault," said the mother.

At that moment Grandpa returned. "I've turned the motor on and let the boat go on a course for the mainland." The darkness, the burning smell, and the cold in the living room made him break off. "What's happening?"

"They're trying to set the house on fire," replied the man.

"Come on," Grandpa reacted. "Quick."

"What're you going to do?" asked the daughter.

Grandpa saw his granddaughter on the stairs, but paid no attention to her. "Come on," he whispered to the others from the kitchen door. "Come with me."

"What're you going to do?"

Nobody answered her question.

"C'mon, c'mon, c'mon," Grandpa insisted.

A constant crunch of glass accompanied the family's movement as they used the glow from the fire to guide them. First Grandpa took his wife's hand. The man, woman, and boy then reached them. They went into the kitchen.

The daughter remained in the living room, still halfway up the stairs, silhouetted against an increasingly orange background. *All your fault.* Those were the last words that her mother had said to her. She hoped they would really become her last words. As far as she was concerned, they could all burn to death in there. The lighthouse could fall on top of them.

In the kitchen, Grandma hugged her husband. "I'll serve you a plate at every meal, every day," she whispered into his ear. "To imagine you're with me."

"You won't have to imagine," he said. "Just promise me you'll be strong. Strong as a—"

"Cactus," she said, completing the sentence they'd repeated so many times during the toughest periods of their marriage. "Strong as a cactus."

"Let's go," said the man. "We have to do it now."

The woman positioned herself in front of the boy. Holding hands, they were the first to go down the stairs that led to the basement. The man went up to his parents. He stroked his mother's lower back.

"Mom," he whispered.

She nodded. She kissed Grandpa's cheek, then walked toward the staircase still holding his hand.

"Mom," her son insisted. His parents' fingers came apart. The man spoke to his father, barely a shadow in front of him.

"Delay going out as long as possible," he said to him. "Then tell them what we discussed, and . . ."

A sudden realization took his breath away.

"Dad, what if they come down to the basement? We have to build the false wall, the door's still visible, they're going to—"

"Son," he cut in. "We've both seen the fire upstairs. This lighthouse is coming down. They'll find nothing but rubble. From now on all you have to worry about is what happens in the basement. I'll take care of everything up here. It will all be fine."

The two men pressed their foreheads together, Grandpa with his hand on the back of his son's neck. They breathed in synchrony.

Then the kitchen door opened.

"You say that all this is my fault," the daughter called out, "but it wasn't me who hid an innocent girl's body."

Her mother heard her from the basement. She handed the boy to Grandma and pointed at the door that led to the main room of their new home. "I'll be right back," she said.

She went back up to the kitchen, the timber stairs shaking under her feet.

"But it was you that ended the life of another innocent child," she screamed at her daughter. "Your own brother!" The stairway creaked again on her way back down to the basement.

A final bottle crashed against the kitchen window. It hit the wall like a missile, then dropped down the stairs, the whole family holding its breath each time it hit a wooden step. Each time the glass clinked on the concrete floor. The bottle withstood the pounding. It remained in one piece when it landed at the bottom of the staircase.

"You're going to pay for what you've done!" the voice yelled outside. It wanted to say more, but a police siren interrupted it from a distance. The missing girl's father fled from the lighthouse, down the gravel path that crossed the plot.

The man kissed his father's cheek. Pieces of glass that had rained on them dropped off them onto the floor with the movement. He didn't look at his daughter before going down.

"No *way*!" she said when she understood what was happening. Her singsong tone made it clear she was mocking them. She moved Grandpa out of the way so she could see down into the basement. Only the rickety stairs separated her from her parents, who turned away without listening to her.

"This is what you're plotting? For all of you to go down into the basement? To hide forever?" She feigned a contained guffaw. "You've got to be kidding, right?"

"We have no choice."

"You and your choices," she answered. "Just one thing." The daughter gestured for silence. "Hear that?"

The police siren was now taking the last bend before reaching the lighthouse.

"Do you really think I won't say anything?"

"Please," Grandpa said behind her, "you don't have to—"

"Shut up," his granddaughter interrupted. Then she addressed her parents. "Ask me not to say anything."

"Don't do it," her father pleaded from the darkness underground.

"Please . . ." her mother begged, unable to say another word because fear took her breath away.

The daughter laughed at them. "Poor things," she said.

And that was when, without having made a decision to do so, Grandpa pushed his granddaughter, who rolled down the stairs. A deep grunt emerged from her stomach when an eyebrow was cut open on the splintered edge of a step. Not even when he heard his granddaughter's moans did Grandpa consider himself responsible for that shove. Which was why he closed the door at the top of the stairs with no remorse whatsoever, and left the kitchen through the swing door. A wave of heat welcomed him in the living room. Discovering the intense glow at the top of the stairs, he smiled. It was what they needed. "They'll find nothing but rubble," he said again.

Sweat pearled his face. He heard the police siren approach and the timber split on the floor above. He felt the rise in temperature in every part of his body. Sweat soaked his back. It moistened his eyebrows. The wind from outside lifted the curtains as if they were the veil of a bride's ghost trying to flee through the window. The draft fanned the fire on the floor above. A bluish light tinted the floor. The siren was on the other side of the door. A policeman banged on it. He shouted something.

Grandpa took a deep breath to relax his body.

He thought of the warmth of Grandma's face on his chest. He thought of her frantic prayers, which had woken him each morning since the night they'd hidden the body in the septic tank. And of the thousands of sighs that had consumed much of both of their lives. He thought of her fingers separating from his. And he thought of the fact that the lighthouse was coming down. The lighthouse where he'd worked for years, the home where he'd brought up his only son, and where his two grandchildren had grown up. He thought of all of that, and a profound sadness was set off inside him.

Then he advanced toward the front door. Feeling the wave of sorrow wash through his body. He gripped the key his wife had turned not long ago. He waited for the tide to bring a new current of pure sadness with the memory. He turned it when it was about to surface. The emotion inflated his stomach. He let it sit there. His chin began to tremble. He didn't stop it. He sobbed. He opened the door just before the fiercest waves rushed over him.

In front of the officer, he let it all out in a heartbroken crying fit.

Like a storm breaking at sea.

And he used that state to tell his story.

The man fought with his daughter on the floor, in front of the basement door. The fall down the stairs had disoriented her, but she was still aware of what was happening. What they intended to do with her. A fingernail separated from the flesh when she tried to cling to the concrete floor. She screamed. Her father's hands closed around her ankles. He remembered lifting the missing girl's body in the same way. He pulled hard on his daughter's legs. She kicked. She tried to grip the floor with sweaty palms that squeaked when they slipped. Another tug from her father took her even closer to the basement's threshold. She let out a desperate scream. The adrenaline that ran through her body in that final surge of rage allowed her to reach the bottle that had fallen down the same stairs before her. She held the hot glass while her father pulled her so hard that resistance became impossible. Some sparks still fought to survive on the dry part of the piece of material. They consumed it in nibbles of ash. The concrete floor scraped her face on the final stretch. She smelled gasoline when her nose slid over one of the splashes that had come from the bottle when it fell. With her free hand she tried to grab the doorframe, but her strength failed.

And the door closed with her inside.

The man turned the key, knowing that he might never use it again. Not if Grandpa put up the false wall that he had to build. Then he deposited his daughter's body beside the table at the basement's entrance. She felt the curved form of the hot glass with satisfaction. Praying that her father wouldn't discover it on her.

Grandma wandered around the room. "So, this is the basement," she said.

Her son put an arm over her shoulders.

"It's our house," he said.

He lifted his other arm, inviting his wife to position herself under it. The boy ran up to his father and hugged him from the front, resting his face against the man's chest. The four of them made a perfect family portrait.

Then they heard the glass scraping along the floor. And the grunt the daughter let out from the effort of the throw.

The boy turned to look in the direction of his sister.

Which was why the thick edge of the bottom of the bottle hit him on the mouth. His bottom lip split in half. Blood and saliva streamed down his chin. Pieces of glass opened unnatural mouths on his face.

Then he felt the liquid. The same liquid his parents and grandmother felt. Grandma swallowed some of the gasoline, her mouth open in shock.

That was when the strip of fire and ash turned the liquid into heat.

Then the heat became pain.

The daughter moved away from them, away from the fire. She sat on the floor, her back resting against the door, watching her family beat themselves to put out the flames.

"Why are you hitting yourselves?" she even asked. She was hypnotized by the dancing flicker that set alight her father's clothes. Her mother's braid. Her brother's hands. And all of their faces. She also saw her grandmother direct a final look of hatred toward her, just before the fire turned her eyes into gigantic black pupils.

She lay on the ground, curled up in the fetal position while her family screamed, rolled on the floor, turned on faucets, ran into rooms. Her irises flashed orange as she stared at the floor.

She heard her father ask her for help.

"Leave me in peace," she whispered, while her family burned in front of her. "Leave me in peace."

28

Supporting her by the elbow, the man guided Grandma to the dining table. His daughter was there reading, sprawled out across three chairs.

"Get up," her father ordered. He spat a large quantity of saliva. He still struggled to control the lips sculpted by fire.

"There're three others free." She gestured at them with the book.

"Get up," he said again.

The daughter obeyed the instruction with heavy movements, purposely making the chairs she was vacating screech. She rounded the table and sat in the same way on the free ones. The man pushed a chair in for Grandma from behind her.

"Sit down." His mother felt for the seat before letting herself drop. He sat in front of her.

"We're going to take the bandage off," he said, inserting his legs between his mother's. "But we're going to be OK whatever happens. We're ready for anything. Right?"

There was silence.

The daughter looked up from her book.

"Right," Grandma whispered.

The man undid the knot that kept the gauze in place. Pulling one of the ends, he unwound the five layers of material that covered Grandma's eyes, five turns of the bandage all the way around her head. Before completing the last, the dressing came away by itself. It was left hanging from her nose. He discarded it on the table.

He had to hold back his tears when he saw his mother's hairless eyebrows. And the wrinkled eyelids forming unnatural folds. In six weeks he still hadn't gotten used to the burns that the mirror showed him on his own face, but seeing them on his mother's was even worse. He covered her eyes with his cupped hands, protecting them from the bulb's light.

"Don't open them yet," he said. "Give them time."

The daughter closed her book. She gathered up her legs and rested her elbows on the table, brushing the hair from her face and watching like a spectator as her father took away his hands.

"Now," he said. "Open them."

Her eyelids trembled, struggling to unstick from each other.

"Open them," he repeated. The smile forced on his lips to receive his mother's gaze disintegrated as soon as she'd blinked a few times.

"Are they open?" she asked.

He swallowed. He spoke to his daughter first. "I hope you're proud of yourself," he said to her. Then he answered Grandma. "Yes, Mom, you've opened them."

They both knew what his reply meant. Grandma tried to dry the single tear that she shed, but it took her a while to find the side of the burn that felt wet. She still hadn't gotten used to the topography of her uneven skin. Then she kissed her crucifix.

"We were ready for anything," she reminded her son. She felt for his face with her fingers. She stroked the line of stiff hair that he struggled to shave. "Right?"

He nodded.

"And anyway, I've already spent six weeks not being able to see," she went on. "I wasn't even sure I could be bothered to learn again." Between her fingers she felt her son's lips form into the misshapen layout of his new smile.

The woman, who'd watched the scene in silence, leaning against the archway that led to the hall, took a deep breath, moved by her mother-in-law's strength of mind. She thought about keeping what she'd come to say to herself, but her tongue was burning too much for her not to say anything.

"Bad news," she announced.

Her husband slumped back into his chair. He wanted to bury his face in his hands. As soon as he felt the confusing surface of his skin, he took them away. "Worse news?"

"It's as I thought," his wife replied, annoyed by the peculiar whistling that came from her burned nose. As if it were a murder weapon, she held up the plastic cylinder that had arrived a few days earlier in one of Grandpa's deliveries.

"We're going to need the second bunk, after all."

The man immediately recalled the afternoon in the mattress store where they'd bought the bunk bed, thinking of a third child who never arrived.

"But not now," he said to himself. He'd covered his face with his hands again, ignoring the strange feel of his unknown features. "Not now."

"Wow, look what things you two find time for down here," the daughter said.

"It wasn't here," her mother cut in. "You know it wasn't in the basement." She held her hand to her belly, her eyes searching for her husband's. Wordlessly they both remembered the only night it could've happened.

"So what does this mean?" the daughter continued. She looked at her father with her eyes wide open. Finding in the baby a reason to finally bring an end to the imprisonment that had gone on too long. Six weeks. The man snatched at her jaw, trapping it like a fly.

"Wipe that smile off your face." He squeezed the healthy skin of her cheeks with loathing. "Don't you see what you've done to Grandma? To all of us?"

"You can't have a baby here," she replied, fighting against the pincers that gripped her.

"You don't get to decide what happens in this basement." He squeezed until he felt his daughter's teeth digging into her skin. Then he let go of her in disgust. She rubbed her cheek.

"You're already holding *me* prisoner," she said. "Don't do it to a child as well." She dodged her father's hand before he could catch her again. The chair fell backward when she escaped. The draft generated when she slammed her bedroom door behind her made the bulb hanging from the living room ceiling swing.

"I can't stand seeing her face," the man said. He pressed his eyes with his wrists. The rough texture of his eyelids made him even angrier. "I can't stand seeing her," he spat through his teeth. Then he finished by yelling it so she could hear it, too. "I can't stand seeing your face!"

The woman went up to him. She soothed him with a hand on his shoulder. The man sobbed.

"I need Grandpa to hurry up and bring it." He swallowed. "I can't stand seeing her face." He pointed at his own burned features. She hushed him like a baby.

Grandma felt for him with her hands. She stroked her son's head until he calmed down. Until he managed to contain his rage, turning it into one of the layers of sediment that had begun to build up on him in the basement, forming the base of future mountains. He stroked his wife's stomach, still flat.

"Are you sure about this?" he asked.

She nodded. An eye closed involuntarily when she gave a thin smile, trying to emulate what would have been her reaction had she found out she was pregnant in other circumstances.

"Now we have to think about what we're going to do," she said.

The spiral of conflicting thoughts that plagued the minds of the three of them culminated in an initial response from Grandma.

"There's one thing we're definitely not going to do," she said, handling her rosary. "No man has the right to take away a life the Lord has given."

"Nobody's suggested that," her daughter-in-law replied.

The man kissed his wife's belly to keep his lips busy, so he wouldn't confess that that had been his first choice.

"Grandpa will have to look after it, then," he offered as an alternative. He looked up to meet the woman's gaze.

"And how would he explain the child's existence?" she argued. "A baby appears exactly nine months after the tragic disappearance of his family?"

The man pressed one side of his face against his wife's body. Another bed of contained desperation settled on top of the previous sediments. He received it, biting his bottom lip.

"So tell me what options we have left," he whispered. "Because I can't think anymore." He rested his elbows on his knees. He shook his head, looking down at the floor. "I can't take it anymore."

"Give it away?" Grandma ventured, with the quiet voice of someone who doesn't believe her own words.

The idea made her daughter-in-law shudder, and she paced around the room to ride out the anxiety it brought her.

"Give it away?" She repeated the words as if she'd just learned them from another language. "For adoption? My child?"

Her voice rose in pitch with each word. She stopped her frenetic pacing and turned around, waiting for an answer.

Grandma moved her lips without finding the right words.

The woman held her hands to her stomach. She massaged it as if she could make out the future baby's anatomy inside.

"I imprisoned myself in this basement so I wouldn't lose a son," she spat out. When she took a step forward to give her words more presence, the beam of sunlight that came in through the basement ceiling was projected onto her body, navel-high, painting a golden circle on her stomach. "And I'm not prepared to lose this one, either."

The man looked his wife in the eye.

"Even if it has to live here?" he asked.

Before she was able to respond, there were booming sounds overhead. A louder bang reverberated in the master bedroom, the one they'd planned to use as a storeroom when the basement was only going to have one occupant. Grandma adjusted her dressing. She also combed her uneven scalp with her fingers, trying to cover the bald patches that the fire had left. Without waiting for anyone to guide her, she made her way to the hall.

"Are you going by yourself?" asked the man.

"This is going to be my life," she answered, her arms stretched out front. "I may as well start getting used to it."

The man put his arm around his wife's shoulder. Together they watched Grandma rush to the metal door, excited that she was about to be reunited with Grandpa. She barely strayed from her path.

"The key," she said from there. "I need the key."

Once in front of the door, the man bent down, holding the key that hung from his neck in the air.

"She's in her bedroom, right?" he said, referring to his daughter.

The original purpose of that door had been to stop any attempts the boy might make to escape, but in the end it was his sister who it prevented from fleeing. If she managed it they would all be condemned. As the daughter herself often screamed at them, telling the world about the basement and its occupants was the first thing she intended to do when she set foot outside. She'd tried it tirelessly during the first weeks.

The entrance in the kitchen was no longer a danger since Grandpa built the planned second wall, so all of her attempts to escape had to focus on the metal door without a handle. Listening in, the daughter discovered the existence of the wardrobe. She also learned of the passage that led to the surface. She was unaware, however, that any plan to get away would be cut short at the final trapdoor, the one that only Grandpa could open from the outside.

"Is she in her bedroom?" repeated the man.

"Open up," the woman replied.

He unlocked the door without taking the key from his neck.

As soon as they went into the room, the daughter's head poked out into the hall. She leapt to the door. She thrust her foot toward the threshold to stop it closing. She arrived late. Again.

"I swear to you I'm getting out of this basement," she muttered to herself. "I'll make all of you pay, for everything."

On the way back to her bedroom, she found her brother standing in the middle of his own room. Motionless, with his arms outstretched on either side.

"Crows everywhere," she told him. "You can't even get that right."

At the wardrobe doors, the man told his mother to wait. He went into the passage alone, and set off up the tunnel bored through the earth. He turned right. Then left. Then right again. At the end of that section he found a giant sack.

"Dad?" he asked into the darkness. His voice traveled up through the passage, muted, chewed up by the earth. There was no response. This time Grandpa hadn't come down. Sometimes it was better not to take the risk. Better to just drop the package and get away from the lighthouse before anyone could see him. The man grabbed the sack's knotted drawstring. He dragged it. After he turned the second corner, the glow from the bedroom was visible at the end of the passage, filtering through the wardrobe.

"Is he with you?" asked Grandma when she heard her son return.

"No."

Grandma's face darkened even more than it had when they'd taken off her bandage. As if coping with Grandpa's absence saddened her more than a future of darkness. In reality, the two things were the same to her.

"Sit down," her daughter-in-law said to her. She wanted to take her arm to guide her to the foot of the bed, but Grandma evaded her. She found the mattress by herself. And by herself she unknotted the bandage that covered her eyes. She made a ball with it, which she deposited on the bed. Then she gathered her hands between her legs. She rubbed her fingers. A continuous but almost inaudible groan vibrated on the roof of her mouth. The woman sat beside her to accompany her in her sorrow.

The man undid the knot on the sack. Although they urgently needed toothpaste, painkillers, rice, vitamin D, and Grandma's medication, he was only worried about finding one thing. The cord untwined into threads with his frenzied attempt to untie it. When he'd achieved a large-enough hole, he inserted a finger. Then three fingers, and then both hands. He opened the bag, holding his breath.

He peered into the sack.

His burned lips spread into a broad smile across his face.

"What's in there?" his wife asked.

The man took out what he'd hoped to find.

"We won't have to look at her anymore," he said.

He showed the woman a white mask.

THE PRESENT

THE PRESENT

29

In one step I positioned myself in front of my sister.

I kicked the mask that she'd just thrown on my bedroom floor out of the way.

I stroked her face, lingering on each curve. Feeling skin so similar to mine. It was the first time I'd touched an adult face that wasn't burned. She just let me do it, holding her breath. Experiencing something that was new to both of us with the same intensity as me.

"Your face," I whispered. "Your face is OK."

She nodded.

"Why aren't you burned?" I asked.

She swallowed, containing her emotion.

"You were all together when the fire happened," I went on. At least, that was what Mom and Dad had always told me. They never said much more about it. And they'd never answered any of the questions I'd asked them.

"Why aren't you burned?" I said again.

My sister stopped my hand. She separated it from her face. She closed her eyes. I observed her heartbeat in her eyelids, such soft eyelids, with fascination. I discovered the even coloring of her healthy skin. Amazed, I witnessed a faint flush light up her cheeks.

"Because I wasn't with them," she answered. The eyelids opened. She fixed her eyes on me.

"You weren't in the basement?"

"No." Her eyes wandered for a fraction of a second. She gripped my wrist harder than she had before, but she didn't seem to know she was doing it.

"Where were you?"

"I shouldn't be here" was the response she offered. "And you don't have to be here, either. We can get you out. Because you want to go. You just said so."

"There's no way out," I replied. "The kitchen door's locked. There're bars on the windows. And Mom says we can't be anywhere else."

"But, do you want to go?"

Mom had asked me the same question a few nights before, when we talked about the big pale-green moths. Then, the memory of my nephew's hand gripping my finger and the smell of carrot soup had been reason enough to not want to leave the basement. But now all I could think of was what my sister had confessed to me about the baby's real father. And the fact that she'd tried to poison the little boy. And that Mom and Grandma had referred to him as the worst of their sins. And that they'd forced my sister to wear a mask when her face wasn't really burned.

"I want to get out," I said.

My heart sped up. I felt it beating in my neck. I relived the dream in which the kitchen door shrank until it disappeared and a beam of light illuminated my face as if I were a cactus. I felt the dream's heat on my cheeks.

"I know how to get out," said my sister. She wetted her lips while, hypnotized, I watched her unscarred features functioning. "With my help, you can get out."

The beating in my neck stopped. The heat suddenly vanished. The imaginary door closed to become the same door it'd always been. The locked door in the kitchen. Because I remembered how my sister's fingers had moved like cockroaches in her blouse pocket, just a few hours earlier. And how she'd painted her breast with the pale blue of the poison cubes and offered it to the baby to stop him living with me in the basement.

"Yeah, sure," I said. "As if I can trust you."

I grabbed the sides of the metal ladder. My sister had fought against Dad so she didn't have to sleep in my brother's bed, so I'd given her mine. On the third rung, a hand grabbed me by the underpants.

"I'm not listening to you," I said. "I don't like what you did to the baby."

I managed to tug myself loose and I climbed onto my brother's mattress. The springs, softer than mine, gave way to my weight without much resistance. The pillow also felt weird. Too thin.

My sister poked her head over the side of the bed.

"Listen to me," she said.

Her breath felt like a crane fly's legs on my face. I turned away from her.

"Switch off the light," I said, looking at the wall.

"You don't have to be shut away down here," she whispered.

Her words fanned the flame that had been lit inside me that night. The desire to see the place the fireflies came from.

"We're here because we want to be," I said.

"I heard you crying. You just said you don't want to be here."

I considered her words.

"You told me off for leaving the firefly jar in the bed," I reminded her. "You said it was dangerous for the baby. But you don't care about the baby. You're not going to trick me again."

My sister's hand climbed up my back. It stopped on the shoulder that wasn't resting on the mattress.

"It's them who're tricking you," she whispered. "Your parents. And Grandma. Why do they make me wear a mask? Why do they tell you I'm burned?"

"Leave me alone," I answered.

"Why did they tell you the kitchen door was unlocked?"

I lay in silence. Reliving the night so many calendars ago when I went up to that door for the first time. When I didn't even try to open it because I was happy in the basement. With my family. Where a little boy should be.

"Poor boy, you don't even know why you're here," she went on. "Do you know why we're here?"

"Because we can't be anywhere else." I reeled off the words that Mom had taught me. "It's the same for everyone."

"That's not what I asked," she said, squeezing my shoulder. "I asked whether you know why we're here."

I opened my mouth to answer but couldn't find the words. I really didn't know.

"Do you know?"

It was a while before she answered.

"No," she finally whispered. "I don't know, either. They have me tricked just like you." She moved her hand to the back of my neck and stroked it. She played with the uneven little hairs that Mom never managed to cut. The skin on my back reacted with a pleasant shiver.

"They have us both tricked," she continued. "Held prisoners. But you don't want to be here anymore. They like this place. Living underground. With no sunlight." Her fingers now sailed along the imaginary canals in my hair.

"Your brother even acts like a cricket when he makes that noise with his mouth," she whispered.

I froze.

"When he makes what noise?"

"You know," she replied, "that noise he makes with his mouth." My sister made her lips vibrate while whistling. I didn't understand why she was spitting on me. Then, for a second, she got the sound she was trying to mimic just right.

"The Cricket Man?" I had to swallow before I could go on. "My brother's the Cricket Man?"

"You didn't know that, either?" she asked. "Wow, they have you even more tricked than I thought."

I covered myself in the sheet. I trembled under the material until I realized that something didn't fit.

"It can't be him," I said. "I've heard the Cricket Man on top of the ceiling while my brother was sleeping here."

My sister tutted. She was silent for a few seconds.

"I didn't say it was him," she corrected me. "But it's him who summons the Cricket Man. He makes that noise with his mouth to call him."

She repeated her slobbery imitation.

"He does it better," she said, "even with his split lip." My sister grabbed my wrist through the sheet.

"But don't be afraid," she said. "From now on I'm going to sleep here with you. You're safe from that Cricket Man now, whoever he is." She pulled back the sheet.

I turned on the mattress until I was lying face up. I said out loud something that wasn't more than a thought. "They're all tricking me."

My sister breathed right near my ear.

"We don't even know if this is really a basement," she whispered.

The heat in my chest rose when I heard her words. The firefly jar glowed at the foot of the bunk bed. Its light radiated from there like a green sun rising. My sister stroked my neck. It was a nice feeling.

"And the poor baby," she went on. "Do you want them to trick him as well? Make him grow up in this basement full of lies?"

I shook my head.

For the first time I saw my sister's eyebrows move. "Of course you don't. And that's why you have to listen to me. Nobody can know you've seen me without the mask on. Swear you won't say anything."

"How shall I swear it?"

"Like you swore not to tell what Dad did to me. They're both very important secrets."

I remembered the words from the other night.

"I swear on the One Up There," I repeated.

"Good boy," she said. "Between us, we can get out of here."

"But Mom says we can't be anywhere else. And that no one can know we're here."

"Another one of their lies. What you have to do is get out of here. Tell someone that the baby's here. They'll come get him. And you and I can go."

"But I want to keep seeing the others . . ."

"They'll still live here in the basement. Where they like being."

"Will they be able to stay here when the people know where we live?"

"Of course they will." My sister's lips made a smile that didn't seem happy. "Do you want me to tell you how to get out or not?"

"You can't get out. The kitchen door's locked. There're bars on the windows."

"But there're a lot of things you don't know," she said. She paused on purpose to make me impatient.

"What things?"

"That there's another door in this basement." My hair brushing against the pillow was all we could hear in the deep silence that followed her words.

"Another door?" I asked.

"Another door," she repeated. "But I'll only tell you where it is if you show me that you deserve to know."

I was silent for a while.

"How do I show you?"

"By only listening to me," she answered. The smile that wasn't happy returned to her face.

30

My sister was last to appear at breakfast. She wore the mask as if nothing had changed. She winked at me with one of her hidden eyes, renewing our alliance from the night before. When she approached the table, Dad fanned his face with a hand. And he coughed.

"What a stink," he said. "Go take a bath. Go on." The smell was a mixture of dry sweat, fresh sweat, and a chemical whiff that made it more pungent. It must've been some of the poison exuded in the night.

She pulled her chair out, disobeying Dad's order. "I'll take a bath when I've had my breakfa—"

Grandma pushed the chair in. The back hit the table. Some of the teaspoons clinked against the cups.

"Go take a bath," Grandma said.

"Before breakfast?" My sister was still holding the chair's ears. "It'll make me feel ill." She tried to regain control of the chair, but the movement of her arms barely budged the piece of furniture.

My brother laughed like a donkey. I thought of him as the traitor who ratted me out to the Cricket Man.

"Go take a bath," Grandma said again.

Behind the mask, my sister's eyes scanned the table. I saw them stop on my mother, who was holding the baby against her chest. She'd found an old baby bottle in her room and was giving the little boy an improvised mixture of water and milk from the carton that we drank. It hadn't been easy getting the baby to suck that strange teat, but when he finally took it, he fed hungrily.

"I can see I'm not needed for anything," my sister said. Her eyes came to rest on me. I remembered parts of the conversation we'd had in the night. Then she let go of the back of the chair. With a quick movement she swooped on the table to pick up two slices of toast. She also snatched my cup of milk. She ran out into the hall before Dad had time to do anything. He was left half-standing with his fist resting on the table, the napkin poking out from inside it like the folds of my sister's blouse had poked out before he'd dropped it on the floor by the bunk in my bedroom.

She slammed the bathroom door shut behind her.

The teaspoons clinked again.

"Just like when she was eighteen," said my mother, getting up and bringing me another cup.

"Your mother's made eggs for you," Grandma said, "like you wanted."

"But boiled this time," Mom pointed out. The egg wobbled on my plate.

I looked at my nephew sucking. He was drinking milk that wasn't from his mother. The rubber teat only just fit in his mouth. His scrunched-up face still showed some kind of inner suffering. I thought of his future. I imagined him learning to walk in the basement. Wondering, like me, where the spot of sun in the living room came from. Asking questions into the air that neither Mom nor Dad was going to answer for him. Thinking his mother had a burned face when he saw the mask she shouldn't be wearing. And gripping the bars on the window at the end of the hallway to breathe in the air that smelled different. Dreaming of getting out.

I had to know where the other door was.

I could ask my sister while she was alone in the bathroom.

I peeled the egg as quickly as I could. I gobbled it down and poured milk into my second cup. I drank it in one gulp.

"I'm not surprised you're so hungry," my mother said. She pinched my cheek.

"Do you want to talk about what happened last night?" asked Grandma. "Do you have any questions?"

I shook my head. I couldn't trust their answers anymore.

I left the empty cup on the table. Mom ran her thumb over my lips to clean off the remnants of milk. A smile creased her face unevenly.

"Can I go to my room?"

"Why such a hurry?"

"I want to make space for my sister's things," I lied. "She's going to stay in my room, isn't she?"

Mom gave me permission to leave. On the way, before I reached the arch that led to the hall, Dad stopped me.

"Isn't it your turn to ride the bike today?" he asked.

He was right. It was one of the three days when I had to do exercise. I let my shoulders drop. I turned toward the bicycle.

"Work a bit harder," my father said. "Exercise is important."

I climbed onto the bike. I pedaled hard so I'd finish before my sister came out of the bathroom. As if time would pass more quickly if my legs moved faster. I counted the number of times the pedal brushed against the contraption's frame. When I reached a thousand, my usual goal, I jumped off the bike.

"Already?" asked my father. He was finishing off his fourth or fifth coffee at the table. My mother was clearing the dishes. Grandma, sitting in a dining chair, was staring at the wall. I heard the faint but constant moan that got caught in her throat when she took up that position. The unconscious murmuring triggered by a bad thought. She was holding the baby on her lap.

"I did a thousand," I said.

"Are you sure?"

"I went"—my breathing was labored—"faster."

Dad doubted my words. "And what if I tell you that you have to do another thousand?"

There was silence.

"Leave the boy alone," Grandma then said.

I ran to the hall while he was undecided. I went into the bathroom still panting.

"Where is the other door?" I asked my sister.

"Open your eyes," she said. "You can open them now, remember?" I'd closed them out of habit. I still took a while to follow her instruction. It isn't easy to give up a habit maintained for years.

"Open them," she said again. I did it unhurriedly. The mask lay on the sink. She was in her underpants and bra, sitting on the edge of the bath that was emptying. I avoided the pile of clothes on the floor.

"Are you sure?" she asked. "Do you really want to know how to get out?"

I sat opposite her on the toilet lid. "If I leave . . . will I be able to come back to the basement to visit Mom?"

"Of course you will," she answered.

"So they'll come get you, me, and the baby out, and they'll leave the others in the basement?"

She nodded with her eyes looking somewhere else.

"Then yes," I concluded. Outside there were lots more fireflies than there were in the basement. Outside I'd see my chick. Outside I'd have the chance to find a real *Actias luna*. And then come back to the basement to show it to Mom.

"Tell me where the other door is."

My sister slid along the bath's edge nearer to me.

"In a wardrobe," she said. She whispered the three words very close to my face. She blinked, trying to read my reaction.

"What is it?" she asked.

I crossed my arms. The reply to her question was obvious.

"What?" she persisted.

"I've read that book," I finally said. "I'm not so easy to fool."

"Huh?"

I glared at her.

She shrugged.

"Narnia," I said. "Narnia's where you get to through a wardrobe."

Her mouth opened on its own. When she got over her amazement, she asked, "How did you turn out so clever shut away in this basement?"

"I *knew* it," I said. I tried to get up, but she trapped my legs with hers, like Dermaptera shut the pincers they have at the end of their abdomens.

"You'd better start believing me if you want to get out of here," she said. Her chest rose and fell quickly. Her breath smelled of milk. "Believe it or not, the way out is in the wardrobe in your parents' room."

I weighed that information. I'd never been in that room for more than two minutes. The night I ran to find Mom so she'd witness my chick being born may have been the longest time I'd ever spent there.

"So why haven't you escaped if you know where there's a way out?" I asked without looking away. "Why've you never tried to get away?"

"For the first few years it was all I did," she answered. "You don't know the half of what's happened in this basement. These people want to see me suffer."

"These people?"

"Your parents," she replied. "And your grandmother. She's no better, even if she seems like she is."

The Dermaptera's pincers gripped my legs, anticipating another escape attempt.

Paul Pen

"What they're not expecting is you wanting to get out," she went on. "We have to take advantage of that." She narrowed her eyes before asking, "Because you haven't told anyone, have you?"

I shook my head. "We swore on the One Up There," I reminded her.

The baby cried in the kitchen. The soles of Dad's brown slippers dragged along the hall. When they went into my room, I was afraid he'd discover the firefly jar in the drawer. Then he neared the bathroom. He stopped on the other side of the door. Listening.

My sister leapt to the washbasin. She jammed on the mask. "I'm in here," she said. She put a hand in the water that was left in the bathtub. She slapped it so he could hear, splashing the wall.

"And your brother?" Dad asked.

The door handle shook. He'd grabbed it outside. My sister made an urgent gesture with her head.

"I'm on the toilet," I said. "I'm fine."

The rub of his footsteps continued in the direction of his bedroom. My sister let out the air she'd kept in. She sat in front of me again, leaving the mask on. She wasn't finding it easy to give up the habit, either.

"Does the wardrobe lead outside?" I asked.

"Not quite," she said. "There's a tunnel that leads to the surface."

I remembered Mom's lesson on the Earth's layers. She'd drawn an arrow pointing at the blue-and-white crust.

"But Mom told me that we live on the surface. On the blue-and-white part of the Earth."

My sister's mask tipped to the side.

"And there was me thinking you were clever . . . Have you seen anything blue when you look out of the window?" she asked. "Or anything white?"

Through the window there was just a lot more darkness. A box inside another box.

"No," I replied.

"Your mother's told you a load of lies," she said.

266

"And how do I get to the tunnel?"

"The tunnel's not difficult to reach. The hard bit is opening the door that's after it."

"What?" I was confused.

"The question's not what," she answered. "The question is how."

My sister looked down at the floor. She murmured something I didn't understand. I could only make out a numerical figure among her mumbles. Then she said something that threw me off.

"Go count the potatoes in the kitchen."

I remained still. Not understanding.

"Go on, go," she insisted. "Then tell me how many there are."

She gave me a slap on the thigh. Then another. I didn't get up until the fourth. I walked backward through the bathroom without taking my eyes off her. My heel hit the glass of milk that she'd stolen from me at breakfast. It rolled along the floor, already empty. I backed into the door handle.

Only my mother was in the kitchen. Grandma was still staring at the wall. I went up to the cupboard where the potatoes were kept.

"Are you going to try again?" Mom asked when I opened it. She was referring to one of the experiments from the *How to Be a Spy Kid* guide, which consisted of making electrical energy by connecting three potatoes to each other. I tried to do the experiment once, but the components available to me in the basement were very different from the ones used in the book. In the illustration, the three potatoes lit up a tiny bulb the size of a bean. I had to try with one of the bulbs that hung from our ceiling. Mom unscrewed it with a cloth. When I connected it to the potatoes, there wasn't even a spark. The experiment was a failure, but Mom still made mashed potatoes with them.

"How many do you need this time?" she asked. She put down the plate she was holding and knelt beside me to take out the potatoes. "And tell me when you want the lightbulb. I don't want you touching it."

"How many are there?" I asked.

"How would I know?" she answered. "Lots, can't you see?" She gestured toward the inside of the cupboard, which was full to the top. Bits of soil fell off when Mom rummaged through the potatoes.

"Are three enough?" She showed me them first. Then she covered her hand with my T-shirt. "Don't let Dad see them." She stretched the material to hide them completely. "Go, run, while he's in his bedroom."

I ran to the bathroom with the potatoes hidden.

"How many?" asked my sister when I went in.

"Loads," I said. "There're loads. The cupboard's full."

She clicked her tongue.

"I knew it," she said. She looked down at the floor again. She began to move her leg, resting it on the toes of her bare foot.

"What should I do?" I asked.

"Let me think."

I heard a constant clicking from one of her foot's bones. I put the potatoes I didn't need for any experiment back under my T-shirt. Their sandy texture scratched my belly.

Then my sister's foot stopped with a final click of the bone. The mask tilted up to look at me.

"We have to wait for the Cricket Man to come."

I dropped the three potatoes onto the floor.

31

We moved from the bathroom to my bedroom before Dad came out of his room. Still in her bra, my sister walked around the bedroom with the potatoes in her hand, not finding anywhere to put them down. She went up to the drawers at the foot of my bed.

"Move that," she said. She was referring to the cactus. I moved it out of the way. She left the three potatoes there.

"I don't want to wait for the Cricket Man," I said, unable to accept what my sister was proposing. "I don't want him to take me away."

"If you do what I say, he won't take you away in his wheelbarrow."

"Wheelbarrow?"

My sister looked at me in silence.

"Sack," she then corrected herself. "In his sack. Come here." She pulled my T-shirt to drag me to the bookshelf. A bump of material was left in the piece of clothing when she let it go.

"Take one," she said. She chose one herself. She crossed her legs to sit down, the book open on her lap. "Go on, take any one."

I ran my finger along the spines, reading the titles. Trying to decide which one I felt like reading most. My sister pulled on my T-shirt to make me sit opposite her.

"Take this one here," she said. "Pretend you're reading."

She passed me *The Wonderful Wizard of Oz*. The book opened by itself on a page that had its top corner folded over. It was number twenty-one.

"Did you see the Cricket Man?" my sister whispered near my face.

"Yes, I did. I saw him in the kitchen." I pronounced the words with emphasis, tired of having to make myself believed. "The Cricket Man really exists."

"Of course he exists," she said. "*I* believe you."

I was going to challenge what she said almost without hearing it.

"You believe me?" I asked when I'd processed her words.

"Sure I believe you."

"Mom says he doesn't exist."

My sister gave a loud sigh. "What did I tell you about your mother?"

I didn't want to answer that question. I looked away, but she straightened my face with a finger.

"What did I tell you about her?" she repeated.

"That she tells me a load of lies."

"That's right," she said. Her lips stretched out behind the mask. "And if you saw the Cricket Man, it was because he came in the house, right?"

I nodded.

"And if he came in the house he must've come in through the only door there is."

"The kitchen door's locked, it won't—"

"I mean the only real door," she cut in. "Which is the only real door?"

I ignored the question again.

"Which is it?"

"The one in the wardrobe in Dad's room," I replied.

"So . . ."

She said the word in a high tone, inviting me to complete the sentence. Like she did when she read the factors of a multiplication and waited for me to calculate the product. I usually solved sums in no time. I didn't know how to finish that sentence.

"So that man came in through the wardrobe in your parents' bedroom," she said, completing the sentence herself after a silence.

I felt a sudden coldness when I imagined the Cricket Man walking around in my parents' room. Scraping the ceiling with his antennae. Prowling around their bed, his legs bending backward on each step. I rubbed my thighs.

"I don't want to wait for the Cricket Man," I said. I raised my voice without realizing it. "He scares me."

"Wait," she said, hushing me, "I haven't finished." Her eyes moved behind the orthopedic material.

"Can you take the mask off?" I asked. "I don't like seeing you in it anymore."

My sister hesitated. Then she pushed it back, leaving it on her head, like a second face looking up at the One Up There. I was relieved to see the smooth skin of her features.

"But when we hear someone walking in the hall," she whispered, "I'll put it back on."

"OK."

She resumed the conversation.

"For the Cricket Man to reach your parents' wardrobe he must've come through the tunnel that leads to the surface. Which means that—"

"No," I interrupted, "that's not right."

"How come?"

"The Cricket Man lives underground," I explained. "The Cricket Man never goes up to the surface."

"What do you mean, he never goes up there? So what does he eat?"

"He eats children," I replied.

"But he must have to breathe," she said. "Don't you think?"

I opened my mouth to say something. But I couldn't remember what my insect book said about how crickets breathe. I knew that caterpillars breathe through holes in their skin, but I didn't know how crickets did it.

"Listen to me," my sister said. "The Cricket Man comes down through the tunnel from the surface. Which means that he has to open the other door. The outer one. The one we can't open. That door's only open while the Cricket Man's inside."

I hunched over even more. I lowered my voice.

"Another door?" I asked.

She smiled. "I told you there're a lot of things you don't know," she said. "It's the trickiest door. That's why we need the Cricket Man. He's the only one who can open it."

I shifted on my backside to move closer to her.

"And if he doesn't come back?" I asked. "If I'm good, he won't have to come back. He eats bad boys."

My sister straightened her back. She held a finger to her mouth, thinking. After a silence, she relaxed her spine again.

"But he will come," she sighed.

"How do you know?"

"Because you still have that jar in your drawer."

I lowered my head, knowing that she was right, that I hadn't been good, that the Cricket Man would keep looking for me until he found me. A shiver ran through my body. My sister must've realized because she swooped on me. The books hit each other between our legs like the tectonic plates that Mom had told me about. She put her arms around me, her breasts squashed against my body.

"Don't be afraid," she said in my ear. "We'll be ready when he comes. We'll make sure the Cricket Man doesn't catch you with his legs."

Then I told her a secret.

"I peed myself in the living room," I said. "Last time he came. He almost got me in the living room. And I peed myself."

My sister squeezed harder with her arms. Her body shook in spasms.

"What is it?" I asked.

She couldn't contain her laughing fit and let out a cackle.

"You peed yourself!"

She separated from me, pointing a finger at me while she laughed. At first it made me angry. Then her noisy laughter became contagious. She hit my shoulder to coax me to laugh with her. And there was something comforting in her reaction to my secret. She managed to make me feel like it wasn't a secret to be ashamed of. I let out a first solitary giggle. She was holding her hands to her belly.

"Peed your pants!" she yelled. The last sound stretched out until it became another fit of laughter. She also tried to imitate the sound of a stream of pee, letting out air through her teeth. That really was funny. I laughed again. This time I couldn't stop. I surrendered completely to it.

We laughed together until we ran out of air, while she gestured with her hands for us to control the volume of our laughter.

After a few deep breaths we calmed ourselves down. My sister picked up the books that'd fallen on the floor, and opened them on our legs. She combed her hair with her fingers. She glanced at the bedroom door to make sure our laughing hadn't attracted anyone's attention.

"There's nothing to be frightened of," she said. "The Cricket Man won't find you."

"How can you know that?"

"Because you'll be hidden in Dad's wardrobe."

The heat from the laughter vanished in an instant. The momentary chrysalis of tranquility split open to let out a black moth of absolute terror. A death's-head hawk moth, the lepidopteran that has a skull tattooed on its thorax.

I shook my head.

I tried to get up. I didn't even want to listen to any explanation my sister might have for those words. She grabbed me by the T-shirt, using the bump of material that she herself had marked in the fabric before.

"You'll hide in the wardrobe before the Cricket Man arrives," she said. I opened my mouth, but she whispered more loudly to assert herself. "And when he comes down to find you, you'll leave through the tunnel. There's a passage and a ladder on the wall. All going up. When you get out, you'll head toward the lights. You'll look for some people. Look for the houses. You'll tell them that you want to save your little nephew. And you'll bring them here." The last word stumbled in her throat. Her eyes went shiny.

"You're going to bring people to this basement." One end of her mouth lifted as if she was going to smile, but for some reason she made an effort to remain serious.

"What's outside?" I asked.

She pressed her lips together. She blinked faster than usual.

"You'll see," she said.

I imagined myself poking my head out to see what was above the basement, making myself visible to the rest of the world. Emerging from the depths with my firefly lamp held high. Tapping the jar's lid to tell them to use their flashing light to make the SOS signal I'd been teaching them. Three short, three long, then three more short flashes. They almost had it. The thought of going outside made me remember something. Or someone. An uncontrollable feeling started in my stomach. It pushed the thought to my mouth. The words escaped before I could contain them.

"My chick!" I cried. I covered my mouth with my hands. I'd let out the secret in front of my sister. With my eyes wide open, I watched her reaction.

"Your chick?" she asked.

I remained silent. My eyes began to dry out from keeping them open so wide.

"Poor thing," she said. "You don't understand a thing." She looked at me in silence for a few seconds. Then she took my hands from my mouth. She wrapped them in hers. "That chick—" she began.

"I didn't mean chick," I interrupted in a late attempt to deny its existence.

"I know what chick you're talking about."

My neck went soft. My head fell forward.

"I was in the bedroom that night, too, remember?"

I recalled how one of my sister's arms had emerged from under her sheets to grab the mask and put it on when Dad came in to tell me off for sneaking into his bedroom. I nodded.

"I heard what Grandma had you believe," she said. Her words left me confused. "Poor boy, look at your little face." My sister rested a hand against my cheek. "It must be tough finding out about so many lies at once."

The corners of my lips pulled downward. I felt pressure on top of my eyes. And an itch in my throat. My chin began to tremble when I thought that my chick could be another invention.

"My chick . . ." I didn't know what else to say.

"Another lie," confirmed my sister. "I told you that Grandma appears better. But she isn't."

"But I saw it," I managed to say. "It was yellow. With feathers. And it tweeted." I relived the excitement of the birth of the little bird in my grandmother's bedroom.

"Grandma put it here," I said, pointing at my shoulder, "and the chick ate from her hair. And then she passed it to me."

"And then what happened?"

"Dad came. Angry because I'd gone in his room," I remembered without difficulty. "I hid the chick behind my back. I had it in my hands. Dad made me show them. And the chick . . . the chick . . ." I had to breathe through my mouth to stop myself from crying. I looked at my sister, struggling to understand.

"The chick wasn't there," she said, finishing my sentence. "Because there is no chick. It never existed. Grandma lied to you. Chicks can't hatch from an unfertilized egg."

"But I saw it . . ."

"Covered in yellow feathers as soon as it hatched? Climbing onto Grandma's shoulder? Eating from her hair?" She raised the pitch of her voice with each new question. "You don't know how a bird's really born."

I'd never seen it. Not even in a photo in the many books we had in the basement. So I shook my head.

"They come out wet," she went on. "And clumsy. With their feathers stuck to their body. Like your nephew when he was born, but in bird form," she added. "Grandma hid the egg under her pillow. And I bet she crushed it with her head."

I remembered how Grandma had asked me to close my eyes just before it hatched. *They don't hatch if they know someone's looking,* she'd said. Then I'd discovered a wet patch on Grandma's pillow, similar to the one left by the clot of liquid that fell onto the floor when Dad squashed my other egg.

I thought about the piece of shell I'd kept in my drawer since that night, protected in its T-shirt nest. A string of dribble overflowed one side of my mouth.

"No, please," I said to my sister. "No . . ."

She hugged me. She stroked my head, hushing me, repositioning herself so that she was sitting beside me. I lay down over her lap. "Don't worry," she said to me. "Things will be different very soon."

That night, I waited for Grandma in her room after dinner. I stood peering into the baby's crib, my chin resting on the edge of his little shelter. Listening to him breathe. The bedroom door opened. Grandma headed to her bed without noticing my presence.

"I'm here," I told her. She turned toward my voice, holding a hand to her chest.

"Don't give me frights like that," she said. "I'll start thinking your father was right about you being like a ghost."

"Don't say that," I whispered.

"Do you want to talk about what happened last night?"

I shook my head.

"Do you want to?"

"No."

Grandma sat on the side of her bed. She took off her rosary and began to flick through the beads with both hands resting on her knees. I went and stood in front of her. I smelled the talcum powder. I bent, intending to give her a kiss, but I changed my mind and straightened my body again.

"Is my chick still alive out there?" I asked.

She said a few more words of her prayer before breaking off. She pinched one of the beads to remember where she'd stopped.

"Your chick?" she asked. "The one that hatched here?"

"The one from the egg Mom gave me."

My grandmother's thicker eyebrow made a few different shapes before she answered.

"Sure," she said, "it'll be tweeting happily out there." My sister was right. Grandma lied, too. She stretched out a hand in search of my belly. I took a step back to move away. She clawed the air. "Where are you?" she asked, moving her arm.

I took another step back. "Goodnight, Grandma," I said.

She raised her sparse eyebrow. She opened her mouth to say something, but at that moment the bedroom door hit the wall. My brother came in making the floor shake as usual. He marched around the room with exaggerated steps, lifting his knees high. When he started humming his song, we understood what state he was in. Grandma shushed him.

"Come on, Scarecrow," she said to him, "get into bed."

My brother stopped his march but kept humming at the same volume. There was a lot of saliva splattering through the gap in his bottom lip. My grandmother waited to hear the squeak of the neighboring mattress's springs before continuing her prayer.

I went up to my nephew's crib. I poked my head over the side. He was sleeping peacefully in spite of the false scarecrow's singing and Grandma's constant mumbling as she prayed. I rested my chin on the top of the wooden frame.

"I'm going to get you out of here," I whispered to the baby. "So they don't trick you like they have me."

He replied with a coo.

Back at the door, I said goodnight again to Grandma.

"And my kiss?" she asked, the prayer stopping, a bead trapped between two fingers.

"Goodnight, Grandma," I repeated.

I closed the door behind me.

32

The potato cupboard emptied as the days went by. The rice, milk, and eggs began to run out, too. Mom had rolled up the toothpaste tube with a hairpin to get as much as possible out of it. My sister said that it was a good sign, that soon we'd be able to put the escape plan we'd devised into action. I lost the desire to see it through whenever I thought about the fact that I was going to have to hide in the same wardrobe where my sister said the Cricket Man would come in. At night, in the dark, she reminded me of the reasons why I had to get out of the basement, persuading me from the bottom bunk. She always kept her mask within reach, on the mattress, in case Mom or Grandma suddenly came into the room.

That was what happened one night when Mom opened the door without warning. She came up to my bunk in the dark. "Are you always going to sleep up here, or what?"

"My sister doesn't want to use this bed."

Although she was lying right under me, she said nothing. Mom brushed my hair with her fingers.

"Son, why've you been so quiet lately? Have we done something to upset you?"

My sister hawked, though it didn't seem like she needed to clear her throat.

"Have you changed your mind about anything?"

"No, Mom," I lied. "There's nothing wrong."

"You sure?"

I confirmed I was with a sound in my throat.

"You can tell us anything." She stroked my head in silence. "Anything." When she kissed me, I felt the wrinkled skin that surrounded her lips on my forehead. Before withdrawing her face, she whispered in my ear, "Even if you think you can't."

My sister scratched the mask with a fingernail as a signal to remind me of the pack of lies they'd told me.

"There's nothing wrong, Mom," I repeated.

She sighed. "All right," she said. She tucked me in and gave me another kiss on the cheek.

Before she left the room, my sister spoke.

"No kiss for me?"

Mom closed the door without answering. My sister let out a chuckle.

On another of those nights, while my sister was putting the finishing touches on the plan from the bottom bunk, I remembered that I'd left the cactus in the living room. I'd spent the whole afternoon pushing the plant pot along with a finger, following the course of the patch of sun. Watching the dust dance between its spines and thinking about how that light could envelop me as well soon enough.

"Where're you going?" she asked when she saw me climb down from the bunk.

"I left my cactus in the living room."

"OK, fetch it. But don't talk to the others too much."

I headed up the hall toward the living room, which was lit like it was every night by the television's glow. I noticed that the intensity of the light didn't change. The movie must've been on pause, two blurry lines of interference traveling up and down a frozen image.

". . . leave because he wants to," I heard my mother say, her voice barely a sigh turned into words. "His father's plan isn't working. We're going to have to tell him everything. He's not so little anymore. We knew that—"

"Quiet," said Grandma. "I hear something."

The floor creaked under my feet.

Mom looked out into the hall. "What're you doing there?"

"I just came out," I lied. "I left my cactus in there."

Mom scanned the floor. "You can get it tomorrow. I'm talking to your grandmother now . . . about the movie we're watching."

Mom never paid much attention to the movies. She just followed them from the kitchen, leaning against the countertop, biting her fingernails so they ended up like little saws.

"Anyway, you should be in bed," she added. "Go before your father gets back."

In the bathroom, the cistern emptied with a final sucking noise. If I wanted the cactus to sleep with me, I had to rescue it before he came out. I heard him turn on the water to wash his hands. I ran up the hall, ignoring my mother's urgent gestures. I dodged her at the hallway entrance, slipping through her hands.

The water stopped running in the sink.

Mom decided to try to overtake me. We both pounced on the plant. Although I was first to reach the pot, she grabbed my forearm. The ceramic container slid between my fingers.

The pot flew.

It broke as it hit the floor in the middle of the living room.

"No," Grandma said when she heard it. She'd listened to what was happening from the sofa.

"Son," said Mom, "no, I didn't want to . . ."

The light from the TV set allowed me to see the soil spilling in all directions. The two balls of spines that formed the cactus rolled to the hallway entrance.

The hinges on the bathroom door squeaked. Dad was coming. He started a sentence before reaching the living room, but was unable to finish it. Just like he was unable to complete his last step. I heard the crunch under his foot, similar to the sound Mom made when she stuck a fork in the pulp of an orange to squeeze it.

Grandma held her hand to her mouth.

Mom squeezed my shoulder in some sort of apology. I moved away from her.

Then Dad screamed. The yelp that follows a flash of pain. The soles of his worn brown slippers had offered little protection against my cactus's spines. He rested a foot on the opposite knee to look at the sole, leaning against the corner that formed the beginning of the hallway, right where I'd hidden from the Cricket Man. Then he scoured the floor with his eyes. When he discovered my mother and me by the table, his hair scar tightened.

"This'd better not be what I think it is," he said. The two of us looked at the squashed remains of my cactus. What should've been a spherical shape was nothing more than a formless lump of waste among triangular pieces of broken pot on a carpet of soil.

"Tell me what this is." Dad raised the volume of his voice. He let go of the corner he was clinging to and swooped on me. When he put down his injured foot, he gave another cry. He had to hop on one leg to reach the sofa. There, Grandma tried to feel for the injured limb, but Dad batted her hand away with the sock he'd just taken off.

"It was me," Mom said.

"Fetch the first-aid kit," he replied. Mom tried to add something, but Dad interrupted her.

"Fetch the first-aid kit, please," he said again. "I'll see to the boy later."

Mom pushed me into the hall. When we passed my cactus's carcass, I stopped. She crouched down beside me. She kept an eye on Dad on the sofa. His breathing was tense. She took the cactus by one of its spines and lifted it. In the light from the television, we both saw the extent of the damage. Both balls had burst, revealing a soft pulp under the split skin covered in spines, most of which had bent, making the cactus wound itself. A drop of slimy liquid hung from one of those wounds. It sparkled in the light before falling to the floor.

"I'm sorry," Mom whispered. Then the spine with which she was holding the moist remains came off. The cactus hit the floor again.

Mom tried to make eye contact with me, but I shied away.

I looked at Grandma on the sofa. I remembered the words she'd said to me when the cactus appeared in the basement. *While this cactus is OK, we'll be OK.* I picked up a piece of the pot and ran to my room.

"It's starting to work," I heard my father say.

"Nothing's *working*," Mom added.

I closed my eyes before entering the bedroom. But not because I was afraid to see my sister's face as I had been for years, but because I didn't want to cry again. I sat on the floor, resting my back against the door.

"What've they done to you now?" she asked.

I showed her the piece of plant pot I'd recovered.

"No way," she said. "Your cactus?"

Only when I knew that I'd have the voice to speak, I said, "I can't wait for the Cricket Man to come."

The springs on my sister's bed squeaked. I opened my eyes. She was lying on her side, her head supported by a hand, her elbow pressing into the mattress. She smiled.

"He'll be here very soon," she said. Realizing she had the mask on, she lifted it to repeat her words with her face uncovered. "Very soon."

I went to the cabinet at the foot of my bed. I opened the drawer. The fireflies were fluttering around inside the jar. I picked up the T-shirt nest that held the shell of the egg the chick never hatched from. I put it on top of the cabinet and placed the piece of plant pot beside it.

I observed the two bits of important things in my life that had broken. Something much more important had broken inside me.

As I climbed the ladder to my bunk, I looked at my sister through the bars that acted as steps. "How do you know he'll come?"

The muscles in her neck tightened. "I just know," she answered.

And it was true that she knew.

The Cricket Man returned to the basement five calendar boxes later.

33

The night that the Cricket Man returned to the basement my sister woke me up by speaking in my ear.

"He's coming," she said. Sleepiness delayed my response. She shook the bunk bed's frame. "The Cricket Man's coming," she said again.

Then I reacted. I opened my eyes, my stomach tight. I pricked my ears, gripping the pillow, and waited to hear his footsteps. Or the sack dragging along somewhere up above the ceiling. I listened.

"Are you sure? I can't hear him."

"Tonight's the night you've been waiting for," she said.

"But I can't hear anything," I insisted, the sheet up to my chin.

"You still don't believe me?" She returned to the bottom bunk, making the springs squeak in an exaggerated way.

"Oh well, we'll have to abort the plan, then," she said. "Two weeks of preparation for nothing. We'll just stay in the basement forever. Although, I'll let the Cricket Man know you're here. As soon as he comes."

I was aware of the intensity in her voice. She continued to murmur things about how disappointing my attitude was until she fell silent.

I took the chance to prick my ears again, hoping to hear one of the sounds that always gave away the Cricket Man's arrival.

Nothing.

Just the cistern's constant dripping.

Then a bang reverberated inside the room. The wall to my right shook. As did the sheet I was holding in my hands.

"The Cricket Man," I whispered.

My sister's face emerged over the side of my mattress.

"See?"

She freed my hands from the sheet finger by finger, tense as they were from the fright.

"You must keep calm," she said, "otherwise you won't be able to control yourself when he passes by you."

She was referring to the moment when the Cricket Man would go through my parents' wardrobe, almost brushing against me because I'd be hidden among the clothes. I imagined the articulated sound of his limbs as he moved. I thought of all of the parts of the plan I didn't feel prepared for.

"Come on," she said.

I began to climb down the ladder. Halfway down, I molded the pillow to imitate the shape of my body. I made the straight angle of a pair of bent legs and the curve of a back in the fetal position. When I'd finished, I jumped down from the step. I landed on bare feet. "How am I going to walk outside?" I asked.

My sister was pacing around the room.

"Normally. Like you always do."

"All I have on is underpants."

She sighed. Then I heard her rummaging through the shelves of the wardrobe I shared with my brother.

"I can't see a thing," she said into the darkness. Seconds later she knelt in front of me.

"Arms up." A T-shirt came down over them. The garment's neck resisted until she passed my head through the hole.

"Now your feet." I lifted my left foot, holding on to her shoulder. It took her a while to get a slipper on.

"I never wear those," I said.

"What does that matter now? What matters is you can walk up top."

"Dad might suspect if he sees me wearing them."

My sister took off the slipper. "Then you'll have to go as you are."

"Will I be able to walk barefoot?"

"You'll have to." My sister carried on pacing around the room. Murmuring. I went to the cabinet at the foot of my bed and opened the drawer. The pencils inside the jar hit against the glass. The greenish light from the fireflies began to glow.

"What do you need from that drawer?" said my sister.

The light went out. "The jar with the—"

"You don't need anything," she interrupted. "You can get it later when you come back. Along with the shell. And the piece of plant pot. You can take the bunk bed as well if you want. But right now you don't need anything."

I moved my face near the drawer. "Don't listen to her," I whispered to the fireflies. "I'll come back for you. I need you to get out." I tapped the jar a few times with my finger, some taps quicker than others. I knew they'd understood me because they didn't answer.

"Come on," my sister said. "It's time."

I heard her adjust the mask's elastic strap to her head. I recognized the echo that the orthopedic material gave her voice when she said the next sentence. "Fetch the book."

We'd left it to one side in one of the bottom sections of the bookshelf. I found it without difficulty even in the dark. I went up to my sister, kneeling by the door. I stepped on a piece of material.

"Are you dressed?"

"I put on a skirt."

"Which one?"

"You've never seen it on me. I hadn't put it on again until today. It's brown."

"And why today?"

She didn't answer. "We have to hurry," she said. "Before the Cricket Man comes down. There's no going back now."

I took a breath so deep it made me dizzy. The room danced around me.

My sister reeled off the stages of the plan, so we'd both remember it. "I go into the room. I pick up the baby. I scream. You run to the end of the corridor. I take the baby to the kitchen. When Dad comes out of the bedroom, you put the book in the door." She repeated it all from memory in a constant whisper, like I did to learn the Latin names of the insects.

"After leaving the book in the door, you go to the kitchen. You say you're going to sleep. But you hide in the wardrobe." My sister held me by the shoulders. "Is that clear?"

I nodded. Her sweaty hand stroked my face.

"I'm going to turn on the light." I heard her take in air before noisily breathing out through her mouth. "Let's go. One, two, three . . ."

She hit the switch.

When the door opened it hit me so hard that it knocked me over. The book slipped from my hands. The sudden contraction of my pupils only allowed me to see the brown trail of her skirt going out of the room. Then she opened another door, the one to Grandma's bedroom.

I searched for the book on my hands and knees. I got to it just as my Grandmother yelled something. I leapt to my feet. I had to be in position before Dad came out of his room.

I crossed the hall in the direction of the window with the bars, the one that most of the fireflies had come in through.

The baby burst into such a high-pitched wail that it forced whoever heard it to go to his aid. Grandma yelled again. My sister responded with an even louder scream. The floor began to shake. My brother had also gotten up. I positioned myself by my parents' door, on the opposite side to where they would head when they came out. I held the book in my hands.

My sister emerged from the bedroom with the baby in her arms.

"I can't stand it anymore!" she shouted. "I hate this baby!"

She made for the living room. When she turned on the light, I could see the brown skirt she was wearing flying behind her. The old material was torn in several places. Grandma ran behind her, barefoot. A breeze smelling of talcum powder floated to where I was. Then my brother appeared.

That was when my parents' door opened.

I pressed my back against the wall.

First he came out. Then my mother soon after.

I heard my sister turn the faucet in the kitchen.

"I'm going to drown him!" she yelled. Her voice reached the end of the hallway clearly over the racket that broke out in the living room.

Before my parents' metal door closed on me, I put *The Wonderful Wizard of Oz* by the frame. The door hit the book and bent it, but it managed to stop the latch from clicking into its slot.

Then I ran to the living room.

My father, mother, and grandmother had surrounded my sister. The constant burble of water as the sink filled blended with the baby's high-pitched screams.

"Let me take care of this!" my father shouted.

He moved my mother aside. Grandma retreated without being told. My brother watched from a distance.

With the boy still in her arms, my sister jammed her elbows in the sink to put up more resistance. Water brimmed over. The baby's diaper was soaking wet. Dad slipped on one of the puddles that formed. He was left sitting on the floor, gripping my sister's skirt. He grunted and pulled on her to get up. One of the tears in the skirt opened up horizontally along her backside. Dad fell backward onto the floor again. My sister was left barelegged. I saw her underpants. The creased material disappeared between her buttocks, leaving the left one in sight.

The baby ran out of air. His crying stopped for the instant during which he hiccupped. Then the snotty screams returned with more force.

Watching the scene, I feared for the baby's safety. I thought about revealing that it was all playacting. Confessing to Mom and Dad that my sister and I were staging a gigantic lie.

But then I looked at the kitchen door. One of the biggest lies they'd told me, when they said it'd always been open.

Dad tried to get up again. My sister kicked out to stop him. She managed to make him slip again.

I approached Mom. I tried to get her attention by touching her shoulder.

"I don't want to see this," I said. The sad face I was supposed to feign as part of the plan came naturally. "I'm going to my room."

"Yes, son, you go." She pushed me to make me leave.

"I'm going to bed," I said again.

"I heard you," she said. "Go on, go. I don't know what you're still doing here."

"Good-bye, Mom."

She pushed me again with her eyes fixed on the struggle.

I pulled her arm. I got her to look at me.

"Good-bye, Mom."

Her nose whistled. I was struck by a feeling I couldn't remember having since the first night I wanted to open the kitchen door. An unexpected feeling of loss. As if the good-bye I'd just said was final. Then I remembered that my sister had promised me that I could come back to the basement after leaving. That my family would still live here after the other people came to find us. I didn't have to be sad. This good-bye wouldn't be the last one.

I hugged my mother.

A scream from my sister interrupted the hug.

"I can't hold on much longer!"

I understood the meaning of her words: I had to carry on with the plan. I separated myself from Mom, and once more I repeated what my sister and I had agreed I had to make clear. "I'm going to bed."

Dad had managed to get up, and he was covering my sister's body completely. I ran to my parents' room. The book was still keeping the door ajar. Before going in, I remembered something. The firefly jar.

"Don't take me to my room!" my sister yelled in the kitchen.

They were coming.

But I couldn't leave the basement without my fireflies. I'd always imagined that they'd be the light that would make me visible to the world. I returned to my bedroom. I leapt to the cabinet and opened the drawer with trembling hands. I took out the jar and held it under my arm.

Positioning myself by the door, I heard Dad shouting in the living room. I had no way of knowing whether he was somewhere he could see the hall from. And I had no idea where Mom was. Or Grandma. Or my brother.

My sister screamed. "Let me go!"

A hurried series of bangs crossed the main room diagonally, from the kitchen to the place where the television was. My sister had managed to slip from Dad's grasp. And she knew where the best place to go was. In that corner, the entrance to the hallway wasn't visible.

It was time.

I crossed the hall.

I pushed the door that the book had kept open. I went into my parents' room just before their voices were amplified with the characteristic echo that the hallway made.

"Leave me alone!" my sister cried.

"Be quiet," Mom whispered. "Your brother will hear you."

I did hear her. Not from the bunk bed like she thought, but from the other side of the door to their bedroom. My mother's words took effect. For a short period of time, a cloud of silence muted the basement.

A loud bang up above the ceiling broke it apart.

The Cricket Man.

"He's coming!" yelled my sister.

My mother shushed her.

I ran to the wardrobe. I wanted to hide from my parents, but, most of all, I wanted to hide from the Cricket Man. On the way there, doubt stopped me. I couldn't remember whether my parents had left the light on or I'd just flicked the switch when I came in. I turned my head as if I could find the answer somewhere in that room. Something caught my attention on my mother's bedside table. It was her photo on the rocks. The one that I found her looking at once in the kitchen. The one that showed her about to be soaked by a big wave. I observed that smooth, unfamiliar face as if it belonged to a stranger. But this time it sparked off a different feeling from the one I'd had the first time I saw it. I took just a second to understand why: it was a very similar face to the one I'd discovered behind my sister's mask.

I heard my bedroom door close.

My sister's screaming was muffled. Even so, I could make out a sentence from the imaginary conversation she had with me inside the room.

"And look at you sleeping there as if nothing's happened!" she screamed. She continued to speak, but I didn't understand anything else. It didn't matter. My parents would be hearing it. And that was the reason for her performance: to make them think I was in the bunk bed with her.

But in reality I was in the middle of their bedroom, unable to decide what to do with the light. I remembered one of the rules in the manual. Act quickly. I chose to turn it off. I reached the switch in one leap.

In the hallway, my mother was talking to my father about what'd happened in the kitchen.

They were about to come in.

When I tried to grab the wardrobe handles, the firefly jar slipped. It rolled toward the bedroom door, the pencils hitting the glass in a perfectly audible rhythmic sequence.

I froze. Listening to the voices in the hallway.

Another of the Cricket Man's bangs made me react.

Barely touching the floor, I grabbed the jar by the lid and escaped into the wardrobe.

I disappeared inside.

I closed the door behind me just as my parents came into the room. They turned on the light without suspecting. I'd made the right decision.

A draft of moist air blew among the hanging clothes. I felt it on my skin. I knew then my sister hadn't lied to me. It was much more than just a wardrobe.

Another noise up above the ceiling gave away the Cricket Man's position.

"Something always has to happen when he's coming," Mom said in the bedroom.

It became clear to me at that moment. Mom knew, too, that the Cricket Man really existed. Even though she'd always denied it to me.

Then, from a place lost in the vast darkness of the wardrobe, the creaking of some unknown hinges reached me.

The ground shook with a loud bang.

A light shone in the distance. Much farther away than what should've been the length of the wardrobe. The light glimmered, sifted by the clothes. It had to be the oil lamp Dad had told me about.

The next thing I heard was some knees clicking.

The Cricket Man's knees. As they bent back-to-front with each step he took toward me.

34

The Cricket Man reached the wardrobe. The light from his oil lamp was so close it could've burned me with its flame. I lowered my head to make myself invisible, certain he'd spot my legs among the hanging clothes. I held my breath. I could hear my own skin tightening. My heart thundered in that confined space. I wished I could silence it.

Some coat hangers slid along the wardrobe's rail above my head. The Cricket Man was pushing his way through, moving obstacles aside with his legs.

Dad spoke in the room, on the other side of the doors. "What's that book doing there?"

"What book?" Mom asked.

"This one."

My heart stopped. I'd spent several seconds deciding whether to leave the light on or off, but I'd forgotten about something much more important. The book. *The Wonderful Wizard of Oz.* I'd left it by the doorjamb when I escaped into the wardrobe. I hugged the firefly jar.

A blouse covered my face.

A few inches away the Cricket Man's body palpitated. I could feel his heat. I could make out his pulse in the slight vibration of the sphere of light that his oil lamp projected. I bit my lips. A drip soaked into my underpants. I pressed my legs together to stop what was about to happen.

"Did you open the door?" Dad asked in the room. "When we got back from the kitchen. Did you open it?"

"It was open. You opened it. I didn't even . . ." Mom didn't finish the sentence. She just gave a frightened yelp.

Something hit the wardrobe door.

Then it fell to the floor.

Dad had thrown the book.

I managed to stay still despite the unexpected bang because my body was so stiff with fear, but the wetness in my underpants continued to spread toward the sides. The Cricket Man reacted to the shock with a flinch. His movement made some clothes dance along the rail. The shadows that his light cast inside the wardrobe stretched, shrank, stretched again.

The book's impact marked the beginning of a bigger racket.

The floor in the room shook under Dad's quick footsteps. He yelled something I couldn't make out. The bedroom door opened.

He was heading to my room. Where he'd discover that I wasn't in bed.

The hangers overhead stopped moving when the Cricket Man recovered from his fright.

Motionless, I imagined myself making him open the wardrobe door. *Come on, come on, come on.* I needed him to get out. To clear the way so I could run up the tunnel and get out before Dad got back from my bedroom, aware of the escape plan. *Come on, come on, come on.*

Then he opened the wardrobe. He went into my parents' room.

"Something's going on," Mom said to the Cricket Man. And although she continued speaking, I couldn't make out anything else. The sound of my own breathing enveloped me completely when I let out the air I'd been holding in. The out-breath woke up my pinched muscles.

A hidden strength exploded in my feet. It impelled me to run in the direction the Cricket Man had come from, the clothes hitting me in the face.

I headed into the darkness, going with this new instinct.

First my bare feet discovered a texture that was new to me. Then an unknown feeling covered me completely, brushed against my ankles, twisted itself around my legs, hit me on the chest, and seeped under my armpits. It was moist air. Like the air I sometimes felt on my face when I peered through the window at the end of the hall, but now it was traveling all over my body. My panting, as I ran, muted the sounds coming from the bedroom.

I very soon ran straight into a soft surface. It felt strange to me. Something scratched my face before the force of the collision propelled me backward. I fell onto my backside. Now it was my buttocks that detected the new texture I'd felt before. I leapt to my feet, frightened by the sensation.

I was afraid the firefly lamp had broken with the impact. I ran my fingers around the jar's contour. It was intact. I felt stupid for not remembering them earlier.

"Glow," I said to the fireflies. "Light the way." I repeated the command with a series of taps on the lid. Before they could obey my instructions, I no longer needed their light, because the wardrobe door opened behind me. The glow from the Cricket Man's oil lamp was bright enough for me to see the dark wall that stood in my way.

I heard him breathe behind me.

A current of stinking air reached me from my right. I ran in that direction. I saw another wall that appeared in front of me just in time, and I avoided the collision. I followed the draft, making another turn. The light from the oil lamp wobbled with each step the Cricket Man took in my direction, warping the space. My shadow on the ground was stuck fast to my feet, as if it, too, wanted to escape the basement. Or as if it was the shadow of my reflection in the window, that part of myself that sometimes looked at me from outside, from the other side of the glass. I gasped. Tears flew behind me.

Another obstacle came into view when it was too late to stop. It was a giant sack made from a brown material. The Cricket Man's sack. I stumbled over it and was thrown forward. One of the soft walls of the passage stopped me from falling. I fell silent, expecting to hear the whimpers of the children trapped in the sack.

What I heard was a loud crash behind me. The chinking of metal objects. The crunch of glass as it broke. And a deep groan from the Cricket Man.

The light he carried went out, leaving me in total darkness.

I began the sequence of taps in Morse code on the jar's lid. I stopped as soon as it dawned on me that the glow from the fireflies would give me away. I was better off staying in the dark. I stretched an arm out in front of me, like Grandma did sometimes to navigate her surroundings. All the surfaces had the same moist texture. I groped the walls with a trembling hand. I couldn't find what I was looking for. What my sister had told me I'd find without difficulty. One afternoon, in the bathroom, she'd held the shower hose in her hands, making a curve with it that she made me touch a few times. She explained to me that, on the last wall in the passage, I'd find some metal things with that shape. Fixed to the wall, one above the other, from bottom to top. She told me they were steps, and that I'd have to climb them like I climbed the ladder to my bunk.

I felt the damp walls without finding anything resembling steps. Then I thought that my sister had tricked me. That it was all a trap. She wanted me gone from the basement so she could do what she wanted with the baby. Poison him without me coming out from under a bed to ruin her plans.

I kept touching the walls, certain I'd been tricked.

The deception magnified in my mind. I imagined that my entire family was part of my sister's plan. They'd all wanted to lead me to that strange passageway. In the dark. They all wanted to get rid of me. Free themselves of the boy who'd disrupted their life together with questions about the patch of sun in the living room. The boy who hid things in his drawer. They wanted to cast me out of the basement for distrusting the Cricket Man, who they weren't scared of. I imagined them in my parents' bedroom celebrating how successful their plan had been. Closing the wardrobe door. Leaving me outside. Forever. Turned into my own reflection in the window. Into the ghost Dad said I was.

Surrounded by darkness, unable to see even a single body part that confirmed I existed, I felt as if I was disappearing. As if I was vanishing into nothing. To become just a bad memory that my family would soon forget.

That was when I touched it. Above my head. Something similar to the shower hose. It was thicker. And it was cold. But I ran my fingers along it and found that it curved, much like my sister had shown me.

I smiled in the dark.

I wanted to grip on to that thing, but it was impossible to do so without letting go of the firefly jar. Holding it under an arm like I was, there was no way I could hang on to the rung with both hands. I tried to stretch my underpants, with the idea of wedging the jar between my body and the elastic, but the container was too wide. I didn't want to leave the basement without my fireflies. They had to glow to show me the world with their light. To perform the sequence of flashes I'd taught them.

I heard footsteps.

And another click of a back-to-front knee.

I was forced to leave the fireflies on the ground.

"I'll be back to save you," I whispered as I crouched down. "You and the baby."

When I crouched I lost track of where the ladder was. I began another search with my arms outstretched. Each time my hands hit the wall, moist stuff fell on my face.

The Cricket Man's breathing sounded too close.

I scratched at the damp texture. Bits of the wall went under my fingernails. I hit something metal with my elbow. I grabbed the step with all my might.

Then I heard an unknown voice.

"Don't go," it said.

It was deep. Full of crackles. Like you'd expect from a throat that was only half-human.

Fear turned me into the perfect prey. So immobilized by the shock that I wouldn't resist. I shook my face to get the bits of wall off my eyes.

When I blinked I discovered a line of light in the distance.

Up above.

It was a purple line, barely visible, but different from anything I'd seen in the basement.

Still gripping the step, I kicked out, trying to find footing on the wall. If the Cricket Man wanted to stick me in his sack, or eat me right there, he'd have to fight for it. I wasn't prepared to let myself be beaten without seeing what was outside the basement. Without knowing what it was like beyond the purple line I could see way above.

Though I'd never performed a movement like it, pulling with my arms to lift my body, I managed to get my elbows to the height of the metal handle. I didn't hold on for long. The pain in my back and shoulders made me fall.

A desperate sob escaped through my nose as I sat up.

"Are you all right?" the voice asked.

I jumped up to reach the step again. I hit the wall.

The Cricket Man spoke again.

"Come with me," he said.

I scratched like crazy at the wall.

Until I heard Grandma's voice.

"Come with us."

Mom joined the chorus of voices. "Come to the bedroom."

"There're a lot of things we have to explain to you," Dad added.

In the dark, I began to make out the shapes of my family in front of me. Someone took a step toward me. The click of the knee gave away his identity.

"Don't eat me," I begged.

Mom's nose whistled.

"It's not the Cricket Man," said Dad.

"Don't be afraid," said Grandma.

The unknown silhouette held out a hand that wasn't a front leg.

"Are you the One Up There?"

He laughed. "I'd rather you called me Grandpa from now on," he said.

35

Mom hugged me in the bedroom, on her knees. She made a visor with her hands over my eyes to ease the pain from the change in light.

"Why are you running away?" she asked. "Why haven't you told us you want to go?"

I broke away from her hug without answering. I sat on the bed with my feet hanging down, the firefly jar on my legs.

"Because you want to keep me locked up," I replied. "And keep telling me lies."

Mom looked at Dad, wanting help. He put an arm behind her back, inviting Grandma and Grandpa to join them. The four of them observed me like I'd observed the fireflies in the jar on so many nights.

"Son," said Dad, "we want you to go, too."

I blinked a few times without understanding. My jaw dropped.

"Your grandfather's going to need help," Grandma said. She kissed him on the cheek.

I hesitated for a second before looking the One Up There, the Cricket Man, in the face for the first time. I discovered features so wrinkled they might've been burned. But they weren't. A sack of saggy

Paul Pen

skin hung from his chin. The eyes behind the glasses seemed buried in the flesh of his eyelids.

"I can't do this on my own anymore," he said. His two eyebrows, white like the only one that Grandma still had, relaxed. It was an expression of calm that was reproduced in the scarred faces of the rest of my family. As if they'd waited a long time for this moment to come.

"But I was about to go," I said. "You stopped me."

"Because we want you to leave, not escape," Dad explained. "We've been hoping for a while that you'd come to the decision yourself. But not even making you sleep in the bathtub made you want to go." A hint of a smile curved Dad's hair scar. "Son, you're going to have to forgive us for many things. I just wanted you to stop liking this place. So that leaving wouldn't be so difficult."

"Leaving?" I hugged the jar, trying to process what Dad was saying. "You're going to let me go?"

"I asked you myself not long ago if you wanted to leave," Mom broke in. "In your bed, when we talked about those green butterflies. It was a serious question, and you told me you didn't want to go."

"Because I didn't."

"And why do you want to escape now?"

"Because I've found out about a lot of things."

The serenity on Dad's face cracked. "What do you mean?"

I swung my legs in the air. I wanted to list all of the terrible things I'd discovered. That Dad had put the baby in my sister's belly. And that Mom and Grandma had allowed it to happen, and that was why they considered it the worst of their sins. But I bit my bottom lip to stop the words from coming. Because I thought that what they were saying to me now could be another trap to keep me in the dark. Another lie to make me stay in the basement. Like the chick. Like the mask. Like the blisters in the outside world.

"I want to leave," I said. "Let me go."

"We're going to let you go," Mom said. "But not like this."

"I want to leave!" The yell caused a spasm of surprise in my family's communal embrace. It also woke the baby in the room next door.

"Tell us why you want to leave."

"Because you've tricked me," I replied, looking Dad in the eyes. "This isn't the best place in the world."

He sighed as he heard me. He freed his arms from Mom and Grandma, then knelt in front of me. He put the firefly jar on the bed. It surprised me that he barely seemed to notice it. "I want you to know that we did it for you."

I frowned, not understanding.

"Making you believe that this was the best place in the world," he explained. He took my hand and pinched the back of it. "Remember?"

He gently twisted my skin like he had the first time I asked him why we couldn't leave the basement. When he explained to me that the outside world was made of blisters like the one made on my skin by an oil burn. The same night when I went up to the kitchen door for the first time.

"Of course I remember," I said.

Mom's nose whistled.

He released the pinch. He kissed my hand, like he'd done then. "That's why you think this is the best place in the world. Because we had to make you believe that it was, so you'd be happy living here."

I held a hand to Dad's face. I stroked his hair scar. I relived the pleasant sensation I'd enjoyed so much when I was little. It triggered other pleasant sensations that made the basement the best place in the world. The heat from the patch of sun on my hands. The pressure of the sheet on my chest when Mom tucked me in. Her wrinkled lips when they kissed my forehead. Grandma's smell. The taste of carrot soup. I finished tracing the line of the scar. The good memories disappeared.

"You've all lied to me," I said.

Dad lowered his head. "I'm sorry."

"It was the best thing we could do," Mom added. "A little boy has to live with his family."

I weighed her words. "But, why do we live here?"

There was a silence. I saw Grandma pressing her forehead against Grandpa's chest, huddling up to him. When Dad looked up at me, the folds of burned flesh cast deep shadows on his face. "Because we can't leave the basement."

"*We* can't," Mom pointed out.

"But you can," Grandpa added. "And the time has come for you to do so."

"And why can't you all leave?" I asked.

Dad's eyes went out of focus. They looked through me into some far-off place. Some past time that must've been left a long way behind.

"There are answers to all these questions," he said in the end. "There'll be plenty of time for that."

I withdrew my hand from between his. I took the firefly jar and pushed myself back over the mattress, separating myself from Dad. I got down from the bed on the other side.

"I want the truth," I said.

"Son . . ."

"You never answer my questions!" I cried.

"It's better if you find out bit by—"

"My sister's the only one I can trust!"

The density of the air changed when I mentioned her. Grandma took a sharp breath. The curve in Dad's hair scar straightened until it became a sharp expression of rage.

"Of course," he said, throwing his hands toward the ceiling. "Your sister. It had to be her behind all of this. What is it she's told you?" Before I could answer his question, he murmured, "In fact, she can explain it herself."

He ran to find her in my bedroom, but when he opened the door, she appeared on the other side stumbling, as if she'd been listening with her ear pressed against the metal. She looked at us one by one as she regained her balance. Then she ran to the wardrobe. Dad got in front of her with an explosive sprint. He threw himself against the doors and closed them with his back.

"Don't even try it," he said to her. "And put the mask on, the boy's here."

"I know the boy's here. I'm not blind. The blind one's your mother."

"Put it on."

"It's not necessary anymore." She seemed to enjoy the silent anxiety that followed her words. "Is it, little brother?"

There was a frantic exchange of looks in the bedroom. Mom leapt to my side. She wanted to cover my eyes, in a useless attempt to prolong the lie, but I resisted, shaking my head. My sister took advantage of my father's confusion to pounce on the wardrobe. He grabbed her by the wrists, and with a turn, held her arms from behind like a straitjacket.

"Don't look so scared," said my sister. "The kid already knows how my face is. He knows you make me wear the mask because you can't bear the fact that the fire didn't affect me."

"And does he know *why* it didn't affect you?" Dad asked.

She didn't answer. She turned to me.

"What've they told you?" She held her chin high to alleviate the pressure Dad was exerting on her body. "That they did everything for your own good?"

I didn't know how to reply.

"It was the best thing we could do," Mom murmured.

"The best?" The smile she tried to feign ended up turning into a grimace of pain. "Well, look what you've achieved."

My sister fixed her eyes on me. Then she aimed them around the room. The whole basement.

"We've managed to stay together," Dad whispered into her ear. "We've given your two brothers the family that you wanted to destroy."

"And now that Grandpa's dying, that's when you want the boy to go."

"Grandpa isn't going to die," Grandma let out in a sob of denial.

Dad's arms tightened like a noose around my sister's neck, making her go quiet. But the words she'd gotten out were enough for me to realize something.

"You knew?" I asked her. "You knew they were going to let me leave?"

She blinked through the mass of tangled hair that covered her face. Her eyelids looked like flies trapped in a spider's web. She moved her mouth but didn't answer.

"Sure she knew," said Dad. "We made the decision when the baby was born. Even before Grandpa came down to tell us what was wrong with him."

The night when I saw the Cricket Man in the basement. When I peed myself hiding in the corner of the living room.

"That just forced us to try to speed up the process," Dad went on. "But it seems like your sister was trying to get in ahead of us."

"You knew," I repeated to my sister. This time it was no longer a question.

"She was using you to get word out about the basement," Dad added.

I held a hand to my mouth.

"Nobody can know we're here," said Grandma.

"But she told me you could keep living here in the basement—" I broke off midsentence when I realized that I was going to repeat my sister's words. Words that had to be false. Just like everything that she'd told me about the Cricket Man. She'd pushed me to carry on with the escape plan without telling me who he really was, even though she knew how scared I was to face him.

I looked at my sister, my eyes filled with the tears of another betrayal.

She squirmed in my father's arms.

"Their lies are much worse!" she screamed. She fought to escape the pincers that held her. I noticed she was focusing her efforts on freeing her right hand. Then suddenly she was still. She spat out some hair that had gone in her mouth. One of her smiles that weren't happy appeared on her face.

"You know what Dad's capable of doing," she said.

"What I'm capable of doing?" he asked. "What're you talking about?"

I knew what she was talking about. The night I spent in the bathtub. The scratches I discovered on his back when I spied on him from behind the curtain.

My sister flung her bare legs into the air. She unbalanced Dad. She kicked like she had on the kitchen table the night she gave birth to the baby. She stamped on my father's feet with her heels, and caught one of the arms that gripped her in her mouth and bit it. My father fought to control the raging insect that my sister had turned into. The two of them fell to the floor, coming away from the wardrobe door.

She fixed a dark look on me.

"You know what he's capable of doing," she said again.

I remembered the tear that I'd seen behind her mask that night.

I took a step toward the wardrobe.

"Run!" she screamed. "They're not going to let you leave! They have to cover for Dad! Get out of this basement and tell everyone what's happening down here."

Dad crushed my sister with all his body weight. He squeezed her face between his hands. The veins in his forearms swelled. I saw my sister trying to regain control of her right hand, but Dad trapped the arm under his knee.

"What have you told him?" he spat through his teeth. Their noses were almost touching.

When I took another step toward the wardrobe, Mom took me by the shoulder.

"Fight!" my sister screamed, her lungs crushed. "They're not going to let you go!"

"We are going to let you leave," Mom said.

"Then prove it to him," she whispered. "Let him go right now."

I shook my arm.

I waited for Mom to let go of me so I could leave.

But what she did was press harder with her fingers.

"I'm sorry," she said. "I can't let you go like this." She pulled me toward her.

I was going to stay in the basement forever.

I fought for my freedom by shaking my body with all my strength. My mother gave me a slap to control me. She scratched my face with those fingernails she nibbled, sculpting them into little saws. I felt the warm bumps they left across my cheek.

And that was when I discovered the biggest lie my sister had told me.

I stopped struggling with Mom.

I looked at my sister's eyes hidden behind locks of hair, her head pressed against the floor.

"You lied to me about Dad," I said.

Her eyes, sunk into her face wet with sweat, pulsed with rage.

"Go, now . . ." Her words whistled in her throat. "Or you'll never get out . . ."

"You lied to me about Dad," I repeated. "The night I spent in the bathtub. You told me you'd gone to the bathroom to wash because of Dad. That you'd made the scratches on his back. But you were quiet for a long time before telling me. And you did this with one of your nails." I copied the gesture she'd made on her bed, running her thumb over the curve of her fingernails, before resting them on my back and admitting that Dad tried to put babies in her belly.

"What a clever boy you are," my sister whispered, struggling to breathe.

"Mom's nails are much scratchier," I went on. "Because she bites them. They're like little saws." I pointed at the scratches they'd just made on my face. "Dad didn't do anything to you that night. And your nose didn't bleed because of him. It bled from the poison. I read it on the box. That night, you came into the bathroom to wash off the poison. You'd put it on your breast like you did later. That's why the baby wouldn't wake up the next day."

"What's he talking about!" Dad sprayed my sister's face with saliva. The veins in his neck swelled even more than the ones in his forearms.

A deep groan escaped from the depths of her stomach.

Mom knelt in front of me.

"What has she told you?" she asked. She used her stretched T-shirt to dry my eyes.

"She told me Dad put the baby in her belly."

Grandma cried when she heard that.

"You wouldn't dare!" my father yelled at his daughter.

My sister's profile lifted above the puddle that her hair had formed on the floor. She smiled at him. "You really think I wouldn't?"

Dad's hands shot to her neck. He squeezed them to keep her from saying another word. He didn't let up until Grandpa told him to stop.

"Son, your father hasn't done anything like that," Mom told me.

"But you and Grandma say the baby's a sin." I sucked in snot. "That it was the worst thing that has happened in this basement."

"And it was," she said. "Every day we regret not having stopped it. But not because it was your father."

I took a deep breath before asking. "Then who was it?"

An earthquake started in the room next door. The trembling advanced down the hall. My brother pounded the metal door, asking to come in. Mom took advantage of his timely appearance to answer.

"The one banging away out there." A veil of tears blocked out her eyes.

"It's not good for a family of mammals to have babies among themselves," I reminded her.

"It's not good," she said, "but sometimes it happens." They were the same words she'd used to explain it to me that time in bed.

"Deep down they think I deserve it," said my sister in a rattling voice. "That my brother owed it to me for what I did to him when he was little."

My father's hands returned to her neck.

"Don't listen to her," Mom whispered.

My sister gave me a final look that I didn't know how to interpret. Then she closed her eyes.

Her tensed arms relaxed under Dad's knees. She stretched out the bent legs she was using to try to unbalance him. Her fists opened. Her entire body relaxed like an insect exposed to potassium cyanide. Her head fell to one side.

Dad observed the process with his mouth open.

In total silence.

"Have you . . . ?" asked Grandma.

My sister's right hand then twisted like a viper, escaping from the knee that Dad had just lifted. It was the same hand she'd tried to free before. I understood why when I recognized the handle that poked out from the frayed waist of her brown skirt. The handle of the knife that Dad had used to imitate the cowboys from the movies one night, stabbing the table between the fingers of his open hand.

"A knife!" I yelled.

She grabbed it before Dad could do anything.

She raised her arm over his back.

"I'm going to get out of this basement!" she screamed.

That instant, Mom separated from me. The firefly jar vanished from between my fingers. I watched her swoop on my sister.

First she stopped the knife that was bearing down on my father.
Then she raised her arm toward the ceiling, the jar held high.
"No!" I cried. But Mom let her arm drop with all its weight.
The firefly lamp smashed on my sister's face.

Her nose caved in, turning her profile into no more than a right angle. Like they'd always told me it was.

A new mask of hair and blood covered her face.

All the fireflies flew out into the room.

36

It was a while before Mom and Dad arrived back in the room. They'd taken my sister away wrapped in a sheet. My brother, who was still banging on the door when they left, took the chance to slip into the room. Grandpa also brought the baby. While I tried pointlessly to reconstruct the jar, we waited for my parents to return.

"Is she all right?" Grandpa asked them when they came in.

Mom shook her head. Seeing me kneeling by pieces of glass, she crouched beside me.

"Be careful," she said. She waved her hand between mine to stop my work.

"What are all of these things?" she asked. She felt the floor with her fingertips. "Why were you keeping peas?"

She continued to feel the floor.

"And this tooth? Did you take it from my sewing box?" Among the glass, she found one of the colored pencils that'd been in the jar. She handed it to me.

"This *is* yours," she said. She carried on searching the floor. "But this screw's from Dad's toolbox. What were you keeping in there?"

"You already know," I whispered to Mom.

"No, no, I don't know," she said. "I thought you had pencils in there, but a screw?"

I gestured at Dad with my head so that she'd understand why I couldn't speak openly.

"Son, your father's not the dad he's been these last few months," she explained. "Your real father's the one who had you riding him like a horse in the living room. The one who fetched you your insect book. Do you think he cares about this jar full of stuff?"

I remembered him taking it from my legs just before, when I'd sat on the bed after returning from the tunnel.

"My fireflies," I said then. "They're my fireflies." I could see them flying around the place, though they weren't glowing because the bedroom light was on. They were perching on the walls and on the bed. They were fluttering around Grandma.

"What fireflies?"

"I had them in the jar," I said.

"This jar?" Mom showed me the lid.

I nodded.

"Look." I pointed at one flying over our heads. "They're everywhere." I followed the insect's flight with my eyes. Mom copied me.

"See?" I asked.

"I can't see anything."

"There's another one, there!"

"What's he talking about?" she asked my father.

Dad came beside us, moving some glass out of the way before resting his knee on the floor. He laid a hand on my shoulder. "Son, there's nothing here."

"There. There're lots of them," I insisted. "They started coming ages ago. They bring me light from outside."

Dad picked things up from the floor and then showed me the palm of his hand. There were a few pieces of the gravel that built up in the space between the window and the second wall.

"These fireflies you're talking about," Dad began. He shook the contents of his hand. "Are you sure they're really here? You've always loved that photo in your book." Dad picked up one of the pieces of gravel between his finger and thumb. He moved it around in the air in an irregular line, imitating an insect's random flying.

"It's just a stone," he said. He dropped it.

It rolled along the floor.

I watched the piece of gravel. I remembered how the first firefly had walked over some identical little stones when it came into the basement through the hall window. I examined the remains of the smashed container. I saw Dad's screw, the same one he'd trod on in the hallway the night the baby took so long to stop crying. The night when the second firefly appeared. Then I noticed the two peas. The ones that fell off my plate when I was having dinner, just before I discovered two more fireflies near the jar. One of them had shown up squashed in my hand one morning. My eyes filled with tears when I saw two of the teeth that I spilled onto the floor when I took them one afternoon from Mom's sewing box. Because that day another pair of fireflies had appeared.

I examined the floor, my eyes coming to rest on each of the little objects contained in the jar. I didn't want to count them, because I didn't want to confirm that there was exactly the same number as there were fireflies in the lamp.

"But don't cry," said my mother.

I looked up to the ceiling. I followed the flight of one of the fireflies until it vanished in the air, disappearing in front of my eyes. Like the chick that never existed had disappeared from my hands that night.

Because the fireflies had never existed, either.

I took a deep breath to fill the void I felt in my chest.

Then Grandma spoke.

"I think I know what's happening," she said. A smile appeared on her face. "Come here."

She held out her arms, inviting me to approach her. She stroked my face when she knew that I was in front of her.

"These fireflies that you say you see are like the chick that hatched in our hands," she explained.

"Huh?"

"I gave you a very special power the night you brought me the egg. I taught you to see things like I have to see them," she said. She laid a wrinkly finger on my forehead. "Imagining them. And I see you've managed to make good use of that power."

I let out a sigh of wonder.

"There's no creature more amazing than one that can make its own light," Grandma went on.

I ran to the light switch at the bedroom door.

I turned it off.

All the fireflies glowed to celebrate the fall of darkness, leaving trails of magical green light in their wake. I swiveled with my arms held wide, traveling all around the room among the intermittent flashes that had been there with me during my last days in the basement.

"What's their light like?" Grandma asked. "Describe it to me."

"Green," I answered.

I took the baby from Grandpa's arms.

"It's the fireflies," I whispered to his little face. "Look at them glow. They slept with you one night."

My nephew held out his arms. He opened and closed his hands in the air. As if he wanted to catch the lights that floated above him.

Grandma got up.

She left the room.

She returned a few seconds later.

"Here," she said. "Get them back." She gave me a new glass jar, while she took the baby.

I leapt onto the bed with the jar open.

I held it up.

"Come back," I said. The fireflies swirled in a cloud of light, a galaxy of flashes, before returning to the container by themselves.

"Is that all of them?" asked Grandma.

I confirmed it was, closing the lid.

There was silence.

"So," Dad murmured. "Can I turn on the light? Or are you two going to do some more of your magic with invisible things?"

Grandma laughed. "You can turn it on," she said.

It was a few seconds before I could open my eyes without it hurting. When I got down from the bed, my family positioned themselves in front of me. Grandma took my father by the hand. Grandpa put his arm around her. Mom stood beside him, holding my brother.

"So, do you want to go out?" Dad asked.

I looked at the wardrobe. I remembered the line of purple light that I'd seen at the top of the tunnel that led outside.

"I want to know what it's like out there," I answered.

My mother lowered her head. My brother stroked her face without much care. He kissed her cheek, covering her in drool.

I left the jar on the bed.

I hugged Mom.

"Will I be able to come back?" I asked with my mouth pressed to her belly.

"You'll have to," Grandpa answered. "Unless your family stops needing food."

Mom ruffled my hair with a hand. I stroked the wrinkly fold between two of her knuckles. The circle of burned skin at the base of the thumb. The wide, smooth scar near the wrist.

Then I stood in front of Dad.

He held a hand out to me like the cowboys did in the movies.

When I shook it, his hair scar curved.

I went up to Grandma, who was holding the baby in her arms. I enjoyed the smell of her talcum powder.

"And what if I want to stay with you?" I asked.

She smiled but shook her head at the same time.

"The world's waiting for you," she said. "You're needed up there."

I looked at the baby's face. He was cooing with pleasure in his characteristic way. Like a purr. His nostrils opened and closed, no doubt recognizing Grandma's smell. I clutched him by the sides.

"What're you doing?" my mother asked. She stretched out a hand, gripping the baby's body. When I tried to pull on the little boy, Mom pushed him toward Grandma, stopping me from taking him.

Dad's fingers closed around her wrist. "Let him go."

"Not yet," she said. "He's my grandson. Just until the next delivery. A few more weeks."

"A few weeks?" Dad gestured at me with his chin. "Or ten years?"

Mom contained a sob. Her fingers separated from the baby like the legs of a butterfly taking flight. Then she hugged my brother.

"You'll always be with me," she whispered in his ear. She kissed his temple a few times in a row.

"Good-bye, Scarecrow," I whispered. He laughed with a guttural gurgle. I tucked one of the legs of his pajama bottoms into his sock.

Grandma handed me the baby.

I rested his head near my elbow, like Mom had shown me.

"We're going to see the sun," I told him. The little boy smiled.

"Can you take the jar?" I asked Grandpa. "I want to go out with my fireflies."

He picked up the container. "Then go out with them," he said. "I'll trade you." He handed me the jar while he took the baby.

"Will I like living out there?" I asked.

"I'm certain you will," he replied. When he got up, I recognized the Cricket Man's clicking in his knees. A shiver threatened to run down my spine, but it died when Grandpa rested his hand on the back of my neck.

"Will I be able to live here if I don't like what I see?"

Mom's nose whistled. "Sure you will," she said.

"But you won't want to," Dad added. "It's too nice outside for that to happen."

I filled my chest with a deep breath. I turned toward the wardrobe. "Shall we go?"

The first thing I touched was the grass that grew around the trapdoor opening. I stroked it with the palm of my hand, feeling the edge of each blade. I still had most of my body underground, supported on one of the steps in the tunnel. I put the firefly lamp down on that damp surface.

I lifted my face.

A breeze stroked me from my forehead to my feet, roaring in my ears.

"Come on," said Grandpa.

I barely heard his voice, absorbed as I was in the air's hum. I gripped the grass to pull myself up, but my feet didn't respond.

"Open your eyes," Grandpa said.

I'd closed them without realizing it.

My hands were frozen.

My legs trembled.

I breathed in a smell so intense I thought I'd go dizzy.

"Open them," Grandpa insisted. "You have to see this."

When I mustered the courage to open them, all I discovered was an immense black expanse. Another ceiling. I'd come out to more walls. To a bigger basement.

"There's nothing here," I said.

"What do you mean, there's nothing? Look at the sky."

I blinked, my face aimed toward the nothingness. I began to make out dots of light. Intermittent flashes up above.

"Are they fireflies?" I asked.

"They're stars," Grandpa replied. "And what you can hear in the distance is the sea."

I stroked the ground with my hands.

Touching the grass.

I tried again to get out.

My legs didn't respond.

Then I remembered the power that Grandma had given me. I could make the outside world what I'd always dreamed it would be.

I wished my chick was there to greet me.

Then I heard it tweet.

Wanting to see it was the encouragement I needed to get out. Once there, I picked up the firefly jar that I'd left on the grass.

"Glow," I told them. "We're outside." The lamp lit up more brightly than ever, illuminating everything around me. Showing me at last the world that was up above the basement.

A world that was like I'd always imagined it.

The chick, small and yellow, walked between my legs, beating its wings and tweeting to welcome me. Lots of green butterflies, their lower wings in the shape of a kite, flew among Grandpa, my nephew, and me.

I unscrewed the jar's lid.

I held it over my head.

The fireflies flew up into the sky, free.

I watched them until I could no longer tell them apart from the stars.

FIFTEEN YEARS
LATER

37

I like leaving the lighthouse when the sun disappears but it's not yet night. It's the only time of day when the world has no shadows. My son walks along holding on to my leg. I know his little hand will let go of my pants one day, because he'll want to know what there is beyond the life that his father has shown him, so I try to memorize each of these moments when his fingers squeeze the fabric as if he was afraid to leave my orbit. My wife has stayed in the kitchen. She was still chopping carrots when the last patch of sun vanished in front of our eyes. The patch that dies on top of the fridge at the end of each day, near the *Actias luna* magnet that we bought on one of our trips.

I crouch down when the boy points to what must seem to him like a bubble of cotton suspended in the air. I've learned that a finger stretched out toward something, along with two tugs on my pants, is the equivalent of a question. I pull the dandelion from its stalk, careful not to shake the ghostlike head left by the flower. After a gentle puff, the bubble of cotton bursts in front of him, dozens of seeds floating in the air all around. There's no happier sound than the one my son knows how to make with his throat. I pursue two of those seeds with my eyes, two tiny parachutes standing out perfectly against the dark background of the sky. They fly with their filaments interlocked. At one point, the seeds are no longer visible in the growing darkness. Although I can't see them, I know they are there, much like Grandma and Grandpa these last few years.

Grandpa hung on much longer than the doctors predicted when they gave him the bad news. He stayed with me long enough to teach me how to find my way out here, in this other world, which I've never gotten used to. Some nights I still go down to sleep in the basement. With Mom and Dad. My brother still marches through imaginary cornfields from time to time. My sister was killed by a blood clot caused by the wounds that the glass jar made on her face and neck. She died in my bed the same night I left. I know Dad didn't go near her, that he watched what was happening from the door, but Grandma didn't let go of her hand until the end. My sister directed her last look at my mother, who asked for forgiveness as the light of life in her daughter's eyes went out in front of her.

The finger now points at the empty jar I left on the ground when I crouched down.

"Not long now," I say. At that moment, the top of the new tower lights up. It's the light from an ordinary bulb, not the big lens that gave my grandfather work. I see my nephew peer out from up there. Until a few years ago I didn't let him go up those stairs. I wave so he can locate me, and his figure vanishes in an instant. He likes to think that he lives in a lighthouse, that there are still ships that need to be guided by its light. We inherited the property as distant relatives of Grandpa's, the ones who came to visit him one day and never left. As a precaution I always say I'm three years older than I really am.

There're still people on the island who look away when they cross paths with me in the street. Others don't understand how I can live in the house where such terrible things happened. Some ask me if I know the real story about what happened back then. About what those people did. I always answer that I've heard something, but that you can't live in the past.

I struggled to forgive my family when I learned what they did with the girl. But when I look at my own son, walking with his legs arced like a cowboy's, laughing as he discovers the world and its dandelions, I wonder whether I'd have done the same thing. Whether I wouldn't do anything in my power to protect him. Anything good. And anything bad.

A short time ago, when I returned from the greenhouse where I work controlling insect infestations, an elderly woman who was strolling at sundown along the jetty where I moored my boat told me that the two moles on my face reminded her of someone. She narrowed her eyes to rewind the tape of her memory, but my son made that happy sound with his throat that only he knows how to make, winning all of her attention. When the elderly woman bent down to pinch the boy's cheek, the tape stopped at some other memory.

Each step we take makes the nearest crickets fall silent. The rest continue their singing, encouraging the moon to appear, perhaps. The windows of the nearby houses paint yellow squares in a navy blue world when the lights come on. I scan the plot of land until I recognize the spot I'm searching for. The weeds grow very quickly around the trapdoor. The nights when I have to open it, I pull out entire plants without intending it, the roots hanging from the stem like bundles of veins outside a body. It's not time to go down tonight, so I let the boy play among the flowers. The blue ones sway each time he bats them. I take a seat on the rise in the land where the entrance is hidden, my legs in the same place they were when I set foot in the outside world for the first time. When I imagined the world was as I'd always dreamed it would be. Filled with the fireflies, the green butterflies, and the chick that never existed.

I cross my legs while my son fights with a poppy plant. His hand is still gripping my pants. I pull on it to get him to sit between my legs, his back against my belly, my chin on his head. His hair smells even better than the field around us. When I put the glass jar on his lap, he hugs it like he hugs the glowworm toy he sleeps with.

There's a solitary flash in the air.

A dot of light, cleaving through the growing darkness. I don't think my son has seen it, because his hands are still investigating the jar's contour.

A second flash flies in front of us.

Followed by two more.

Joy springs up in my son's throat.

"See them?" I ask.

A cloud of fireflies hovers over the blades of grass swaying in the sea breeze. They're real fireflies, not like the ones in the basement. The moon has answered the call of the crickets and is beginning to tinge the sea's surface with silver. The garland of green flashes captures all of the boy's attention. He's absorbed in the magical, intermittent lights that float in the darkness enveloping us.

Then my son stands up.

And his hand releases my pants.

Maybe the day has come when his desire to know is stronger than his fear of the unknown. I hold out a hand over the metal surface of the trapdoor when I see myself reflected in my son's silhouette. I imagine Mom's hand coming up from underground. I stroke the wrinkly fold between two of her knuckles. The circle of burned skin at the base of the thumb. The wide, smooth scar near the wrist.

Behind me I hear some accelerated footsteps. My nephew appears beside me, panting from the effort of his running. I let him sit next to me, over the entrance to the basement that he doesn't remember. My mother's imagined hand becomes the real hand of my nephew, who squeezes mine with a smile. They're the same fingers that grabbed at the darkness on the other side of the bars the night I imagined that we'd gone out, looking at our reflection in the window.

"We're outside now," I tell him, repeating the phrase I'd said to him back then.

He gives me a mocking look because he thinks I've said something obvious. I catch him by the neck with my arm and kiss his temple before turning my attention to my son.

Emotion blurs my vision when I see him advancing with his arms outstretched to touch the fireflies, a miracle happening for the first time in front of him. Although a tear slides down the side of my nose, I smile when he waves his arms among dozens of dots of light.

Because I know the light will always belong to people like him.

And those unwilling to look beyond their own little world will be left in the dark.

ABOUT THE AUTHOR

Photo © Eduardo P. V. Rubaudonadeu

Paul Pen is an author, journalist, and scriptwriter. In 2014, he won the Gonzoo Prize for author of the year from Spanish newspaper *20 minutos*, awarded by popular vote. His first novel, *The Warning*, also earned him the title of Fnac New Talent in 2011 and has been translated into German and Italian. Pen's short stories include a digital-format collection of suspenseful tales titled *Thirteen Stories*. *The Light of the Fireflies* is his second novel and is available in English for the first time.

ABOUT THE TRANSLATOR

Photo © 2013 Thomas Frogbrooke

Simon Bruni is a literary, academic, and general translator of Spanish texts. He has translated everything from video games to sixteenth-century Spanish Inquisition manuscripts to literary novels. Bruni is a two-time winner of the John Dryden Translation Prize, first in 2011 for Francisco Pérez Gandul's cult prison thriller *Cell 211* and again in 2015 for Paul Pen's harrowing short story "The Porcelain Boy."

For more information, please visit www.simonbruni.com.